MW01089324

PARALLEL

THE PARALLEL SERIES, BOOK ONE

ELLE O'ROARK

1st Edit: Jenn Wood, All About the Edits

2nd Edit: Kathy Bosman

Cover Design: Emily Wittig

ISBN: 978-1-956800-00-5

To Patrick, Lily and Jack,
who will always be the best thing I ever created.
Oh, and stop reading here. No matter how old you are.

PROLOGUE

I had a nightmare as a child. A nightmare that visited me again and again. I've never forgotten it, not a single detail, although if my parents hadn't kept the psychologist's report, I'd probably assume the years had added and detracted from it in various ways. But they didn't. It's all in writing, exactly as it rests in my head.

QUINN, age four, was brought into our clinic due to recurrent nightmares. Parents report that patient wakes several times a week, crying for her "husband" ("Nick"), and claiming they've been separated by someone. Patient insists she "isn't supposed to be here" for hours and sometimes days afterward. There are no further signs of psychosis.

AT FIRST THOSE NIGHTMARES—THEIR weirdness, their specificity—made my mother scared for me. Over time though, she also became scared *of* me, and that taught me a lesson I'd continue to find true over the coming years: the things I knew, *real* things, were safest kept to myself.

1

QUINN
2018

Déjà vu.

It translates to *already seen*, but really it sort of means the opposite: that you *haven't* already seen the thing, but feel like you have. I once asked Jeff if he thought they actually call it *déjà vu* in France or perhaps keep a better, more accurate expression for themselves. He laughed and said, "you think about the weirdest shit sometimes."

Which is so much truer than he knows.

"Everything okay?" he asks now, as we follow my mother and his into the inn where we will marry in seven short weeks. I've been *off*, somehow, since the moment we pulled into town, and I guess it shows.

"Yeah. Sorry. I've got the start of a headache." It's not entirely true, but I don't know how to explain this thing in my head, this irritating low hum. It makes me feel as if I'm only half here.

We step into the lobby and my mother extends her arms

like a game show hostess. "Isn't it cute?" she asks without waiting for an answer. "I know it's an hour from D.C., but at this late date it's the best we're going to do." In truth, the lobby reminds me of an upscale retirement community—baby blue walls, baby blue carpet, Chippendale chairs—but the actual wedding and reception will take place on the lawn. And as my mother pointed out, we can no longer afford to be picky.

Jeff's mother, Abby, steps beside me, running a hand over my head, the way she might a prize stallion. "You're being so calm about this. Any other bride would be in a panic."

It's posed as a compliment, but I'm not sure it is. Losing our venue two months before the wedding *should* have made me panic, but I try not to get too attached to things. Caring too much about anything makes perfectly reasonable people go insane—just ask the girl who burned down the reception hall her ex was about to get married in...which happened to be the reception hall *we* were getting married in too.

My mother claps her hands together. "Well, our appointment with the hotel's events coordinator isn't for another hour. Shall we get some lunch while we wait?"

Jeff and I exchange a quick look. On this point we are both of one mind. "We really need to get back to D.C. before rush hour." *Are my words coming out as slowly as they feel?* It's as if I'm on delay somehow, two steps behind. "Maybe you could just show us around?"

My mother's smile fades to something far less genuine. She wants giddy participation from me and has been consistently disappointed with my inability to provide it.

She and Abby lead the way, back to the porch where we entered. "We've already been discussing it a bit," Abby says to me over her shoulder. "We were thinking you could walk down the stairs and out to the porch, where your fa— *uncle*, I mean, will wait." She pauses for a moment, blushing at the error. It shouldn't be a big deal at this point—my dad's been gone almost eight years—but I feel that pinch deep in my chest anyway. That hint of sadness that never quite leaves. "And then we'll do a red carpet out to the tent."

Together we step outside. It's a gruelingly hot day, as are most summer days anywhere near D.C., and this thing in my head only gets worse. I vaguely notice my surroundings—blinding sun, a technicolor blue sky, the rose bushes my mother is commenting on, but all the while I feel displaced, like I'm following this from far away. *What the hell is going on?* I could call it déjà vu, but it's not really that. The conversation occurring right now, with this group of people, is wholly new. It's the place that feels familiar. *More* than familiar, actually. It feels important.

They're discussing the lake. I'm not sure what I've missed, but Abby is worried about its proximity. "It would just take one boatful of drunks to create chaos," she says. "And we don't want a bunch of looky-loos either."

"Most boats can't reach this part of the lake," I reply without thinking. "There's too much brush under the water on the way here."

Abby's brow raises. "I didn't realize you'd been here before. And when did you ever sail?"

My pulse begins to race, and I take a quick, panicked breath. They know I haven't been here. They know I don't sail.

I don't know why I let it slip out.

"No," I reply. "I read up a little before I came." The words sound as false to me as they are, and I know they sound false to my mother too. If I were to glance at her right now, I'd see that troubled look on her face, the one I've seen a thousand times before. I learned early in life it bothered her, this strange ability of mine to sometimes know things I should not.

Jeff's phone rings and he turns the other way, while my mother walks ahead, frowning at the ground beneath her. "I hope they're going to water soon," she frets. "If it stays this dry, that carpet will be covered with dust by the time the ceremony starts."

She is right, unfortunately. I can see the soil shift loosely before me, the grass burned and threadbare beneath an unrelenting sun, all the way to the pavilion. If there were even the slightest breeze, we'd be choking on it right now.

We round the corner of the inn, and the lake comes into view, shimmering in the early July heat. It looks like any other lake, yet there's something about it that speaks to me. I stare, trying to place it, and as I do, my gaze is compelled upward, beyond its sapphire depths, to a cottage in the distance.

It's a tap, at first. A small tap between my shoulder blades, like a parent warning a child to pay attention. But then something shifts inside me, invisible anchors sinking into the ground, holding me in place. My stomach seems to drop as they go.

I know that house.

I want to look away. My heart is beating harder, and the fact that people are going to notice makes it beat harder still, but already a picture is forming in my head—a wide deck, a long, grassy slope leading to the water's edge.

"How can the grass be so dry with all this water around?" Abby asks, but her voice is growing dim beneath this sudden ringing in my ears.

And then, her words disappear entirely. There is no ground, no light, nothing to grab. I'm plummeting, and the fall is endless.

WHEN MY EYES OPEN, I'm flat on my back. Soil clings to my skin and the sun is beating down so fiercely it drowns out all thought. I'm in some kind of field with a house in the distance, and a woman is leaning over me. Have I met her somewhere before? It feels like I have but I can't place her at all.

"Quinn!" she cries. "Oh, thank God. Are you okay?"

The light is too much. That drumming in my head turns into a gong. I need it to stop, so I squeeze my eyes shut. The smell of parched grass assaults me.

"Why am I here?" I whisper. The words are slurred, the voice barely my own. *God, my head hurts.*

"You fell," she says, "We're at the inn. For your wedding, remember?"

The woman is pleading with me as if I'm a child on the cusp of a tantrum, but nothing she says makes sense. *I* am already married. And since when did London get so *hot*? It's never like this here.

A man comes jogging toward us. His build is similar to Nick's—tall, muscular—but even from a distance, I know he's not Nick, not even close. My eyes flutter closed and for a moment, I feel like I'm with him again—watching the smile that starts slowly before it lifts high to one side, catching the faint scent of chlorine from his morning swim. Where is he? He was *right* next to me a second ago.

The man drops to the ground beside me, and the women scurry out of his way. "She must have tripped," one of them says, "and now she's really out of it. I think she may need to go to the hospital."

I'm not going anywhere with these people, but I feel that first burst of fear in my chest. The throbbing in my head is growing. What if they try to force me to leave with them? I don't even know that I'd be able to fight them off with my head like this.

"Where's Nick?" The words emerge wispy and insufficient, needy rather than commanding.

"The hotel manager is Mark," says another voice. "Maybe she means Mark?"

"Can you sit up?" the guy asks. "Come on, Quinn."

I squint, trying to see him better in the bright sun. *How does he know my name*? There's something familiar about him, but he also just has one of those faces. "Are you a doctor?"

His jaw sags open. "Babe, it's me. *Jeff*."

What the hell is happening here? Why is this guy acting like we're old friends? I focus on him, trying to make sense of it.

"Your fiancé," he adds.

For a moment I just stare at him in horror. And then I begin scrambling backward, a useless attempt at escape. "No," I gasp, but even as I'm denying it, praying this is a nightmare, some part of my brain has begun to recognize him too, and remembers a different life, one in which Nick does not exist.

Nick does not exist.

I roll face down in the grass and begin to weep.

2

QUINN

My memory has mostly returned by the time they've gotten me into the car. My mother and Jeff look at each other carefully, but say nothing about the fact that I, for a period of time, did not recognize either of them. I rest my aching head against the seat as they quietly argue outside. God only knows what my mother is making of this.

"It will take you an hour to get back to D.C.," she says. "There's a state-of-the-art hospital in Annapolis."

"Even a state-of-the-art hospital is not going to be as good as Georgetown," he replies. "Look, just finish up with the contract here. I swear I'll take good care of her, and I'll let you know what they say the second I hear anything."

I swallow hard, willing away this desperate thing in my chest, the one I woke with. They tell me I collapsed, but the things I saw seemed so real—*Nick* seemed so real—that it's hard to believe I imagined them. A dream, a hallucination—it should be shadowy, vague. This is not. I remember our first date, our second date, the weeks that went by afterward. I don't see Nick as some blurry figure I could only describe in generalities. I remember his eyes, his mouth, that dimple of his. I remember how familiar he seemed from the moment we met, that I knew before he'd even opened his mouth how he would laugh, how he would smile, how he would kiss. It was as if our relationship wasn't new at all. It was a path so well-tread we could run rather than walk.

My eyes open. Two feet away, Jeff and my mother continue to discuss me, and my chest pinches tight. Jeff's the person I've loved for the past six years. The man I wake up next to each morning, the one who made crepes for my birthday and gave up a day of fishing to walk through the Hirshhorn with me last weekend. I *hate* that I'm sitting here right now wanting someone I've never met.

Someone who doesn't even *exist*.

But on the way home, the motion of the car lulling me to sleep, it's not Jeff who's in my head. It's Nick, just as I imagined him when I fell.

~

I WAKE in Nick's flat just before he does. His hand is on my hip, possessive even in his sleep, and I'm smiling at that when his eyes flicker open. I'm also smiling at the view, given that a sheet is only covering his lower half, leaving the rest of him—bare, tan, flawless—on glorious display. Last night he said he'd stopped swimming competitively in college, but he's obviously still doing a whole lot of something.

"You stayed," he says, his grin lifting high on one side. My heart flutters at the sight of it. I can't believe I crossed an ocean only to fall for a guy who grew up a few hours from me.

"I did. Although to be fair, I kind of had to since I have no idea how to get back to my apartment from here." Given that I could

easily have called Uber or pulled up a city map on my phone, this doesn't make much sense, but he's kind enough not to point it out.

That dimple of his appears. I want to marry him based on that dimple alone. "All part of my evil plan to keep you here."

I glance around his flat, which I saw little of last night because it was late when we got in and the two of us were, um, a little occupied. It's bachelorish—bare walls, windows in need of curtains, ash-gray hardwood. I decide I'm open to the possibility of being kept.

"Evil plan?" I ask. "So this is something you've been working on for a while?"

"Absolutely. Though 'meet gorgeous female with no knowledge of London' was a surprisingly difficult first step."

We are both smiling right now. How can it be so comfortable? How can I already feel so connected to him? From the moment we met yesterday, it was as if I was meant to know him, or perhaps, somehow, already did. "So far I sort of like your evil plan."

He raises himself up, leaning on his forearm. It brings him closer to my mouth. "And I was a perfect gentleman as promised, wasn't I?"

Our eyes lock. He kissed me for hours the night before, until I was on the cusp of begging him to undress me, but it went no further. His gaze flickers to my mouth. He's remembering it too.

"You were a perfect gentleman."

He leans over me, broad, tan shoulders sculpted by God himself. "You can't kiss me until I've brushed my teeth," I warn.

"Then I'll focus on other parts." His lips brush against my jawline and move to my neck. He pulls at the skin just hard enough to elicit a sharp inhale, my body arching against his without thought.

"Jesus," he groans. "I'm trying to behave here, but you're not making it easy."

Since he's only wearing boxers, that fact was already clear to me, but I don't care. My hand skims down his broad back to his waistband. I want to slide my palm over his hard ass, and let my nails sink into his skin...

"I want you to make that noise again," he says, his voice husky and low. He pulls at my neck in the same place he just did.

"Oh God, I like that way too much," I murmur. "Just don't give me a hickey."

He laughs apologetically. "I think it's too late."

"Then," I reply, pulling him back down, "you might as well do it again."

"HON," says Jeff, shaking my shoulder. "Wake up."

I blink, trying to make sense of the fact that Nick is no longer with me. And then I look over at my fiancé, at his sweet face and his furrowed brow, and feel sick with guilt. It couldn't have been real, with Nick, but I still have the sinking feeling that hits when you discover you've done something very, very wrong.

"Where are we?" I ask, my voice raspy with sleep. We're surrounded by the cement walls of a parking garage, deep underground and lit only by flickering fluorescent light. It provides no clues.

"The hospital. You fell at the inn, remember? Hurt your head?"

Argh. It comes back to me in a rush. Planning the reception, the sense of déjà vu, the sight of that white cottage in the distance. And then the time I spent with Nick—the time I *thought* I spent with Nick—during which Jeff didn't seem to exist. It was so real. It still feels real. It would be enough to make me believe in reincarnation, except it was all happening *now*, or close to it. I remember his iWatch on the nightstand. I was thinking about Uber. It was recent. And the very last thing I want is to be poked and prodded by some doctor while skirting around the fact that part of me still thinks it happened.

"I think we can skip it," I tell him. I'm sure to Jeff this whole thing seems monumental, but my childhood was littered with bizarre little episodes none of us could explain, and this seems likely to fall in the same category, if a thousand times more extreme. "I'm fine now and I don't feel like sitting in a waiting room for hours just to have some doctor tell me he thinks I'm okay."

His jaw swings open. "You seem to be gravely underestimating the seriousness of this. You had no idea who I was." His voice is strung tight—concern or hurt feelings, I can't tell. "I already called your office and told them you won't be in."

I lean my head back against the seat and allow my eyes to shut for a moment. "A few hours of sleep would do me more good than any doctor right now."

His door opens. "You didn't even recognize your own mother. We're getting it checked out."

I'm too tired for this, but also too tired to argue. I follow Jeff into the hospital, petulant as a teenager. It seems like an even worse idea once we're inside. While Georgetown the *city* is a haven of the wealthy and privileged, Georgetown *hospital* is not. I walk in expecting private school kids with lacrosse injuries or socialites with adverse reactions to Botox but find chaos instead: police restraining a screaming woman just inside the doors, a guy with an abdominal wound dripping blood off to the right.

Jeff shields me through all of it, placing his broad shoulders between me and the blood and the screaming woman, with no concern for himself. If my father is somewhere watching us right now, he's smiling. He was so certain Jeff would always keep me safe, and he was right.

Eventually, my name is called, and we are led back to a room with cinderblock walls and a poster that asks me to describe where my pain rests on a scale between the smiley-face emoji and the crying one. A resident appears moments later to complete an exam of my reflexes, orientation, and medical history. *No, this has never happened before. No, I don't use drugs. Yes, I drink socially, but not much.* And then the attending comes in and does it all over again.

I'm not in the mood to go through it all twice. And it's exhausting, telling half-truths, keeping so many things to myself. "I just fell," I tell her. "It wasn't a big deal."

Jeff frowns at me. "She didn't recognize me or her mother when she woke. She had no idea where we were and was asking for someone named *Nick*." There is a hint, just a hint, of outrage when he says the name. *He's jealous*, I realize at last. That's why this bothers him. He probably thinks Nick is some ex of mine I've never mentioned, and I could attempt to reassure him on that point, but the truth is almost worse. If he could picture what I do—Nick looming over me with that *look*, the one that even now makes me want certain things more than I've ever wanted them before—I doubt he'd be relieved. Especially since it all seemed to be happening recently, during the time I've been with Jeff.

"So, you had a little memory loss and recovered quickly?" the doctor asks.

I try to smile, the way a perfectly normal person who isn't fantasizing about a stranger might. "Yeah, it took a minute and then I was fine. Just a headache, and that's gone now too. I skipped breakfast and wasn't feeling great anyway."

"We'll get an MRI just to be sure," she says.

My shoulders tense. She's probably checking for concussions and it will come to nothing...but I don't love the idea of anyone looking too closely at what's in my head. "I'd really rather not. Honestly, I don't think it was a big deal."

"It's best to be on the safe side," she counters. "Are you sore anywhere?"

I shrug. "Not really."

"Let me check your lymph nodes." She moves in front of me and places her hands just beneath my jaw. Her palm hits the base of my neck and I wince. "Sorry," she says. "I pressed on your, uh—" She trails off.

"My what?"

Her smile is so awkward it's physically painful. "You've got a, um, bruise...on your neck." I struggle to understand why, exactly, she's being so weird—until I realize that by *bruise* she actually means *hickey*.

"*What?*" I scoff. "No."

"Look in the mirror," she says, with another awkward smile. I glance at my reflection and there, glaring back at me, is a small purplish-red mark. My pulse rises as Jeff steps forward to take a closer look. His face falls. Whatever is there, we both know he's not responsible for it. He's never given me a hickey in my life, and he's been out of town for most of the past week.

I put these things together and a quiet kind of fear creeps in, spreads icy fingers inside my chest.

Because all that comes to mind is the memory of Nick's mouth on my neck.

~

When my exam is complete, a nurse directs us upstairs, to neurology. Jeff's silence on the way is unnerving. He hasn't said a word since he saw the bruise. "Tell me what you're thinking," I say. "You know it's not a hickey."

"All I know," he says without inflection, "is that I didn't give it to you."

I groan quietly under my breath. Despite the dream about Nick, there's no way it's *actually* a hickey. And I can't believe he'd even question it. "You've been with me all day long. And last night too. If I really had a bruise on my neck the entire time, don't you think you'd have noticed it by now? I probably just hit a rock or something when I fell today."

The doors open and his hand goes to the small of my back

as we step out. Even as upset as he is, he still wants to take care of me, guide me, shield me.

I guess this is what my father saw in him, long before I did. I was only 20 when I came back home after my father's diagnosis, and to my mind, Jeff was already an adult—out of college, back in Rocton working as an assistant football coach. Toward the end of his life, my father's hints turned into pleas. *Jeff will keep you safe*, he would whisper, squeezing my hand, the morphine making his words nearly unintelligible. *Marry him and you'll always be safe*. I nodded only to comfort him, not really meaning it. But the way Jeff took care of me and my mom after my father passed made an impression on me, and once he really set his mind to winning me over, it was impossible not to fall in love with him. So I guess my dad was right all along.

"We're looking for imaging," Jeff says to a nurse passing by.

She doesn't even look up from her phone. "Sixth floor."

We glance at each other and return to the elevator, facing forward. His hand remains on my back. I think there's probably nothing I could do to him, really, that he wouldn't forgive—not that I've actually done anything that requires forgiveness. And that loyalty of his is one of many things I love. My friends come to me with story after story of men behaving badly, and it just confirms what I already know: I got one of the good ones.

He shifts beside me. "Look, put yourself in my shoes. You wake up asking for another guy. You don't even recognize me. And it turns out you've got this hickey on your neck I didn't give you..."

"You know better," I reply. "Whatever the explanation is, you should know me well enough to realize I would never cheat, and if you don't, then you shouldn't be marrying me."

The elevator doors open. When we get on, I push the button for the first floor.

"What about the MRI?" he asks.

"I'm totally fine and I'm tired," I tell him. "I just want to go home."

He turns and wraps his arms around me. "I'm sorry. You're right. You've never given me one reason to doubt you."

I allow my head to rest against his chest. "I just don't get where it even came from."

"Sometimes…" he begins, and the gust of his exhale ruffles my hair. "You're the smartest, most beautiful girl who ever came out of our town. And sometimes I wonder how I got this lucky, like it's just a matter of time before you figure out you could do so much better than me."

I ache for him. His issues with work may have taken an even greater toll than I realized. "That's crazy," I whisper.

"Can we just forget this happened?"

I nod and give him one last squeeze as the elevator doors open. I'd love to forget it happened too. I'm just not sure I can when the proof it did is staring back at me every time I look in the mirror.

3

NICK

Meg's alarm wakes me, and my first feeling is regret. I was having the dream again—a girl standing on a boat, seen from a distance. Lithe, golden-skinned. Her husky laugh echoing off the water, sun-streaked curls blowing in the breeze.

Meg's alarm continues shrieking. "Hon," I groan. "Alarm."

She mumbles something, reaching for her phone to hit snooze.

In the ensuing silence, suspended somewhere between sleep and wakefulness, I think of the dream and feel a pang in the center of my rib cage. It's the same one every time, and I never remember much of it. Mostly, it's just the sight of her standing there, nothing but smooth skin and a tiny red bikini I long to remove, and the way she makes me feel—as if my heart is exploding in my chest.

Meg's alarm goes off again and I give up on sleep, padding quietly to the closet for my gym bag. I was at the hospital until after midnight and it feels like I just shut my eyes five minutes ago, but birds are chirping so I figure it'll be dawn soon enough. I don't mind waking up early during the summer anyway. At least with all the students gone I won't have to fight for a lane at the pool.

"Why are you up?" Meg asks, yawning again as she moves toward the stuff she keeps on the left side of my closet. "I thought you went in late on Tuesdays."

"It might have something to do with the fact that you hit the snooze button three times," I reply. I'm crankier than normal. That dream about the girl on the boat always leaves me feeling dissatisfied with my life, and guilty at the same time. I have an amazing girlfriend. I shouldn't be dreaming about someone else. "It's fine. I'll get in an extra-long workout."

She winces as she pulls a clean pair of scrubs off the rack. "Then this is probably a bad time to ask, but do you mind if I crash here for a little while? I want to end my lease but I haven't found another place yet. I promise I'll never hit the snooze button again."

I drop goggles in my bag and look in a drawer for my second pair to stall for time. I know the question should be a no-brainer, but I'm comfortable with what Meg and I have. I don't know if I'm ready for more, and moving in here temporarily seems like the kind of situation that turns permanent before you know it. "I like your place."

"It's just too far from the hospital. I'm here almost every night anyway. What's going to change?"

I sigh, frustrated more with myself than the situation. She's absolutely right, and there's really no reason for me to object. I like having her here. The fact that we share a profession makes things easy with us in a way it hasn't been with other women I've dated. I just really need to stop waking up thinking about someone else. "Yeah, okay."

She wraps her arms around my waist. "You could at least try to sound enthusiastic," she scolds.

I drop a quick kiss to the top of her head and grab my bag. "You know I'm just cranky until I swim."

"Fine, go swim," she replies, pulling me back for a real kiss, content once more. "But I expect enthusiasm when I talk to you later."

I force a smile, hoping I'll be able to drum some up by then.

~

AT THE POOL, I swim hard, longer than normal, building up from a 4x25 to 4x200 before I work my way down. I take long strokes, feeling the water rush past as my arms slice through. What I love about swimming is how scientific it is. Muscle and position and timing, all simple to adjust when it goes off course.

I only wish the rest of my life was as simple, that I knew which parts required adjustment. I've done exactly what I was supposed to, dammit—college, med school, residency—but something is still missing, and it's this constant itch just beneath the surface of my skin, wondering what it is.

My mother claims what's missing from my life is a family, but I suspect that has more to do with her desire for grandchildren than anything else. *You and Meg are both 30*, she says. *Her biological clock is ticking even if yours is not.* But every time I even consider it, the dream about the girl in the boat returns to needle me, to leave me dissatisfied with what I have and suddenly uncertain I'm doing the right thing.

It makes no sense, really. I can't name a specific quality about the girl. I can't really see her face. I don't know what she likes, how she will laugh, if she's rude to waiters or hates dogs. All I know is how I feel—as if I'd swim the ocean to save her, walk into battle on her behalf without a second thought. That when I stand on that dock in my dream, I want to give myself to her until there is nothing left of me.

And I don't feel that way about Meg. I've never felt that way about anyone.

~

My morning is full. It's afternoon before I get in to see Darcy, the patient who kept me here so late last night. Things looked pretty grim fourteen hours ago, but when I walk into her room she's laughing over a cartoon so hard she's got to hold onto her stomach. Her exhausted mother is sound asleep in the chair beside her. Seven year olds bounce back a lot faster than adults.

"*Teen Titans*?" I ask. "Or *Teen Drama Island*?"

"*Teen Titans*," she replies.

I walk over and watch for a few seconds. "And your favorite is the goth one."

Darcy tilts her head. "What does *goth* mean?"

I take the seat beside her and point at the screen. "You know how Raven never smiles and is always wearing all black and looking unhappy? That's goth."

"I want to be goth when I grow up too," she says.

When she grows up. My chest aches, but she's watching my reaction so I force myself to smile as I rise. "Don't tell your mother I gave you that idea."

I go to the nurses' station next to make sure there's nothing pressing to be dealt with. The waiting room is packed, which means I'll be here this evening too. Not a great day to get by on four hours of sleep.

I turn away, but as I do my eyes catch on a couple standing by the elevator. There's something so familiar about the woman, even from behind—about the set of her shoulders, in the way she gathers her long brown hair into a ponytail before letting it fall. I feel a pull toward her I can't explain, and the fact that she's clearly with the guy beside her matters not at all.

"Mr. Jensen's family has called for you twice," says Bev, one of the nurses, thrusting a piece of paper into my hand. "The nursing home wants you to up his meds."

I look back at the elevator but the woman is gone. For a moment I just look blankly at the space where she stood, feeling as if I've lost something.

"You okay, Dr. Reilly?" Bev asks.

I wince. I'm acting like a nutjob today. "Sleep deprivation," I tell her.

Yes, that's probably all it is.

4

QUINN

I dream that night about so many things, some big and some small. Nick's flat in Marylebone, which became *our* flat in Marylebone. Grocery shopping. Trying to make the perfect gin fizz. Sitting with Nick at some pub on a night in late autumn, getting pleasantly smashed, happy in a way I've never been before and didn't even know existed until the day we met.

"Show me," he says, nodding at my laptop bag. In the three months we've been together, there's not been a single project I've completed for my graduate program that he hasn't demanded to see.

"It's just a basic building design. There's no way you actually want to see it," I argue.

"Of course I do," he says, sliding his drink toward me. I take a sip and flinch. I'll never get used to the taste of whiskey. "And then I want you to start throwing out terms like spaciality and cantilevers."

My mouth tips upward despite my every effort to look stern. "You're making fun of me."

"I'm not," he says, placing his palm on my cheek. "I love

watching you talk about architecture. Your whole face lights up. And it amazes me that you can do all this."

I laugh. "You can save human lives, but you're impressed I can draw a building?"

"But I don't create things," he says. "And I love that you're so fascinated by it."

"You'll be just as fascinated next year." During this, the first year of his residency, he's all over the place—like the neurology rotation that led to our first meeting. Next year is when he'll get to focus on cardiology, his chosen specialty.

He takes a sip of his drink. "I hope so. I thought with my dad's heart problem, it would feel more meaningful, but right now I'm not sure."

"Are you worried it'll be depressing?"

"There are worse specialties. Like oncology. You know why they nail coffins shut?"

I prepare myself. Doctor humor tends to be on the macabre side.

He grins. "To keep oncologists from trying to resuscitate the corpse."

I laugh and shake my head. "Just because there are worse specialties doesn't mean it's right for you. I want you to be riveted by something."

His smile is soft. His hand, beneath the table, finds mine and swallows it. "I'm pretty riveted by this patient I met during my neurology rotation."

"Is that right?" I ask, biting down on my grin. His gaze flickers to the movement of my lips. "Maybe you should ask her out."

"You think she'll say yes?"

I smile at him. "I can't imagine there's anyone who could say no to you."

There's something guarded in his eyes...a secret he isn't ready to share with me. "I really hope you're right," he replies.

I learn that secret of his two nights later.

It's just after my evening class. I step outside the architecture building to find Nick sitting on a bench out front, jacket thrown over his scrubs, smiling as he waits. When he smiles at me, it's like his whole heart is in his eyes. I sometimes wonder if it's even possible for him to feel the way I do, this loopy, out-of-control adoration, but when I see him smiling at me like he is right now, it's impossible to doubt it.

He rises as I walk down the stairs. "You move like a dancer," he says. I skitter to a halt in front of him, going on my toes to press my mouth to his.

"I assure you I'm not," I reply. "Two left feet."

He hesitates, then gives me a distracted smile. There's something off tonight, but I can't put my finger on it. "You could swing dance, though. Anyone can."

I grin up at him. "I thought I was supposed to be the wild, impetuous one, and you were supposed to be the driven resident who doesn't know how to have fun."

"Until you, I kind of was," he says softly.

I think of the serious guy I met at the hospital that first day and how much he's changed since then. The fact that he is good for me is something I've known all along. But it's only now I realize I'm good for him too.

He grabs one hand and places it on his shoulder, pulling me off the sidewalk and into the grass. If it weren't late, I'd probably refuse, but the campus is mostly empty at this hour. "One, two. One, two," he says, moving us in a slow circle. "You're a natural."

I laugh. "I seem to be a little better at things when I'm with you."

"That's because we're meant to be together," he says softly.

In our case, it's not a cliché. Ever since we met, we've had a knowledge of the other that was almost intuitive, muscle memory. And I've been having these weird dreams about his childhood even though I wasn't a part of it. Dreams in which I'm his best friend, the little girl next door he shares everything with. I would assume it was wishful thinking if it weren't for the fact that I wake knowing things I shouldn't. I referenced his twin, their treehouse, his parents' place by the lake—all before he ever told me about them. I have no idea how I knew.

My voice is hushed as I meet his eye. "I think...no matter what universe we land in, we land there together."

He stops dancing. Before I can blink, before I can ask why, he's lowering to one knee in front of me. There's a small black velvet box in his hand. "I know it's too soon," he says. "I know this is insane. But I also know that you're the person I was born for, and I don't want to wait to start our lives together."

Inside me there's this new thing, like the start of a sunrise. A dim warmth against the horizon, spreading, spreading until I'm flooded with light. It may be too soon, and everyone will say we're insane, but he's the person I've waited my entire life to find. To belong to. And now I will.

~

I WAKE EARLY in the morning, feeling steeped in happiness, cocooned in it, until I open my eyes and see that it's Jeff, not Nick, beside me. Nothing about Jeff has changed. He has the same sweet face he's always had, mouth open, peaceful and deeply asleep. But there's a part of me that doesn't want him here. That misses Nick so much I could weep at the sight of my fiancé beside me. I inch away, struggling with my disappointment and horrified by it, all in the same breath.

The tightness in my chest propels me from the bed and into the living room. How, *how*, could it have felt so real? How can I remember the feel of his palm on mine, the weight of the velvet box I took from his hand? And the shops outside Nick's flat—I can name them. I can name the streets surrounding them—Marylebone, Harley Street—as if they are familiar when I'm not sure I've ever even heard of them before. How could I see London so *vividly* when it's somewhere I've never been?

Yes, I've known things before, things I should not know. But this is different. I'm seeing the life I might have had, if my father hadn't gotten sick and my mother hadn't fallen apart after he died. Because that was all part of the plan—get my architecture degree, move to London for graduate school. This knowledge... it feels like something I'm *supposed* to know. If feels important, like a life-altering conversation held while drunk, recalled only in small flashes the next day.

I grab my wedding binder, the nearest thing I can find. I skip past all the details about shoes and dresses and invitations, until I get to the blank pages in the back, and then I start to sketch. When I'm done, the interior of our flat—mine and Nick's—sits in front of me. The tiny box of a kitchen, half the wall taken up by a radiator that would wake us with its *clunk clunk clunk* each morning. The bedroom, so small we had to edge around our bed to get in and out, and the garden terrace you could only reach by climbing on top of the radiator and out the bedroom windows. I stare at the drawing, feeling unsettled. It's far too specific to be something I just dreamed up.

The tightness in my chest has gone nowhere. I miss it, that imaginary flat. I miss the icy floors on winter mornings and Nick's broad hand pulling me through the window on a summer night so we could sit on the terrace. I miss the smell of chlorine on his skin and the way he'd look at me when someone made a comment—his eyes light and amused while his mouth didn't give an inch—because he knew what I was thinking when no one else did. I miss being understood.

And I don't want to miss anything. A week ago I was happy with my life, and now, *now*, it's as if I've given something up... something I want more than the life I actually have.

~

My boss is waiting in reception to pounce on me when I walk through the office doors a few hours later. Dee is bone thin, unnaturally tall, and prone to wearing a fur stole whenever the temperature drops below 70, which never fails to make me think of Cruella de Vil. The comparison is, sadly, all too apt.

"Where's the layout?" she demands, tapping her nails on the Lucite console beside her.

"Good morning, Dee," I reply. "I'm feeling so much better, thanks."

Not that I expected her to ask how I was after yesterday's hospital visit. In six years at this magazine, she has never even managed to say *good morning*. For her to inquire about my health would require stronger mood stabilizers than modern medicine has discovered.

Her nose crinkles. "The layout, Quinn," she says between her teeth. "Where is it?"

"I made the changes from home last night. I just need to print it out."

"And where's the Resort Wear preview?"

I sigh deeply. Lots of the people I graduated with love what they do and salivate at the idea of beginning a project. But graphic design was never my first choice, and I'm reminded of that every time Dee assigns me something new. "It's not due until next week."

Her mouth tightens. "Just because I give you a due date doesn't mean you have to wait *until* the due date."

"Hmmm," I reply, walking past. As in, *hmmm, how interesting you think so*. I've learned over time that the best way to handle Dee is mostly by pretending she hasn't spoken at all. I should have expected it, really. Do anything so egregious as take a vacation or a day of sick leave, and Dee will always come after you with sharpened fangs when you return.

Trevor, Dee's lovely but beleaguered assistant, and my closest friend here, appears at my desk moments after I've opened up my Mac.

"*Hmmm*," repeats Trevor, imitating my airy tone before he

gives me a wide smile. "You already aggravate her enough by being so cute, you know, without *also* failing to kiss her ass."

"She'll fire me eventually."

"Never," he says decisively, perching on the edge of the file cabinet. "You know what she wants before *she* knows what she wants. What I don't understand is why you stay."

"I stay because she pays me more than any other graphic artist I know." The move to D.C. has been hard on us—Jeff's quit two jobs since we arrived six years ago and was let go from two others—and it's made my tenure at *Washington Insider* last far longer than I'd have liked. For the foreseeable future, I need to know I can pay our bills by myself, because there's no reason to think I won't be doing so again.

Trevor generally manages to keep his opinions about my personal life to himself, but I see the response he's holding in flash across his face—*you wouldn't have to stay here if Jeff could keep a job*—before he blinks it away and grins at me. "Anyway, aren't you going to ask me about my date?"

I groan. Trevor always shows me his dates' Grindr profiles before he goes out—in part, because he's excited, but mostly so I can avenge his death if something awful happens. Last night's date—the guy with five different photos of his greased-up chest, the one whose profile read simply *I'm here to fuck*—actually looked slightly *less* creepy than most.

"I'm scared to ask, but how was your date?"

He closes his eyes, the smile on his face absolutely indecent. "You know when you're messing around with someone and you want him so much you think you'll die if you don't get it?"

I assume the question is rhetorical, but when I don't answer, he elbows me. "Come on. Jeff's boring, but he's still hot. At some point in your relationship, he's had you ready to beg."

I stiffen. "Not *everyone* is like that, Trevor. And Jeff isn't boring. You just prefer guys who oil their chests over guys who call when they're supposed to call and show up when they've promised they will."

He pets my hair as he leaves, like it's a fur coat or a cuddly pet. "Pretty, pretty Quinn. You break my heart sometimes."

It's nothing Trevor hasn't said before, but given that I've been fantasizing about an absolute stranger for the better part of twenty-four hours, it's sort of poorly timed.

After he leaves, I send the most recent layout to print and call my mother, who's already left three messages so far this morning. Because she tends to handle uncertainty poorly, I told her yesterday's blackout was the result of a pre-wedding diet. Only now do I realize this means I'll spend the next seven weeks being interrogated about my food intake.

"You had breakfast, right?" she asks.

"Yes." A nice big breakfast. Of coffee, but it had creamer, so I assume that counts.

"What are you having for lunch?"

I laugh. "Mom, it's not even nine a.m. I'm not thinking about lunch."

"But you're not going to forget to eat, right?"

"I promise I won't."

"Why on earth would you be on a diet anyway?" she demands. "You don't have a pound to lose. Just please stop doing whatever it is."

"Okay, I promise."

She hesitates. "When you woke yesterday, you asked for someone named Nick. Do you remember?"

Crap. I was really hoping she wouldn't bring it up. "Yeah."

"That was the name you used to mention when you were little. Those nightmares you had. I guess it was just a coincidence?" There's a hint of pleading to her voice—she desperately *wants* it to be a coincidence—but my God I wish there was one person I could discuss this with. To say *I miss someone I've never met. I grieve for him.* My mother, however, will never be that person. "Yeah, I guess."

"It was...shocking...hearing you ask for him," she says quietly. "Just like it was when you were small. You seemed so certain it was true."

I hesitate. I remember little about the year I spent in therapy, aside from the strain on my mother's face each time she brought me in. I was her miracle baby, the child she never thought they'd have, and I was flawed. I wanted to become normal for her, but at the end of most sessions my mother seemed a little more hopeless than the time before. "Did the psychologist ever tell you why it was happening?" I ask cautiously.

"She just said you had a very active imagination. But it finally stopped. And the other stuff..." There is a long, awkward pause. We really don't discuss *the other stuff*. "Well, after what happened with the Petersons, you seemed to grow out of it, mostly." Her words end on a whisper. Perhaps she thinks saying it quietly means she's admitted to less. "Anyway, the nightmares stopped, and that's what matters."

I wish I shared her certainty that this is over. But when I think of Nick—of his laugh and the way he looked at me, as if he knew me in a way no one else ever has—a sort of panic thrums in my chest. I didn't want the nightmares. But I don't want this either. In some ways, it scares me even more.

THAT NIGHT, Trevor and I head out for drinks, swinging by my friend Caroline's office to grab her on the way. Though Caroline was my friend first, she and Trevor have been attached at the hip since I started throwing her work for the magazine.

"Quinn," she says, shaking her perfect, jet-black bob as I walk in, "*what* are you wearing?"

I sigh. I never take her comments too personally—as a stylist, she has a far higher bar for clothing choices than most people—but occasionally, I wish she'd just let it go.

"Instead of telling me how I've chosen wrong, just go ahead and dress me."

She squeals and claps her hands. "I love when you let me dress you," she sings. She grins at Trevor. "It's like having a grown-up doll to play with. You should make her come see me every morning."

Trevor's palm shoots out. "No. Absolutely not. Dee already resents her just for being young and pretty. You start putting her in nice clothes and makeup every day, and we will all suffer."

Five minutes later, I walk out of her bathroom in a Dries Van Noten dress that could pay my mortgage, and Caroline is appeased. "So much better."

I have to agree. I wouldn't say I'm *frumpy* under normal circumstances, but when Caroline gets her hands on me, I wind up feeling like Gigi Hadid, which is an experience words can't sufficiently describe.

"If only Lindsay could see you now," says Caroline. "You could tell her to shove that Hermes purse right up her ass."

I laugh. I cannot believe Caroline is still holding a grudge about the purse incident nearly a decade later. I'm not sure I'd even remember it if she didn't reference it so often.

"Who's Lindsay?" asks Trevor.

"This girl on our floor freshman year," I reply. "She was awful to everyone but she hated me the most because I was there on a scholarship."

"No," corrects Caroline, "she hated you because you were her first experience of not being the hottest girl in the room. That's why she went out of her way to throw her money in your face." She turns to Trevor. "You know that Hermes Kelly bag? Real ones are like ten grand, but we found the best knock-off and I talked Quinn into it. And then we get back to the dorm, and Lindsay says, 'Bless your little heart. It almost looks like a *real* Kelly bag.' And then the bitch goes and buys a real one, just to show she can."

I shrug. "Well, I'd suggest karma would get her eventually, but she's got this amazing job and she's married to some millionaire, so I guess she won in the end."

Trevor and Caroline glance at each other. "You could have that too, if you wanted," says Trevor cautiously.

I roll my eyes. "I *don't* want that. You know I was just joking. And you're in my wedding in seven weeks, remember?"

"But the job," Caroline says. "You're only twenty-eight. You could still go back to school."

I wrap an arm around each of them and pull them close for a moment as we walk down the street. "I appreciate your concern, guys, but I don't need Lindsay's life. The one I have is just fine with me."

I force myself not to think of Nick as I say these words. But inside, it sort of feels like a lie.

~

When I finally get into bed, I'm exhausted and a tiny bit buzzed, which I hope means there will be no dreams of Nick. I want to have nonsensical, boring dreams—the kind where the toilet floods and I have to fix it using a car engine, or where my boss is at my wedding demanding I return to work to correct something, although the latter seems completely within the realm of possibility. But even as my eyes shut, I already feel Nick calling to me, as if he's been waiting for me to find him again, somewhere inside my head.

Nick stands on the dock, shirtless and surrounded by sunlight, like some kind of mythical figure. Watching me float away.

"Hey!" I call, just a hint of panic in my voice. "I don't know how

to sail this thing."

I don't know how to sail anything, not even the tiny Sunfish that the current took as soon as he untied it from the dock.

"It's okay," he calls out. "Just pull the sail to the left."

I do what he says, but that seems to send me farther. I stand, balancing in the center and waving to him. "SOS!"

He smiles, sweet and sheepish in the same moment, and that dimple appears. God, I love that dimple. It makes me feel as if my heart has swelled until it is pushing against my sternum—my ribs stretched to the point of pain. I watch him dive in, all lean muscle and easy grace, the sunlight glinting off his back. His strokes as he swims toward me are long and even. He reaches the boat in no time at all, which amazes me, though it shouldn't. He got a full scholarship based on that particular ability of his.

He pulls himself up and over the side of the boat in a single fluid move. We lean toward each other, and when he kisses me, I forget we're on a boat, in the middle of a lake. All I know is him, warm and sweet and whole beside me. The past few months have been hard, for both of us, but I know in this moment we will be fine. There is something about the two of us that seems to survive all things. Tragedy strikes and we wobble like bowling pins but return to our places, upright and beside each other.

"Thank you for swimming out to get me," I whisper.

His words are low and warm against my ear, his voice serious and perhaps a little sad. "I'll never just let you float away," he replies.

WHEN I WAKE, Jeff is asleep, draped heavily around my back like a blanket, and for the first time in all the years I've known him, the feel of him against me brings with it a deep swell of panic. While I refuse to feel guilty about dreams I have no control over, the fact that I can't stand my fiancé touching me afterward? Yes, I can *and should* feel guilty about that.

I quietly extricate myself, as my head starts to throb, and go to the living room. It's still dark out, and in the dim light the room feels sort of foreign to me. Nothing has changed, yet it just isn't mine somehow. I look around the room and try to remember why I chose this stuff—the staid furniture, heavy wood, dark colors. But then, I guess I didn't really *choose* any of it. I just didn't argue against it.

A traitorous voice in my head asks, for the first time, if that's how Jeff and I ended up together too. It's a ridiculous question, of course, because Jeff and I were bound to end up together eventually—our parents were best friends and he was our rock after my father died. But at the same time, it seems like part of a pattern: my life consists entirely of things that occurred by default or were chosen by someone else first.

I lie on the couch but remain awake until it's light out, wanting only to be rid of this unsettled feeling, this sudden discontentment with everything. Jeff emerges from the bedroom just as I'm rising and regards me through half-lidded eyes, scratching his stomach.

"You having another headache?" he asks.

I am, actually. I've gotten so accustomed to them I barely noticed. "Yeah, they're pretty much a constant at this point."

He wraps his arms around my waist and I lay my head against his chest. His skin is clammy. Wiry chest hairs poke at my cheek.

"What's going on, babe?" he asks. "Is it the wedding?"

I can't tell him the truth. I can't. "Maybe. It's been a stressful couple of weeks."

"Not having second thoughts, are you?" he asks, laughing. Of course he would laugh. Because it's unthinkable. We are not the kind of people who have second thoughts. But we also aren't the kind of people who fantasize about others. And now, it appears, I am.

5

QUINN

On Monday, it is Caroline who drives me out to the inn to finalize wedding plans, since Jeff was busy and I was nervous about driving alone, given what happened the other day. Caroline is able to take off work without a ration of shit since she's her own boss, and not for the first time, I wonder what my life might be like if I hadn't left school to take care of my dad. Would I have a job I love? Would I be able to set my own hours? If he hadn't gotten sick, if my mother hadn't fallen apart so completely...but what's done is done. You can't change the past.

"I love Trevor," she says, "but his ideas for your bachelorette party leave much to be desired."

"Such as?"

"*Prostitutes*, Quinn. I'm not joking. He wants me to bring in prostitutes."

"Oh my God. To strip?"

"No. You hire *strippers* to strip."

I give a choked laugh. "So for *sex*? How would that even

work? Is he thinking I'd just, like...go into the bathroom with one of them?"

"He said 'guys do it, so why shouldn't she? I want her to see what she's missing.'"

I sigh. "He seems to be under the impression that just because I'm not all 'do me, Jeff, right now,' that we're missing something."

I expect her to laugh but she's oddly quiet. "But you're like that *sometimes*, right?"

I slant a glance at her. "*Et tu, Brute*? Please don't join the last-minute chorus of people telling me I'm making a mistake. I mean, you've had *years* to tell me this, so mere weeks before my wedding is just...rude."

"I'm not," she argues. "You know I think Jeff's great. And to be fair, I have asked you about this before. Right before you moved in with him."

I broke up with Jeff to move back to D.C., but when he followed me here—showing up on my doorstep with this impassioned speech straight out of a romance—it felt like fate, like the kind of thing I was supposed to give into. I was torn at the time, but it's all kind of romantic, in hindsight. "I thought you just wanted to make sure I'd thought it through. I didn't think you were trying to dissuade me."

"I wasn't, necessarily. I just didn't...I wasn't sure he made you happy."

"Of course he does," I reply, shocked she'd even think it. Jeff might not be the most exciting guy, but that's fine with me. What matters far more is that he is cute and kind, reliable and steadfast. While Caroline and Trevor sit around bemoaning men who forget to call, who change plans without warning or hook up with the blond at the gym, I've found someone who remembers every anniversary and doesn't even seem to realize other women exist. "Where is this coming from? The other day you guys are telling me it's not too late to change my mind and now this?"

She gives me an apologetic smile before she looks back at the road. "I know you love him, and I know he's a good guy, but when was the last time you were happy with him?"

My head jerks back. "I'm happy now! And if I don't seem happy that's not his fault. It's just who I am."

Her eyes flicker to me once more and she frowns. *But it's not who you were*, her look says.

I turn up the radio and change the subject, because I cannot think about this right now. There are times in your life when you just have to focus, get through something and leave all the considering and mulling over behind. And despite the dreams about Nick, this is that time. I'm getting married in a matter of weeks. It'd be too late to change my mind if I wanted to. And I don't want to.

I really don't.

~

WE SIT in the inn's small restaurant with my mother, going over the guest list. The din of their lunchtime service grates, though it probably has more to do with how on edge I've felt ever since we got to town, just like I was the last time. It's driving me crazy, this feeling. As if I'm supposed to know something I don't.

"Jeff's friends from college," my mother says, "do we keep them all together or split them up? And do you know yet if his friend Tim is bringing the baby?" She clicks her pen, poised for an answer I can't provide. It's easily the tenth question she's asked about Jeff and his friends about which I have no clue.

I groan. "I should have made Jeff come for this."

"Well," my mother says with a fond smile, "he had to work."

"So did I," I reply.

She pats my arm. "When push comes to shove, you need someone who puts work first."

Of course, she would say this. She's spent her entire life on a farm, where work has to come first, where it begins early and ends late and doesn't offer four weeks of paid vacation. And perhaps that's why the transition to D.C. has been so hard on Jeff—because he was raised to believe that putting your nose to the grindstone is the path to success, and it hasn't panned out for him here. No matter how hard he works, there is always someone craftier or cannier taking his clients, stealing his thunder.

My mother puts the guest list aside, apparently tired of asking me questions I can't answer. "Let's walk outside and look at the space again," she says. "I think we need a feel for how it will all be laid out, and you barely saw it the last time."

I feel a twitch, a tremor, in my chest, even as I agree. I realize the little white house in the distance didn't *cause* what happened the other day, much like stepping on a crack will not actually break your mother's back, but...it happened. And I don't want it to happen again.

Outdoors it is stifling, and painfully bright, the very air tinged a harsh gold, making things seem ominous in some way I can't name. But my mother and Caroline are oblivious to it, so I push myself forward, alongside them. They're talking about valets and overflow parking, but I can't seem to follow the conversation.

We pass the edge of the inn. The lake is spread before us, so deep blue it appears bottomless. I inhale and then force my gaze up to the right, to the white house I wish wasn't there.

I cannot look away.

My mom and Caroline politely disagree about table placement and if we need one bar or two, and my eyes are locked, unmoving, on that house, seeing it in my head, though it's at least a quarter mile away—a wide deck, a dock with a tiny boat bobbing alongside it. I see Nick there too, younger than he was in London. That dream I had last night...it took place there. I'm certain of it. Images sharpen in my mind, and I begin to shiver, hugging myself for warmth.

"Goodness, Quinn, what's wrong with you? It's almost ninety degrees," my mother says, but her voice is distant, tinny, and then there are no sounds at all.

I LAND ON THE FLOOR, hard, my legs tangled in sheets and butt naked aside from them.

I have a single moment in which I am utterly blank. Unsure of the month or the year, or why I'm in this room with high, arched windows, winter sunlight illuminating dust motes in the air. And then a face appears over the side of the bed. Blue eyes flecked with gold, broad shoulders, the flash of a smile.

"I'm trying not to laugh," Nick says.

I grin. "This is very sexy, isn't it, the way I'm all splayed out on the floor?"

There's a gleam in his eye that wasn't there moments before. "Honestly? Yeah. A little."

He reaches one long, perfectly formed arm out to hoist me into bed. I land on top of him, smiling as I take in his face. God, I love him so much it hurts.

"Good morning, Mrs. Reilly," he says, nuzzling my neck.

I breathe him in. "Good morning, Dr. Reilly."

Outside, Paris waits, but neither of us care. We are drunk on the novelty of this, waking up married. I've been a bit drunk, truthfully, on the novelty of having found him at all. Two Americans who chose London at the same time. If I hadn't gone to the hospital for a migraine days after arriving, if Nick's rotation hadn't gotten messed up, so that he was in neurology rather than peds that week—I can't even imagine. There is obviously something greater at play with us, something more than mere fate. But whatever it is, even if we can never explain it, it's something good.

"We'll need to call home and tell our parents today," he says. We've avoided this, knowing it would meet with nothing but objections on both sides. I'd like to keep avoiding it, personally.

"They're going to think we're crazy."

He pushes my hair behind my ear. "It is a little crazy. But they'll get it once they see us together. We'll go back to the States over break, charm everyone, and they'll be fine."

I sigh. "I'm not sure my mother will be as easily won over as you think. But then, I wasn't easily won over either, and look at me now."

"I am looking at you now," he says. He flips me so I'm flat on my back and then looms over me, his gaze on my mouth. "And it looks like you need to be won over a little more."

I pull him down, waiting for the delicious weight of him settling against me, but before it happens, there is this din in my head, sudden and loud.

The dull throb of a migraine, and a voice—shrill, unrelenting as an alarm. I'd give anything to silence it.

"Quinn!" a woman's voice cries, the pitch rising. My head feels as if it's splitting open from the inside, as if it will cleave into two perfect halves like a watermelon. I groan and push at my temples as I force my eyes open. I'm standing in the grass, beside a lake, being shaken by this panicked woman and Nick... is gone.

The memories flood my brain: the quick wedding in London, Nick and I unable to stop smiling through the whole thing, fully aware it was insane to marry someone you'd known so briefly. The honeymoon itself, spent mostly naked in our hotel room. The dread I felt at the thought of calling my mother.

My mother. It comes to me with a startled gasp—she's the woman standing here, shaking me. My eyes open and fill with tears. Nick is not my husband. He's not *anything*. How can he possibly not exist when I remember him in such detail? When I feel so much for him?

"You just completely went blank there, like you were asleep standing up!" my mother cries. "You looked like a corpse! We're going to the hospital."

The pain is unbearable, a pendulum of it swinging through my brain, bruising me a little more with each rotation. Before I can argue that a trip to the hospital is unnecessary, I drop to my knees and throw up in the grass.

~

I KNOW it's different this time, that it's serious. After the longest, most arduous car ride of my life, Caroline and I arrive back in the same emergency room I sat in last week. This time I'm taken straight to neurology, where a nurse says she's going to give me something for the pain that will put me to sleep for a while. *Will I even wake up from this*? I wonder, as the needle goes into my arm. *Do I really care if I don't?*

"What's going to happen?" I ask. My words are slurred, my brain sinking somewhere dark and hazy.

"You'll be just fine," she says with a pat on the shoulder. "I'll make sure Dr. Reilly is there to see you as soon as you wake up."

My eyes flutter closed before I can ask if I've heard her correctly.

6

NICK

I get to the cafeteria just after Meg does and slide my tray next to hers at the salad bar. She watches me make my salad and turns away. "Just once, I'd like to see you live a little."

"In what way?" I ask, loading a second chicken breast on my plate.

"That," she says, nodding toward my tray. "You probably burned a thousand calories swimming this morning, but it's like the world will fall apart if you actually use dressing or cheese, or anything that would make your meal pleasant instead of merely healthy."

I shrug. "You see people die every day. Isn't it enough to be alive without needing everything to be *fun* on top of it?"

"I'm not saying everything has to be fun," she argues. "But the minute you seem to enjoy yourself, it's like you feel guilty about it or something. It's okay to have a *little* fun."

"Believe me, if I was in the mood for fun, it would not involve blue cheese dressing." I grin at her, but she doesn't smile back. There's a shadow to her eyes I've seen before, a warning sign that she's unhappy about something.

I pay and we take our seats, but she remains silent, grim. I pinch the bridge of my nose and brace myself for the relationship talk that appears to be coming. "What's up?"

Her eyes are on the table instead of me, her palms pressed against it, trying to rein herself in. "You were talking in your sleep last night."

Fuck.

I'm generally an open book, but there are two recurring dreams I've had for years that I'd prefer to keep to myself, for Meg's sake as much as my own. There's the one about the girl on the boat, obviously, and a similar one in which I'm dancing outside with that same girl—I know it's her though I can never quite make out her face—and trying to summon the courage to ask her something. I've always wondered if it's a metaphor for my fear of commitment, although in the dream I want that commitment as much as I want my next breath. But it's sure as hell nothing I need Meg to hear about. "Yeah?"

She continues to avoid my eye. "Yeah. And it was like you were talking to someone you were *with*. You were promising her she'd be fine and then you were..." she swallows. "You were yelling at someone to get away from her."

I have no idea what she's talking about, but it sounds like an accusation, which leaves me feeling both annoyed and guilty at once. I force a laugh. "Maybe I was dreaming about the EMT that kept asking you out."

Her lips press tight. "You weren't dreaming about me."

I blow out a breath, suddenly tired. Meg and I have known each other a long time. She knew the deal when I returned from London. She knew my romantic history consisted only of brief, relatively meaningless relationships, and that I couldn't promise ours would be any different. And things are going well, much better than I thought, but she can't start scrutinizing what happens in my *sleep*. "How could you possibly know that?"

"Because," she says, "you sounded like you were in love with her. And you've never once sounded like that with me."

Another accusation. It bothers her that I won't say it, that I can't say it. It bothers me too, but I just need to be sure about things and I'm not there yet. "Meg—"

She holds up her hand. "*Don't*. I know you said you just want something casual and you can't make any promises. What bothers me is that you made it sound like you don't think you're *capable* of more, and obviously you are."

"It was just a dream."

She nods. I've never seen her cry but she's swallowing hard now, as if she might, and I hate myself in this moment. I want to be better and do better by her. I've just got to figure out how.

AFTER OUR LUNCH CONCLUDES, I get upstairs and a resident briefs me on my next patient as we walk down the hall. "Quinn Stewart. Twenty-eight-year-old female. Fell last week and suffered some memory loss. Today, she appeared to go unconscious for a few minutes, still standing, and she came to with some memory loss and a severe migraine. The pain was so bad they had to sedate her."

I rub the back of my neck. A migraine *that* severe is not a good omen. I send him off to check on someone down in oncology, and then tap on the door and walk in. The patient is asleep, but her face is turned toward me.

My heart seems to give one long audible thud and my steps stutter to a halt.

It's her—the girl in the dream. I've never seen her face clearly, and yet standing here the experience of it is the same. If

I were standing on a dock right now I'd dive off and swim to her.

I pinch the bridge of my nose. *Jesus Christ, what's wrong with me?* I'm a neurologist. I should know, better than almost anyone in this hospital, that the brain is capable of tricking you into thinking anything is true. It happens to my patients all the time. I just had no idea it would feel this fucking real.

A guy sitting in the corner chair rises and I turn toward him, extending my hand, scrambling to feign normalcy. "I'm Nick Reilly. And you're..."

"Jeff Walker. Quinn's fiancé."

I frown, irritated by him for no reason. *Focus. You're here to do a job.* "I saw in the chart that this happened last week too, so I have to ask: does she have any issues with drugs and alcohol?"

"No," he says. "None. They gave her something for the pain that knocked her out, but she barely even drinks."

I walk to her bedside. She lies there like a beautiful present, waiting to be unwrapped and discovered. Her eyes are closed, but I already know their color—smoky green, like the forest seen through fog. I can picture them in my head, as familiar to me as my own. Her lids flicker and her hand trails along the side of the bed until it finds mine. Her fingers curl there, as if it's something she's done a thousand times. I slide my hand away quickly, hoping her fiancé didn't notice.

"Hey," she says, the word slurred, half-asleep. "How was your swim?"

I freeze, wondering if I've heard her correctly. "I... How do you know I went swimming?"

She laughs, a throaty noise that strikes a chord inside me, like a song I'd forgotten I loved. "You're cranky if you skip it," she murmurs.

My breath comes short. I can name on one hand the number of people who know this about me, so how the fuck does she? Across the room, her fiancé has gone rigid. It's like

I've walked into some soap opera without knowing my part. "Um...have we met?"

Her mouth curves upward but she doesn't answer, so I try again. "Quinn, *how* did we meet?"

"Hospital," she says. "London."

At last something makes sense. I'm still hard-pressed to imagine how I could have treated anyone who looks like her and *forgotten*, but I'm not sure there's another explanation. "Right," I reply. "Sorry it slipped my mind. I was a resident, so I saw a ton of patients."

She smiles as she drifts back to sleep. "That's okay," she murmurs. "As long as I'm the only one you married."

The words hit me like a hammer. Somewhere inside me they land, settle in and feel true, even though I know they can't be.

Her fiancé sits wide-eyed, his frown deepening. "You two know each other?" he asks.

For a moment my mind is blank. *Do we?* No. I know I haven't met her. I know I'd remember her. I shake my head. "People can say crazy things when they're sedated. I have no memory of meeting your girlfriend—"

He cuts me off. "Fiancée."

I'm irritated by his outburst and ignore it. "—but I did my residency in London, so she must have been a patient."

His frown deepens. "One problem. Quinn's never been out of the country."

The hairs on the back of my neck go up. She knew about the swimming, and she knew I was in London. How? I only got back to the States last summer and I've been dating Meg the entire time.

The guy is staring me down like a detective waiting for the perp to confess. I grit my teeth. I have no idea what's going on here, but their interpersonal drama is not my concern. "Like I said before, people say a lot of things when sedated. Anyhow, since this is the second episode in a week, I'd like her to remain overnight. I'll get her on the schedule for an MRI in the morning."

"She's not going to like that," he says. "She's going to want to get back to work."

I glance over at her. I've certainly encountered workaholic patients who insist they're too busy to get a test that could save their lives, but she looks so calm right now, so peaceful, that it's hard to imagine her being one of them. I think she's an architect—I must have seen it in her chart—and not to demean her profession, but it's not like the fate of the world rests in her hands. "She needs an MRI," I reply, my voice hard and unyielding. "So I'd suggest you make sure she gets it."

He looks taken aback, but I don't care. I just need to get the fuck out of this room.

I'M NOT much of a drinker, but I need a damn drink. I call Jace, a friend who was in med school with me and then wound up at the same hospital years later. His wife and Meg have become friends, which should make me happy, but instead makes me feel a little trapped.

I meet him at Clyde's, a few blocks from the hospital. It hasn't changed since we were in school—same wood bar, tightly packed tables, dim lighting. He casts a glance at the double scotch in my hand and grins. "Heard you and Meg are moving in together. Is that why we're hitting the heavy stuff before dinner?"

For a moment, the words don't even register, and then I laugh unhappily. "We aren't moving in together. She's going to stay at my place until she finds something else. But it appears you've heard otherwise."

"Maybe I misunderstood," he says with a smirk. A smirk

that says what we both know, which is that he didn't misunderstand anything at all. "So, what's up?"

I take a sip of my scotch and then set it down, staring straight ahead at the mirror behind the bar. "I'm going to tell you something that sounds crazy."

"I doubt it'll sound all that crazy to me," he replies. Jace is an obstetrician. Of all our friends, he tends to have the most bizarre stories—patients who've contracted sexually transmitted diseases from pets, a woman with a baby hanging between her legs by the umbilical cord as she exits the elevator.

"This may even top one of your stories," I tell him, hesitating before I start to recount what happened this afternoon. It's so surreal I'm starting to wonder if I've gotten the facts wrong. "I walk into a patient's room today. A new patient. She's sedated and her eyes are closed, but when I get to her bedside she seems to know who I am." I pause, taking another sip of scotch. "She knew that I swim every morning. She knew I was in London for my residency. And then she says something about how we were married."

Jace tips his head. "Come on, bro. She's fucking with you."

"How? Her eyes were closed. She'd never even met me."

He shrugs. "You had a million fangirls when you were swimming. She's probably some superfan and knew you'd be the one treating her."

I shake my head. "I really don't think so. She knew way too much, and she said it all in front of her fiancé, who was clearly unhappy about it, by the way."

"What other explanation is there? Unless you believe in psychics."

I stare at my drink. "Here's the thing: I've seen her before. I mean, not in real life. I've dreamed about her." Jace is looking at me like I'm crazy, which I can hardly fault him for. I wonder if this is how I look at my patients sometimes. God, I hope not. "I know this sounds nuts, but I swear I've dreamed about her. And in those dreams we're definitely together, and then here she is today telling me we're married. I mean, I know it's not true, but it's like I'm somehow not connecting to a huge part of my memory."

He raises a brow. "Well, no matter what has happened and no matter what you feel, she's still your patient. You can't act on it."

I scowl at him. "Of course I'm not going to *act* on it," I reply. "Give me a little credit. I'm just trying to figure out what the hell is going on."

He appears unimpressed by this situation, like it's an everyday occurrence to feel intensely attached to a patient you've never met, and then have her claim to be your wife. "Look, you probably had a dream about a girl who looks vaguely like her, nothing more. And then your mind drew these connecting lines where they don't exist. The real question is why you're doing it."

"What's that supposed to mean?"

He leans on the bar, swinging his stool to face me. "Don't you think the timing of it is a little suspect? Your fear of commitment is legendary, and now the minute you and Meg start moving in together, *bam*, you decide you've been dreaming about a patient you've never met. You're freaking out and looking for the escape hatch. Nothing more."

"We aren't moving in together," I mutter, swirling the ice in my empty glass.

"Fine, whatever," he says. "You and Meg are moving forward. Same thing."

Fuck. I want to be someone who can do that, move a relationship forward. I want it to be with Meg. But the fact that I'm now feeling so attached to a complete stranger tells me I'm definitely not ready to do so. And a piece of me wonders if Quinn Stewart is the reason why.

7

QUINN

Nick and I are in our favorite pub. It's a recent find, and though the drinks are overpriced, the music is amazing—it's mostly British bands, but they play a fair amount of older stuff from home. "Everlong" by Foo Fighters comes on and most of the bar starts singing. I've never given the lyrics much thought but as we sing-shout them tonight, I realize how perfect they are. It's a song about love, perhaps a slightly obsessive love, and meeting someone you waited for, maybe before you even knew he existed. I have goose bumps when it concludes.

"I've loved that song since I was a kid," Nick says, holding my eye. "But now I think it's my favorite."

"Mine too," I whisper.

A rotation of British bands starts up next. Arctic Monkeys, Florence and the Machine—music you can dance to. The crowd even manages to dance to Radiohead, though I'm not sure how. "Sofa Song" by The Kooks starts playing and he grabs my hand.

"Come on," he says.

"I don't dance," I whine, pulling back. "Remember? That whole

thing where I was so bad at it you had to propose just to make it stop?"

He laughs. "Yes, thank God I happened to have an engagement ring in my pocket that night."

On the dance floor he gets me in position and coaches me once more, with his "one, two, one, two, rock step". Then he spins me out and back to him. As I land against his chest I feel a shift inside me, and it's as if I'm in two places at once. Here with him now, but also in his childhood treehouse. The treehouse I've never laid eyes on but know intimately. I remember the creak of the floorboards under our feet, the slanted roof he had to duck to avoid. A chill creeps up from the base of my spine. "I feel like we've done this before," I tell him. The words are spoken at a near-whisper. "In your treehouse."

He pulls me closer, knowing this weird knowledge I have of us unsettles me. "All I care about is the fact that you're with me now," he says.

I smile, but my throat tightens at his words. Lately I've had this odd sense that our time is running out, and I have no idea why. "Distract me," I whisper.

With a flick of his wrist I'm spinning away from him, anchored by his hand, and then twirling back. When I look up again, his face is inches from mine. "Distracting enough?" he asks.

"Yeah." My shoulders settle and I smile up at him. "I think we're okay at this as long you're doing all the work."

A feral light is in his eyes that wasn't there a moment ago. "I'm more than happy to do all the work," he says, his voice low and raspy, "if that's what you're worried about."

Desire is like a fist, squeezing tight in my stomach.

"Take me home," I say, going on my toes to press my mouth to his. "You're at your most distracting there."

Jeff is gazing at me just as my eyes open. I swallow down that terrible disappointment I always feel when I discover him in Nick's place, closely followed by guilt over the disappointment. He forces a small smile but seems...irked. "I'll be right back," he says. "I'm supposed to let them know when you're up."

He returns with a nurse a minute later. She asks a number of relevant questions about my accident and my general health, as well as a number of ridiculous ones about drug use and suicidal thoughts. She says they'd like to keep me overnight, but when she asks to speak to Jeff privately, I feel a bubble of frustration pop inside me. I am not a child.

"Aren't there laws that prevent discussing my case with outsiders?" I snap.

Jeff's mouth falls open. "*Outsider?*" he demands. "I'm going to be your husband in a few weeks, remember?"

The nurse looks between the two of us. "I'll give you some time to chat," she says, backing from the room.

I know from Jeff's wounded expression that I need to backpedal, though I feel like doing anything but. "I didn't mean you were literally an outsider. But she's asking all these questions as if I passed out *on purpose*, and then she wants to talk to you alone? I don't need people discussing my case behind my back."

He takes the seat beside me and sits there, his jaw shifting. "Hon," he says quietly, not meeting my eye, "who's Nick?"

My stomach drops. God only knows what I said when I was sedated, but I can certainly imagine how bad it could have been, given how many hours I've spent dreaming about Nick and what we were *doing* during those hours. "I don't know anyone named Nick," I whisper. He doesn't believe me and I can't fault him—it sounds like a lie to me too.

"You asked for him that day, the first day you passed out," Jeff says, the words coming faster, carried by an undercurrent that is undeniably angry. "You didn't even fucking *remember* me, but you were asking for him. And then this doctor comes in tonight, a doctor named *Nick*, and you fucking hold his hand and tell him you're married to him."

My heart has climbed all the way to my throat. I have no idea what he's talking about, but I've kept a pretty tight lid on my words for years, and the possibility that I let the lid come loose is terrifying. I scramble back through my memory, but all I come up with is Caroline bringing me here and a needle going into my arm.

"I have no idea what you're talking about. It must be a coincidence." A bizarre, *humiliating* coincidence. There isn't a bone in my body that believes the Nick who apparently came into my room earlier is the same one I've been dreaming about. Nick is a common name, and, more importantly, it's just not possible. I press my hands to my heated face. "God. That's so embarrassing."

"It's more than that," Jeff says, rising, his fists clenched. "You *knew* him. You knew stuff about him you shouldn't have known unless you dated him."

I grow still. "Like what?"

"You knew that he goes swimming every day and you knew he did his residency in London."

It takes a moment to find my voice, and when I do it's a shadow of itself. "So are you saying I was *correct*?" I whisper.

"Yes," he spits. "You were correct. The guy seemed as freaked out as I was. Which really only leaves a few possibilities. You're stalking him or you've been seeing him."

For a moment, my jaw hangs open, stunned into speechlessness. The fact that the doctor is named Nick could be a coincidence. But the swimming? London? That seems like a few too many coincidences. And if it's him, if it's really him...is he a lot older? I was dreaming about Nick when I was toddler. Which means he'd be pushing sixty by now.

I take a deep breath. Jeff is standing there, waiting for a

response from me and growing paler every second I don't offer one. "Of course I'm not stalking him or seeing him," I finally say. "I don't even know who you're *talking* about."

He presses the base of his hand to his forehead. "Look. I just need the truth. Are you... Is there someone else?"

I blink once, twice, stalling for time. Looking for an answer that won't be a lie. On one hand, I know I've done nothing wrong. On the other, there is definitely someone else, someone who may, possibly, exist. I'm not a dishonest person, but this isn't a time when the whole truth will help anyone. "No. I'm not seeing anyone. Of course I'm not. And this whole thing is hard enough without you trying to make me feel bad about something crazy I said when I was sedated."

His eyes close, and his teeth grind against each other. "It's not just one crazy thing you said. It's several. Plus the hickey last week."

I bury my face in my hands. "It wasn't a hickey! It was just a weird bruise." I can't believe this is still a *thing*, that it's even a question. "My God, Jeff. Is our relationship really so fragile that this is the first conclusion you jump to?"

His shoulders sag. "No, it's not. I'm sorry. Okay? I'm sorry. You just knew a lot about him, and if it was a coincidence, it was a bizarre one."

I nod, restraining a thousand questions I would like to ask right now: *what did the doctor look like? Was he our age? Our parents' age? What was his last name? Did he know me too?* I'm imprisoned by my inability to ask, by the fact that any question at all will trigger suspicion.

There's a knock on the door and my head jerks toward it, my pulse racing. A nurse enters with dinner for me and I fall back into the pillow, struggling to hide my disappointment.

"You can have it," I tell Jeff. "I'm not hungry."

He shrugs and eats the bland meal without complaint, but that is just him—he takes what he's given, he's happy with it and he doesn't ask for more. Nick, at least as I've imagined him, is not like that. He's hungry—for knowledge and experience and competition. He's hungry, most of all, for me. I grow wet just picturing that ferocity of his, the restrained violence in him when he flips me on my back and crawls over me.

Jeff looks up from his tray. "You okay?" he asks. "You're all red."

Jesus. My fiancé is sitting five feet from me in the freaking hospital and I'm fantasizing about someone else. "It's hot in here," I say, waving a hand in front of my face.

My God. What if it's really Nick, my Nick, who walks in here tomorrow? What if he's twice my age now? What if it isn't him at all?

I find each of those possibilities equally terrifying.

~

JEFF HAS ALREADY LEFT for work by the time I wake the next day, and that's probably for the best, given that I've spent another night dreaming about Nick, and London.

Today I wake knowing it costs six pounds to take the Underground to Kensington. I know how to convert currency. I know that Covent Garden isn't a garden at all but an outdoor mall, and that *pants* over there actually means *underwear*. And it's different than things you'd learn from a book, or a show. I know these things, not as if I saw them, but as if I lived them.

I climb from the bed and grab the wedding binder out of my bag. I draw the shops at Covent Garden. I draw a rough map tracing the streets I would take to get to the Underground. The walk to University College. Then, grabbing my phone and ignoring the wealth of angry texts from Dee—who was expecting me back at work yesterday—I go online and type in *Harley Street, Marylebone.*

Before me a map appears, precisely matching my own.

I hit the button to see a photo of the street view and there, on the phone screen, is the exterior I drew a few days ago—Nick's flat, white stucco and brown brick. An arched portico, double doors. I even got the bushes in front right.

I slam the sketchbook shut, feeling like I'm going to be sick. *This isn't possible, this isn't possible. I'm seeing things, or this is some kind of extended dream.* I open my eyes and the photo is still there on my phone, assuring me it happened.

There's a light tap on the door, and Caroline walks in carrying a big bag in her left hand. "Hey, sicko," she says, oblivious to my freak-out. "You scared the piss out of everyone yesterday."

I force a smile. "Sorry. I hear I wasn't such a fun travel companion on the way home."

"No worries. The stories I'll have after your bachelorette will make up for everything, especially since I told Trevor to move ahead with hiring the prostitutes."

I laugh weakly and she swings the bag she's carrying onto the bed. "I knew you'd be too freaked out about Dee's wrath to go home to change, so I brought you toiletries and clothes." She reaches inside it and hands me a smaller bag from Blue Mercury. "Plus a few other necessities."

I peek inside: Bobbi Brown eyeliner, mascara, and gloss. "I love you so much."

"More than Jeff?"

"Obviously. All he's ever given me was this dumb ring." I smile as I say it, but Caroline's known me way too long not to pick up when something's amiss.

"What's up?" she asks. "I mean, aside from the fact that there's obviously something wrong with your brain, that is."

I bite my lip. I've had a long history of hiding my strangeness from people, even her. I know all too well it's something even those who love me most are unable to accept. But I can't keep dealing with this on my own. Sighing, I hand her the sketchpad.

"Look," I whisper.

Her brow furrows. "Uh...it's a nice drawing? But you've always been amazing at drawing buildings."

"It's London. Harley Street, in Marylebone. I keep dreaming about it, but I've never even been there. And you know what? Covent Garden. I thought it was an actual garden, but it's not. It's, like, an outdoor mall."

"Everyone knows it's a mall."

"I didn't. But now I know every store..." I trail off, frustrated by the impossibility of all this. Tears fill my eyes. "I know how to convert the currency. I know how to take their subway from Marylebone to Kensington. I'm seeing my life as if my father never died and it went on as I'd planned it. I'm in London, getting my master's in architecture. I don't remember my classes but I even wake remembering things I learned in them."

She sets the drawings aside and leans back in her chair. "You probably saw this stuff on the Travel Channel. God only knows how much knowledge we've all got stored in our brains."

"That's not all, though." My throat tightens. What remains is, by far, the worst part. The part I'm not sure I should say aloud, even to my best friend. "There's a guy."

Her eyes light up. "*Now* it's getting interesting. What guy?"

"Nick. He's a resident there, going into cardiology. We're married. And insanely in love. I can't even describe it. I had dreams about him when I was little, and they started up again after I passed out last week. But they're not like dreams. It's more like I'm living it all for the first time. I wake up and my brain is full of what I didn't know the day before." I don't tell her my doctor here may be the same guy. I think I'm scared to say it aloud, worried I'll jinx it.

She frowns. "Look, I don't want you to accuse me of being down on Jeff, because that's really not what this is, but... it kind of sounds like you invented the guy who represents how you *want* to feel. He's not real but maybe it's your subconscious' way of suggesting you think twice."

I shake my head vehemently. "But it's *not* how I want to feel. At all. I just need it to stop."

Her eyes go wide. "Why the hell wouldn't you want to feel like that? Everyone wants to feel what you're describing."

I don't, but I can't entirely say why that's the case. I just sense trouble. There's something dark inside me, something I buried so deep I can mostly forget it's there. But it's been whispering to me again of late, ever since I started remembering Nick. And the terror of hearing it far exceeds the pull of wanting something more.

Not that I can say any of this to her. There's a limit to the amount of crazy you can share in one day, even with your best friend.

"Because I already have exactly what I want. If this is my subconscious, I need a doctor who can make her shut up."

Caroline glances at me. "Or maybe one who can tell you why you'd choose to be less happy than you could be."

"You're saying I need a shrink?"

She comes to my end of the bed and wraps an arm around me. "Maybe. Or we just wait and see if Trevor has a better plan," she says with a grin. "Warning: it may involve prostitutes."

There are still tears in my eyes, but I manage to laugh. "In that case, let's keep this between ourselves."

~

CAROLINE HEADS OUT TO WORK, actually looking forward to her day. There are many times I envy her, and this is one of them. She's at a point in her career where she is mostly calling the shots. If she wants to leave in the middle of the day, she leaves.

If she wants to jet off on a safari with an Australian rugby player she met at a bar, she just takes off. It makes me think, once again, of returning to school. But as Jeff always reminds me, the money would be astronomical. It would take me five years, if not longer, before I had the education I need to start making money again, and all the while we'd be relying on *Jeff's* income, which can't exactly be relied upon. He argues that it's impractical, and what can I really say in my defense? He's absolutely right.

A nurse walks in moments after Caroline has left. "How are you feeling today?" she asks. "I have the breakfast menu if you'd like to order."

"No thanks," I reply. I still can't eat. Until I see who Nick is, I won't be able to hold down a single bite. "Will I...be talking to the doctor today?"

She nods. "Yes, the attendings are meeting with the residents right now, but one of them will be in later."

One of them. So even if Nick is here, it might not be him I see.

She mistakes my expression for impatience. "It looks like your friend brought you some stuff if you want to clean up. That way you'll be ready to leave as soon as possible today."

I grab the bag Caroline brought and hop into the shower. When I emerge, I'm clean and dressed in far nicer clothes than any I actually own—designer jeans, a James Perse T-shirt that hugs my curves like it was made for me. Yes, it would be nice to live like Caroline once in a while.

I shove yesterday's dirty clothes into the bag and have just finished tidying up when there's a knock on the door.

Then Nick, *my* Nick, walks into the room.

8

NICK

I've thought about nothing but Quinn all morning. I guess I just forgot she might not be quite as ready for our meeting as I am. She sees me and those stormy green-gray eyes open wide, her whole body swaying toward the wall like a tree in high winds. I lunge forward to catch her, and find I am standing far too close, my hands on her arms. But there's a part of me right now that doesn't care. It's not about her looks, though God knows her looks alone would be enough. This is so much more than that. Something about her just compels me to move closer. *She smells exactly like I remember*, I think, before I correct myself. *You can't possibly remember what she smells like. You just met her yesterday for Christ's sake.*

"I'm okay," she says weakly, eyes focused on my chest.

She lets me lead her to the bed, but perches on its edge, a captive preparing for escape. "This cannot be happening," she whispers. She sounds near tears. "You're real. I just...I don't know how this is possible."

There isn't a hint of guile on her face, so I dismiss Jace's theory that she's fucking with me somehow. But I don't really have a theory to take its place. "I'm trying to make sense of this too," I explain. "We must have met before."

She stares at me. Her mouth is like a peony just before it bursts open, full and round. I want to press my thumb to its center. "I really don't think that's possible."

"You've somehow managed to learn a lot about me," I say quietly. "There has to be an explanation for it. When I checked in on you last night, you knew that I swim. You knew where I did my residency."

Her hand shakes as she pushes the hair back from her face. "That barely scratches the surface of what I know." There's something grave in her voice. An unnerving certainty.

"What do you mean?"

She looks at me for a long moment, searching for something she doesn't seem to find. "You like bananas but won't eat anything banana-flavored," she finally says when I remain silent. "You gave up your shot at the Olympics to go to med school, but every morning you still swim because it clears your head. You had a flat in Marylebone during your residency. On Harley Street."

I blink. "How—"

"Your favorite bar in London was the Golden Eagle. We were broke, but on special occasions you'd order a single malt scotch. You wanted to be a cardiologist because your dad has this heart problem, and it always bothered you that no one could fix it completely. But now you're a neurologist, which makes no sense. I was the only person you ever knew who even needed a neurologist."

I squeeze my eyes shut. It is impossible that she knows these things. If she were to interview every person I'd ever known, she might be able to gather most of this, but not all of it. Meg knows maybe half, at best. I open my eyes to find her watching me again. She glances away, and then reaches for a binder beside her.

"Since I've already completely creeped you out, look at this." She opens the binder and pushes it into my hands. A drawing. Goose bumps crawl across my neck when I realize what it is. She's drawn my flat in London. The *interior* of my flat. I push against my temples, trying to make sense of this. Nothing feels real, almost as if I'm asleep and will wake up at any moment pondering the bizarre dream I just had about a patient. Because it would be easy enough for her to find my old address with a little sleuth work, but how the fuck does she know what it looked like *inside*, down to the cow-shaped kettle my mother sent me as a joke? "How the hell do you know what the *inside* of my flat looked like?"

"I have no idea," she says. She is frowning, lips pressed tight. She seems as troubled by this as I am, so I'm inclined to believe her. At the very least I think *she* believes she's telling the truth. But there has got to be an explanation. I believe in science. I do not believe in reincarnation, ghosts, fairies, vampires, or psychics. I don't even believe in God, for that matter, and I think miracles are just another name for things we don't yet understand. With enough investigation, I can *make* this make sense.

"Okay, I'll play along. How did we meet?" I ask.

She winces. "Don't say you'll *play along*, like this is something I want to be part of," she says. Her tone pleads with me more than it demands. "I'm engaged. Do you really think I want to fall asleep every night and dream about another man?"

"I'm sorry. I phrased that poorly. In your dream that told you all this," I say, lifting the sketch, "how did we meet?"

She toys with the hem of her shirt. "I went to the hospital, right after I arrived in London. I had a migraine because I'd left my meds at home. And you came to discharge me."

"And when would this have been?"

Her teeth sink into her lower lip. My gaze flickers to that peony mouth again. "Late August, probably four years ago. You wanted to watch the World Rowing Championship because you had a friend in it. Matt, I think?"

I gawk at her, frozen aside from my heart, which is thumping so hard it would be impossible to miss. How? How could she possibly know this? Matt Langois was a friend from undergrad. He rowed for the US, and I watched it whenever I had time. "This can't be happening," I murmur. "This has got to be...I'm not accusing you of anything, but someone is fucking with us."

She sighs heavily. "*How?* It's not like someone could climb into my head and make me dream all this up."

I have no answer to that, but it reminds me of the real reason I'm here. I glance at my watch. "Let's table all this for now. I've got you scheduled for an MRI in five minutes."

She stiffens. "Is it necessary?"

"There's nothing to be scared of—you're not claustrophobic, right?"

She inhales and sets her shoulders. "No. I just don't...never mind. It's fine. What are you looking for?"

"There are a couple of things that could be going on, but this is just a precaution. In all likelihood, everything will come back completely fine."

I rise but she does not. "What kind of things?"

"A bleed, a cyst, a tumor. Really, it's probably nothing."

She looks worried. I reach out to grab her hand, and I'm an inch from hers when I realize what I'm doing and jerk it back. *What the hell is going on here?* I've never tried to hold a patient's hand in my life. It's as if it was a reflex.

I'm beginning to wonder if I need an MRI too.

9

QUINN

Nick Reilly exists.

I sit here on the edge of the bed, my mind trying to grasp it all, but the reality of him is too large to be held in one place and made logical.

Nick, in my dreams, was beautiful. In real life, however, he's so much more. He's vital and male in a way I didn't entirely grasp until now. The bump where his nose was broken, the tiny hint of a scar just to its left from a fist fight with his brother—they don't mar the perfection of his face, they emphasize it. They roughen him up just the right amount, make him *hot* rather than lovely. Nick without that scar, without the small asymmetry, would be a face for photographers, for ad campaigns. Nick with those things becomes someone you want to have pin you to the nearest available surface.

Which I remember him doing so, so many times. But to him, I'm simply a new patient. Potentially one who's been stalking him.

It's me, some voice inside my head whispers to him. *Remem-*

ber? Remember our flat? Remember the way I'd wait for you to slide into bed and wrap yourself around me? Do you remember the first time you told me you loved me? The night you proposed?

That same part of me cries out for him, wants to hold him tighter than I've ever held anyone, wants to breathe in his smell of soap and chlorine and skin and just remain there.

Thank God the rational piece prevails. The part that knows this is not real life and remembers I'm in love with someone else. *Just because you dreamed about him doesn't mean it ever happened*, the rational piece warns. *It doesn't make him yours.*

He asks how I know the things I do, and I proceed to recite more of them, my stomach sinking at the wary look on his face. Perhaps he'd appear relaxed to a casual onlooker, but I know better somehow. He's restraining himself. Beneath that oxford his arms are taut, braced...against me? I'm not sure. God, I want so badly to press my mouth to that line between his brows, let it fall to the curve of his upper lip. As if I really need to do one more thing to ensure he sends me for a psych consult.

Our bizarre conversation comes to an abrupt end when he suddenly remembers the MRI, the haze in his eyes clearing. We walk down a long hall, and then he uses his badge to open the doors to another area. I'm 5'7", but next to him, I feel diminutive. His head bows just to speak to me. "So, you dreamed we met and what else?"

I realize he's humoring me. *Of course* he is—it's not as if he thinks any of it is true. Even *I* don't think it's true, so why would he? "It's a lot of just...normal stuff. Hanging out...dating stuff."

"That's it?" he teases. "I must have been pretty boring, if that's all you've got." It's a playful side of him, one I've seen in dreams but not in real life until now. He's trying to take my mind off the MRI.

"We went to Paris for our honey—" I trail off. *God. I cannot believe I just said that out loud.*

He stops. "You're telling me you dreamed about our *honeymoon*?"

I should be too upset by what this MRI might uncover to be capable of humiliation right now, but I'm not. I feel the heat in my face and there is no way to stop it. "No comment."

He raises a brow, holding the elevator door open and following me in. "Oh, you're not getting off that easily. If we had a honeymoon in Paris, I need to hear all about it. What did we do?"

I roll my eyes, trying hard not to smile. "It was December and cold as hell, and we were there on our *honeymoon*. What do you think we did?"

He laughs. "Wow. Any other glamorous trips where we never left the hotel?"

I glance up at him as we arrive at our floor. "Not really. Well, I guess we went to the lake, if that counts."

The elevator door opens, but he doesn't move. "What lake?"

I pause, puzzled by the sudden change in him. There is no longer anything playful about his tone. "I have no idea. It's kind of like the lake where I'm getting married. There's a dock and a big, white house with a deck, and I'm on this boat I can't sail, while you watch me go."

The elevator doors have shut again, and he sags against the wall. His skin looks slightly green under the fluorescent lights.

"Where are you getting married?" he asks.

I hear dread in his voice. For some reason it makes me dread answering him. "Lake Hester? It's outside—"

"Annapolis," he whispers. He leans his head against the wall and closes his eyes. "My parents have a place there. Their weekend house. I think you're describing it."

He can't even look at me. I try to put myself in his shoes—some random patient reciting facts from his life, describing the interior of his flat and his parents' vacation home. I'd have picked up the emergency phone long before now if I were him.

"I'm not stalking you," I say quietly. "I understand why you'd be freaked out, but I swear to God I've never even looked up your name."

"I don't think you're stalking me."

"Then why—"

"I've had that dream too," he says. "About you."

I blink. I've heard him but his words just...don't make sense. This is *my* problem, my messed-up brain. If this is his idea of a joke I don't find it amusing. "*What?*"

He swallows. "I thought...when I saw you here that my mind was playing tricks on me. But I've had that precise dream. You're standing up on the Sunfish, and then I swim out to get you."

I feel lightheaded again and lean against the wall of the elevator, the same way he did just a moment before. *How can we share the same memory of something we both know never happened?* I remember seeing him on the dock, I remember the way he dove into the water and emerged moments later, seal-sleek, grinning. There have been other things in the past, other times my brain somehow misfired. But I've never had someone else's brain misfire alongside mine.

He steps closer, his hands on my arms. "Are you okay?"

I nod. My voice is muted, hoarse. "I just need this to make sense."

"Me too," he says, pressing the button to open the elevator's door. "And I'm not sure a brain scan is going to accomplish that."

~

THROUGHOUT THE EXAM, I keep my body still, but my mind won't stop racing. What was that look he gave me when he left? The part of me that wants to romanticize all this might call it *longing*. And God knows I didn't want him to leave, but what I really *need* is not to feel anything for him at all. I'm hard-pressed to imagine we will ever solve this, but I don't need it solved, I just need it to stop. I can't keep having these dreams anymore.

When I return to my room, the nurse says she'll get my paperwork together so I can leave. "I'd like to see Dr. Reilly before I go."

"I don't know what his schedule is like today. You may have to book a follow-up with him if you need more information."

My nails dig into my palms. "No. I need to see him today. I'll wait if I have to."

"Yes, all the female patients want to see Dr. Reilly again," she says with a smirk. "But he's a very busy man. I'll see what I can do."

She thinks I'm trying to fuel a crush, when I'm really trying to end one.

My stomach growls loud enough for us both to hear. "There's a room at the end of the hall with snacks," she says. "You can grab something while I get your discharge papers ready."

As it turns out, the only snacks I find are graham crackers and juice, but I'm hungry enough I don't even mind. I reach for a cranberry juice, peeling off the foil and drinking it before I've even closed the refrigerator door.

"You have to shut the door," says a small voice. I look over my shoulder to find a little girl with no hair, pulling an IV behind her. "If you don't, an alarm will go off."

"Want one?" I offer.

She frowns. "I'm not allowed until my test is done." I look longingly at the cranberry juices stacked high in the fridge and shut the door. I can't sit here and drink anything else in front of her.

"So, are you here all day?" I ask.

She drops her eyes. "I kind of live here. When I ask my

mommy if we are going home again, she smiles and cries at the same time."

She scans my face, searching for some kind of answer there. I swallow down the lump in my throat. "Do you miss being home?"

She nods. "And I miss being outside. We used to go get cupcakes. They have cupcakes here, but not good ones."

"What kind of cupcakes did you get?"

"Red velvet with the white icing that isn't just white."

"What about this person?" I ask, pointing to the cartoon character on the T-shirt that covers her hospital gown. "If I come back with a cupcake for you, should I bring one for her too?"

She giggles. "That's Raven. She doesn't eat cupcakes."

"Doesn't eat *cupcakes*?" I ask, feigning horror. "That's crazy talk."

"I should have known Darcy would find you," says a voice. I look up and Nick is standing there in all his broad-shouldered glory, crooked smile and dimple on full blast.

My heart flutters and begins beating hard. All my good intentions fade away in his presence—I just want to stay right here and follow him wherever he goes. "Darcy was informing me that Raven does not eat cupcakes. I thought *everyone* ate cupcakes."

"She's *pretend*," says Darcy, dragging out the word and giggling at the same time.

Nick grins at her. "You, Miss Darcy, need to get to your room so they can get you ready for your test. And you, Miss Quinn, need to get to your room so we can go over your discharge paperwork."

I wave at Darcy before she turns away. "Later, Raven. Later, Cupcake Girl." Her smile is so wide it hurts. A patient like that must break Nick's heart. She's breaking mine and I just met her.

When I look up, Nick is watching me in that quiet way of

his. I think if I could peek in his head I'd find a thousand words he'll never give voice to. "So, it looks like you're ready to leave?"

I want to run my hand over the rasp of his jaw, pull his head low enough that I can press my mouth to his forehead. Exactly the sort of thought that needs to stop. "I was wondering if there is something you can give me to stop the dreams? Maybe some kind of sleeping pill?"

He frowns. "There's a drug that could help, but one of the primary side effects is headaches. I'm not sure it's a good idea, under the circumstances."

"I'll risk it," I say quickly. "I need these dreams to stop."

He cocks his head to the side. "Why? You were in so much pain yesterday you had to be sedated, and it sounds like these dreams aren't even bad."

I'm frustrated more with myself than with him, though it probably doesn't come across that way. "Because there's no point. Do you actually think we're going to figure out why this is happening?"

"Probably not, but it's possible. I keep thinking there's some obvious explanation we are both missing."

"There isn't," I reply firmly. "And in the meantime, I have a real life, and these dreams are making it *seem* like a life I don't want. I would rather not know any of this than be unhappy with what I have."

His teeth sink into his lower lip, an action that makes my stomach clench in an unfamiliar way. Both pleasant and unpleasant at the same time. "Maybe your dreams are saying you're already unhappy with what you have."

I look away from him. It's sort of what Caroline said too. "Then I'd like them to stop telling me that."

He sighs. "We'll need to wait on the results before I prescribe anything. I assume you're heading home. I can call you there with results when they're in."

I shake my head. "I've got to get to work. We go to print next week. I've lost way too much time as it is."

"Print?" he asks, frowning. "Aren't you an architect?"

I still. "What made you think that?"

"I'm not sure," he says slowly. "I thought I saw it in your file. But...you aren't? I could have sworn..."

The room grows silent. My voice is a whisper when I finally speak. "I was an architecture major in college, but my father died after my sophomore year and I had to move home where it wasn't an option. But...in my head, when we were in London, that's what I was studying. I was there getting a graduate degree."

The weirdness of it rests between us. "I guess," he says with a faltering smile, "you're not the only stalker of the two of us, then."

~

I WALK INTO THE OFFICE, hoping to escape Dee. No luck—she's just leaving as I walk in. She holds the door but remains still, blocking my path. "We are seriously behind," she says, jaw clenched. "Please try to get caught up. I need proofs before you leave today."

A torrent of words I won't say to her rises in my throat: *we've worked together for six freaking years. You know I was just hospitalized and you know I never take sick leave. How dare you act put upon right now?*

I clench my fists and slide past her into the office. We need this job. I could leave and wind up with half the pay and a boss who's just as awful. And then my inheritance, the one I've refused to touch for the past seven years, will be gone as soon as Jeff loses his job, frittered away on the mortgage and groceries and I'll have nothing to show for it.

The layout is already open on my Mac and has obviously

been tinkered with by someone who has no knowledge of Photoshop. Only Dee would dare, and she's managed to create twice as much work for me as I'd have had otherwise. I let my head sink back against my chair, staring up at the exposed ceiling, at the gleaming metal of heating ducts and maze of white pipes, wondering how I will feel about Dee and this job if Nick calls with bad news.

Will I be glad I sucked it up all these years, managed to keep us afloat all the times when Jeff was out of work? Or will I feel like this place stole six years of my life?

Except, the magazine didn't steal those years. I stole them from myself. I'm the one who listened when my mom begged me to stay at home after my father died. I'm the one who let Jeff persuade me it would be foolish to go back to school for architecture. I'm the one who chose to remain at this desk for so long.

I never fought for a single thing I wanted, and now it might be too late.

The real question, however, is what I will do if it isn't.

~

It's late in the afternoon when I finally hear from the hospital. I'm oddly disappointed that it's one of the nurses calling, rather than Nick. "Dr. Reilly is wondering if you can come in tomorrow for another MRI," she says.

I lay my pen down. "Another one? Was there a problem?"

"I doubt it," she says breezily. "It's a different kind of MRI. It may be that the other one wasn't clear."

I convince myself it doesn't mean anything. It's not until much later, when Jeff and I are having dinner and he asks about the test, that I actually start to worry.

"So what is it again that the hospital wants you to do tomorrow?" he asks.

I shrug as I help myself to seconds, which is something I never do. Poor Jeff probably made extra for his lunch tomorrow and I'm demolishing it, but I've had nothing to eat since that juice this morning. "Some other kind of MRI. They didn't really explain."

There's a crease between his eyebrows. "Do you think it means anything?"

I hesitate, will away the nervous flutter in my chest. "It doesn't sound like it. It sounds like they used the wrong kind of test. Why? Do *you* think it means anything?"

Jeff frowns. "That guy barely looked old enough to be out of med school, so I wouldn't be at all surprised to learn he ordered the wrong test. You need to switch doctors."

I set down my fork, but it remains in my grip, stiffly held. I want to argue in Nick's defense, but it would be poorly received, given what happened in the hospital last night. "I don't know that he ordered the wrong test," I reply, the words spoken carefully. "I'm just saying it might be what happened."

"Well, if this turns out to be something, I still think you should switch."

No. My shoulders are rigid and it takes everything in my power not to snap at him. His concerns have nothing to do with Nick's professional abilities. He's just jealous, and as much as it pisses me off...he's more right than he knows. For my own sanity, for the health of our future together, Nick Reilly is the last person I should be spending time with.

10

QUINN

Nick creeps into the flat, trying hard not to wake me. He always does this, on the nights he works late, but I'm a light sleeper and there are little things that give him away long before he sets foot in the room: the clink of keys against a counter, a coat falling against a chair. He keeps a spare toothbrush at the kitchen sink for nights like this, just so the bathroom light won't wake me.

"I'm up," I tell him when he comes into the bedroom, feeling around in the darkness for the dresser before he stubs his toe on it again.

"Sorry," he says. He pulls off his scrubs and slips beneath the sheets, wrapping cold arms around me, pulling the covers up to my chin. "I tried to be quiet."

"I was already awake." I scoot until I'm pressed tight to his chest. His bare skin, his smell, the weight of his arm—they're all I need in the entire world right now. "I had the weirdest dream and woke up all upset."

His calloused hand squeezes my arm lightly in sympathy. "What dream?"

My legs stretch, tangle with his. "We were together but we were teenagers, I think? And we were trying to elope."

His low laugh brushes my ear. "That does sound terrifying. I'm bad enough now. A teenage Nick wouldn't have left you alone for a minute."

I roll his way, wishing I could laugh with him but I can't yet. It all still feels so real. "We were at this gas station and I called home to tell my mother what we were doing and you were inside, in line. And I started crying because I was never going to see you again. I just knew somehow that it was all over, and I was going to die. And then I woke up."

I can't get it out of my head—the sight of him in the convenience store, smiling at me from his place in line, while I stood there panicked, certain it was over. The distress I feel in dreams normally fades immediately. This one though—it remains unchanged.

His lips press to the top of my head. "Hon, it doesn't require a degree to figure that one out. Call your mom. She's probably going to be less upset with you for getting married than she is that you waited so long to tell her. And you're an adult. It's not like she can ground you and lock you in your room."

I nod, but I'm not so sure he's right.

~

I WAKE MISSING NICK. I close my eyes and can almost imagine the way he fit against me, long arms pulling me tight. The mint from his toothpaste, a hint of chlorine as I buried my face into his chest. Jeff and I don't cuddle like that, and he isn't someone I share my worries with—I suppose because I'm too busy shouldering his. I leaned on Nick in that dream, physically and mentally, and it's something I didn't know I was missing until this morning. My future with Jeff contains wonderful things: a house, kids, a trip to the Jersey shore every summer. But right now I'm aching for what my future won't contain instead.

I dress and head to the hospital. My inappropriate eagerness to see Nick outweighs my dread of what he might say—I've almost convinced myself that the need for another MRI is meaningless anyway.

I've just signed in when his head pops around the corner. Like an idiot, like a teen with a crush, I begin blushing. It's so strange to see him now, to be a stranger to him, when in my head, we were together an hour ago. I can still remember him sliding against me, bare aside from his boxers.

I blush harder. I remember removing those boxers too.

"Come on back," he says, holding the door so I can walk past. We go to his office, which is larger than I'd have anticipated. His diplomas are on the wall and there are photos too. I keep my eyes focused straight ahead, scared of what I'll discover if I look too closely. It's funny it never occurred to me, until this moment, that he might not be single. My gaze shifts to his ring finger. It's bare. My shoulders settle again.

He perches on the edge of the desk, long legs eating up the distance between us. "I'm sorry we had to ask you to come back in. How do you feel today?"

"Great," I reply, "but I'm wondering why I need another test."

He nods, his hands wrapping around the edge of the desk. "I don't want you to panic when I tell you this, but we found something on your scans yesterday."

Found something. I freeze, suddenly aware of my heart, pounding louder than normal, so loud I'm surprised he can't hear it too.

He rises, flipping on a light board just to our left. What I presume is an image of my brain hangs there. I'm oddly relieved to see it looks normal, as if I thought it might be half a human brain and half something wildly improbable, like antennae or another set of teeth. "This," he says, pointing at a black dot in its center, "is what we found. It's so small I'm not even sure it's what's caused your seizures. Something of that size, in that location, should not be symptomatic."

"What is it?" I whisper.

He takes the seat beside me. His eyes are the softest gray-blue, like the wings of a dove. "It appears to be a tumor."

Ice fills my lungs, making a deep breath impossible. "A tumor."

His hand reaches out, and for a moment I'm certain it's going to grab mine. But just like yesterday, he stops himself. "The majority of brain tumors are benign, so I really don't want you stressing about this just yet. You very well could have had this for your entire life."

"And if mine isn't benign? What then?"

He nods, his eyes flickering away. "Operating in this area of the brain is impossible. But again, it could very well be nothing. We need to do another imaging test—similar to what we've already done, but this time looking at the metabolic activity around the tumor. It should help us determine the type of tumor it is and how likely it is to grow."

My mouth is dry. I nod, feeling...nothing. Nothing at all. I dig my nails into my palms but it barely registers.

"Are you okay?" he asks.

"I don't know." What I want more than anything is to dislodge the sense that all of this can't really be happening. I'm only twenty-eight. I'm about to get married. My life is just starting, and out of nowhere I'm missing him and wanting what I've never wanted, and I may be looking at the end of all of it. I don't know how to put this into words. "My life was completely normal a week ago," I finally say.

"Let me take you down to imaging," he says, rising. "Your life may still be completely normal."

This time he sets me up for the exam himself, helping me

onto the table, getting everything into position. He seems to hesitate when it's time to leave. "It's going to be fine," he says.

"You know, even if the tumor is nothing, I'm still having bizarre dreams about someone I don't know and discovering they're accurate."

His smile is soft. "Hey," he says, "I'm not a bad guy. There are worse people to dream about. Unless I'm a jerk. If I am, then your dreams are completely fictitious."

"You weren't a jerk."

"Good." His dimple appears, and I have a sudden memory of him in that convenience store smiling at me through the glass, unaware that my heart was breaking, that we were going to be separated. And as I slide into the MRI to check on my inoperable brain tumor, I can't help but feel history seems to be repeating.

11

NICK

Meg and I both have an hour free. She wants to go out to lunch and is not happy when I tell her I want to swim instead.

"*Again?*" she asks. "You already worked out."

I blow out a breath. I am way too keyed up to sit with her for an hour. "It's just been one of those days." One of those days when I'm waiting for a report from radiology that won't fucking arrive. One of those days when I'm going to put a fist through a wall if I hear, *again*, that it's "on the way." And one of those days when I can't stop thinking about a patient, can't stop picturing her...even though we are both with other people, and, as my patient, she'd be off-limits even if we weren't.

I get over to the pool and dive in without preamble, with no routine in mind. I just need to push, to swim until I'm too exhausted to think about this anymore. I've always hated impossible questions. Medical journals produced nothing helpful, not that I expected them to. There's no answer to what's going on with me and Quinn, but I can't stop pushing and prodding at it, as if something completely obvious will present itself. It spins in my brain until I'm sick of thinking. And thus the need for this swim, which doesn't seem to be doing a damn bit of good.

I thought I was happy with Meg. Maybe it wasn't everything I'd ever wanted from a relationship, but it felt like enough... certainly far more than my brother will ever get to experience. Except spending a morning with Quinn was like being exposed to sunlight after an entire lifetime beneath fluorescent lights. I'm not sure, now, that I can be happy with less.

I HUSTLE back to the hospital with my hair still wet, stopping by Darcy's room on the way. I never see her without thinking about what could have been. If her mother had brought her in when Darcy's headaches first started, we could have saved her. As much as this bothers me, it's her mom who's being destroyed by the knowledge, and it wasn't even her fault. When the pediatrician dismissed her concerns, she listened to him. God, I wish she hadn't. Doctors know a lot less than they want you to believe. Especially that one.

Darcy is in bed when I get to the room, with her mom curled up beside her. She smiles wide, more animated than usual, and lifts a massive cupcake in the air. "Look what Quinn sent me!" she says.

Darcy's mother reaches behind her to a massive box from Sprinkles, where ten of twelve cupcakes remain. "Want one?" she asks. "Darcy's new friend sent six for Darcy and six for Raven, so I feel like we may have more than we need."

Something expands inside my chest. Who learns she has a brain tumor and manages to think about a little girl she just met instead? I decline and head straight to radiology, ready to unleash hell if the results aren't in. Fortunately, that's not necessary. I rip the radiologist's report from the envelope before I've even gotten to my office.

~

SHE ANSWERS on the first ring.

"It's Nick." I pause. "Nick Reilly."

"Hi Ni— Dr. Reilly."

"You've gone on a honeymoon with me, so I feel like we ought to at least be on a first-name basis."

She laughs. The sound is husky, intimate. I have to reach down and adjust myself, which is not exactly typical when calling a patient about her brain tumor. "I'm going to assume," she says, "that you wouldn't be making jokes if I only had a month to live."

This is true, although since I appear to be incapable of behaving normally around her I couldn't say for sure. "It's all good news. We don't see signs of increased blood flow to the area, which indicates it is not growing. It's possible it's been there forever." I've never been so relieved by a scan in my life.

"So I'm okay?" she asks. "Aside from the bizarre knowledge of your personal history, that is."

I grin and lean back in my chair. "Aside from that, I think so. We'll still need to keep an eye on it, but as long as you don't have any more incidents, a follow-up MRI in six months will be fine."

Except, in six months, she could already be married to that tool I met in her room the other night. The thought makes me queasy.

"So if the scan looked okay, does that mean you can call something in for me, to stop the dreams?"

Why does a part of me want to tell her *no*? I sigh heavily.

"We've got your pharmacy on file. I'll call it in and check with you tomorrow to see how it worked."

It takes a minute for us to actually hang up the phone. She seems as reluctant as I am to end the call. And I like her reluctance way, way too much.

12

QUINN

I'm fine. I'm going to live. It's a relief...so I'm not sure why I feel vaguely disappointed when Nick hangs up. I pick up the phone to call my mother afterward but put it down again. She doesn't know about the brain tumor because I didn't want to worry her until I knew more, and I suppose there's no reason to tell her now. Plus, she's worked herself up into a fever over the fact that I've now passed out at the inn twice—which certainly doesn't bode well for the wedding—and I don't feel like listening to any more of her theories about why it's happening. No pesticide or allergy has ever caused the problem I'm currently having. I concocted some theory about the sunlight from the lake affecting my pineal gland, and she's gotten the inn to agree to let us place the tent in front of the main building rather than beside it, so I can avoid looking at the house if necessary.

I pick up the meds on the way to the Metro, bouncing them from one hand to the other during the long ride home. I don't actually *want* to take them. I've seen myself falling in love with

Nick, marrying him. It's like a really engrossing TV show that's just ended on a cliffhanger, and I'm desperate to know what comes next. Except, with each of these dreams, I fall a little harder for him, and that is so much more dangerous now that I know he exists.

Jeff's in the yard when I get home, playing football with Isaac, this teenager who lives a few houses down from us. He's in his element right now, and the sight of it is bittersweet. It's who he was meant to be—a football coach, a big fish in a small pond—and I took it from him by moving here. My friends are less forgiving than I am of his job woes, but that's because they didn't know him back when he was succeeding. They'll never understand how much he gave up to be with me.

My father saw that quality in Jeff. Knew he would always be there, loyal and steadfast in his devotion, willing to follow me wherever I went. I trusted my father's views implicitly, and for good reason—I wasn't the only one of us who sometimes knew things I should not. My father knew I was allergic to shellfish before I'd ever had it. He knew Matisse was my favorite artist before I'd ever set foot in a gallery. So sometimes I wonder if he knew things about my future that I did not, and wanted Jeff to be there by my side when they happened.

I cross the street and Jeff smiles over his shoulder, throwing one last pass to Isaac before following me inside.

"That kid has an amazing spiral," he says. "He's fast too. I could totally have him ready for JV if his mom would just agree."

We make dinner while he continues to tell me Isaac's strengths, and bitches about Isaac's mom's fear of concussions. *That stupid Will Smith movie made everyone paranoid. You know what sport has the most injuries? Cheerleading.*

I was worried my news about the brain tumor would ruin our evening, but the whole time we're cooking he never asks once about the MRI. I try not to let it bother me.

Over dinner he complains about the new asshole at corporate and some policy on travel reimbursement I'm unable to care about. I wait for him to finish his diatribe, resentment churning in my stomach, but when he's done with that he moves on to another topic entirely.

"We need to go back to that development in Manassas," he says, oblivious to my unhappiness. "The agent called today and said the model is open."

I'm already in a bad mood, so the suggestion hits me poorly. "I told you I don't want to live in Manassas. It would take me two hours to get into work."

He shrugs. "Well, it's not like you *have* to work in D.C.," he says. "You can get a job anywhere."

I grind my teeth. I go out of my way not to remind him about his employment history, but the fact that he's managed to stay at his current job for four months doesn't mean my job is suddenly irrelevant. "*Washington Insider* pays me twice what anyone else will," I remind him. "And there have been months when we've needed every penny of it to pay our bills."

"I'm sorry," he says. His shoulders sag and I immediately want to take it back. "I know it's been rough going for a while. But it's not like we're completely screwed if one of us is out of work. You've never even touched your inheritance."

Just like that I'm irritated again. "I want that money to go toward something special. I'm not going to fritter it away on things we should be able afford on our own."

"You thought you were going to use it on school," he argues, "but obviously that's no longer happening. I get not wanting to fritter it away, but let's at least put it toward something like a house. We can't stay here. We need a place where we can raise a family."

Nothing he's said is untrue, but my stomach sinks all the same. Once that money's gone, it's gone. And with it, any lingering hope of becoming an architect. I know it's probably never happening, but the idea of giving it up hurts anyway. "Yeah," I say. "Maybe."

"It doesn't have to be Manassas, but we would get so much more for our money there. We should at least go look at the model when I get back."

"When you get back? You're *leaving?*"

"Yeah," he says. "Day after tomorrow. I told you about it—Albany, and then down to Miami."

Is it unreasonable to expect him to stay home under the circumstances? Perhaps. But this, combined with the fact he hasn't even *asked* about my test results, has me feeling separate from him. As if we are no longer part of a team, but two entities that merely coexist.

I'm in bed, nearly asleep, when he finally slides in beside me. I can't remember a time in my life when I didn't think Jeff was hot. He was Rocton's star football player, and I'm still the envy of half my graduating class for landing him. But tonight, when he starts to tug at my shorts and those wiry chest hairs of his are scraping my back, I feel repulsed. And that's a first in all our years together.

I remove his hand. "Sorry. It was a long day. Dee was pissy about me being out this morning."

"Oh yeah," he says, kissing the back of my head. "I forgot to ask. Everything good?"

Nick wouldn't need to be reminded, whispers that traitorous voice. I banish the thought, but something surly and petulant remains behind. It leaves me unwilling to tell him the whole truth, because he hasn't earned it. "Yeah."

Eventually his breathing deepens, turning into small snores, and I realize I haven't taken the meds Nick prescribed. I creep from the room and pop the pills into my mouth before I can change my mind. But instead of returning to bed, I curl up with my laptop on the corner of the couch and do something I absolutely should not: I search for Nick's name and click on *images*. There are thousands of Nick Reillys in the world, but only mine was a top college swimmer, and those pictures are the last thing I should be looking at right now: Nick, shoulders arched as he does the butterfly. Nick, standing with teammates in nothing but a Speedo, a medal around his neck. *Jesus, those abs*. My stomach spasms at the sight of him.

And since I'm apparently determined *not* to do the right thing tonight, I click on a video. The NCAA 400 Freestyle Relay. "Nick Reilly, of UVA, beginning the last lap at a serious disadvantage," the sportscaster says. "Three seconds behind Paul Diering of Syracuse. I see no way for UVA to win the race at this point."

But then something miraculous happens, something I know will happen because suddenly I'm certain I was *there*, sitting in the bleachers, screaming my heart out. Nick starts to catch up.

"But the race may not be over yet!" the announcer shouts. "Look at UVA. That's Nick Reilly, using that powerhouse kick we've come to expect from him, and he's—oh my God—he's really gonna do it. Look at the way he cuts through the water..."

I don't even have to watch—I remember all of it. The way Nick comes out of the turn an arm's length behind the guy from Florida State, the way he consumes that difference and then surges. I was hoarse from screaming after that meet. I watch as he wins, leaping from the pool to be surrounded by ecstatic teammates.

I have absolutely no memory of meeting him in college, but I know I was there. I remember him searching for me, pulling me in for a soaking wet hug. The camera shows no hug, of course, and when it pans to the bleachers, the place I sat is occupied by someone else...someone I knew well—Nick's mom. The sight of her hurts. She is, I think, another person I once loved but lost.

I set the laptop on the table and pull the throw blanket over me in frustration. It was bad enough when I remembered being in London with Nick, but now I'm remembering times that predate that...and it feels like I was happier in *all of them* than I am now.

Which means a situation that was already fucked up has gotten worse. "I really hope the drugs work," I whisper as I close my eyes.

I do not plunge into dreamless sleep. Instead, I go someplace where I am young. Nick's kitchen, in his parents' home. He and his brother have both been sent to their rooms for the fistfight that erupted at the table, and only his mother and I remain behind.

"I don't know why they were fighting," I tell her. "All three of us can fit in the treehouse at the same time."

She gives me a weary smile. A smile I have seen often of late. "The problem is that there are two of them and only one of you."

It takes me a second to understand what she's really trying to say—that the fight wasn't over the treehouse at all. It makes me nervous. I just want everything to stay the same.

"I don't want them to fight," I tell her. The three of us have been best friends since we were little, and now they're going to ruin everything.

She sighs. "It'll end eventually."

"When?" I ask.

Her smile is sad. "When you decide between them."

13

NICK

My arms slice through the water, fast, but not fast enough. I'm trying to run away from all of this, but the harder I push, the more Quinn fills my head. After we hung up yesterday, I did my best to shake the whole thing off. She's already taken, and so am I. I couldn't be with her even if that weren't the case.

By the time I'm done, I'm so tired I can barely push myself out of the pool. But Quinn remains front-and-center in my brain. I can't seem to outrun her.

~

I DON'T ALLOW myself to call her until after lunch. The moment the clock strikes one, however, I'm in my office with the door shut, dialing her number. It feels an awful lot like the first time I called a girl as a nervous thirteen-year-old.

"It's Nick." I pause. "Nick Reilly."

"I know which Nick you are," she says with a soft, husky laugh.

I inhale, fighting the temptation to make this a social call. To joke around with her and ask how her day is. I've never once struggled to act professional until Quinn came into the picture. "I was just checking to see how you're feeling today, and if you had any side effects from the meds."

"No side effects," she says. "But they didn't work, either."

I sit up a little straighter. "So you had more dreams."

"Yeah," she says, sighing. "They're getting worse. I'm not just seeing things from London anymore. I'm seeing things from college and childhood. I know what your kitchen looked like as a kid. I remember being in the treehouse with you and Ryan, and—"

My circulatory system whirs to a halt. I'm so stunned by the mention of my twin that I cut her off, my voice sharper than I'd intended. "How do you know about my brother?" I demand. He's been gone for over a decade. The only reason I mentioned him to Meg at all was because I had to warn her before she met my mom.

"How do I know about any of this?" she replies, with an exasperated exhale. "I thought we were past the point where you accused me of stalking."

I bury my head in my hands. Of all the things she's known, this is the first one that actually kind of scares me. I don't believe in ghosts but if my dead brother wanted to fuck with me he'd pull a stunt just like this. "We are. I'm sorry. It was just a shock hearing you say his name." Even my parents won't talk about him now, at least not in front of me. I've often wondered if this is because they know I blame myself for what happened, or if it's because they blame me too.

She pauses. "Did...something happen to him?"

"He died. In high school."

"Oh," she says, her voice catching. "Oh, God. I'm so sorry."

"It's okay," I assure her. "Really. You didn't do anything wrong, and it all happened a long time ago. I just was shocked to hear you mention his name." She's silent. It makes no sense, but I know she's grieving Ryan's death, and it feels like she has a right to. "Are you okay?" I ask.

"It's just strange," she whispers. "I had that dream last night, and it's like this whole box of new memories opened up. A lot of them about you, but a lot of them are about him too, as a child. I just can't believe...I'm sorry. Never mind. What were we talking about?"

I run a hand through my hair. There's a whole lot more to unpack here, but I'm not sure I'm ready to hear it. "You were saying the drugs didn't work."

"Right. So is there something else I can take to stop the dreams? Something stronger?"

"We can try something else, but...Quinn, if the Prazosin didn't work, I really doubt anything else will either."

"Okay," she says. "Maybe it will go better tonight."

The conversation has reached its natural end but I'm just not ready to let her go. "Are you back at work?"

She gives a low laugh. "Could you tell by the abject misery in my voice?"

It bothers me that she's at that job. It's just *wrong*. "Why didn't you go back to school for architecture when you returned to D.C.?" I ask abruptly.

She hesitates. "It's complicated."

I want to keep her on the phone, but I've pushed this as long as I can. "Okay, well, give the meds another shot, and if they're still not working, we can try something else."

She thanks me and hangs up. But I sit here, still holding the phone like a lovesick teenager.

14

QUINN

"I'm so glad you're here," I whisper to Nick. He grips my hand hard through the tangle of wires—IV, blood pressure cuff, oxygen monitor—hinting at anxiety he's trying to keep to himself. He's used to hospital rooms, but usually he's the one barking orders, not the one sitting and praying all will be well.

And in this moment, I suddenly feel certain it won't be.

"There's something I have to tell you," I whisper. "It won't make sense, but I need you to—" I'm cut off mid-speech by a pain so sharp it knocks the words from my brain. His hand tightens. I'll be bruised by it when this is done.

"It's going to be okay," he says, but I see in those circles under his eyes, the greenish pallor beneath his tan, that he is no more certain of that than I am. And he doesn't even know everything: all the horrible truths that have come back to me only recently. I picture him and Ryan as boys and I flinch. The things I did in that other life—would he have forgiven me eventually? I'll never know.

The pain hits again, another wave, wiping my brain clear of its mission, leaving only the panic behind. I struggle to focus around it.

"My mother...my mother will explain everything." I cling to his hand so I'm not swept away. "About the Rule of Threes. I'm sorry...I didn't believe her."

"Something's wrong," Nick barks at the staff, his eyes focused on a monitor overhead.

The doctor glances at us. She is setting things on a tray, slow and methodical, without a clue how bad this is about to turn. "She's fine. Everything's fine."

"It's not," he insists, and his voice sharpens. "Check everything. Check every goddamned thing you think you don't need to check because something is wrong."

"Dr. Reilly, you need to calm down," she says sternly, "or we're going to have to ask you to leave."

He leans over me. His concern has turned to panic. "Honey, you're okay," he says, but I feel it already, the dimming inside me. I want to cry out and beg the universe for one more minute, a chance to explain, but I know it's useless.

My lids start to flutter. The world grows thick and slow, too liquid for me to grasp. I start to sink beneath it.

An alarm triggers. "Goddammit!" Nick shouts, rising. "Look at her blood pressure. I need Levophed, stat!"

The door opens, and that's when I see her—the woman who enters silently, her pale blond hair shimmering beneath the hospital lights. The room is in chaos and no one but me even notices her. She is capable of terrible things, just like me, and her presence here means the end of everything. Of this life I wanted so badly. "No," I whisper. "Don't. Please."

"There's no other choice at this point," she says.

I turn to my husband, taking in the face I love so much. "Wait for me," I plead. "I'll find you, but you have to wait."

Nick's panicked, desperate face is the last thing I see.

My eyes fly open. For a moment my limbs are unresponsive, weighted, and I can't even cry out. It feels as if I've been held underwater for too long. A part of me wants to fight and another part is lethargic, ready to sink low.

It only takes a few seconds before it subsides and I pitch forward, gasping for air, limbs flailing. What the hell just happened? It's the same dream I had as a child, but it's the first time I've ever woken feeling as if I was dying.

I climb from the bed with my pulse racing, too scared to fall back asleep, and go to the living room. I turn on the TV and all the lights, wishing Jeff was awake too. What would have happened if I hadn't woken when I did? It terrifies me, the power these dreams seem to hold.

I spend hours pacing or curled in fetal position on the couch. Eventually I'm able to convince myself I only *thought* I couldn't move, but what I cannot shake, even hours later, is the horror I felt—not just of the woman who entered the room, but of myself. I truly believed there was something terrible inside me—something I had to hide from Nick.

I sense it inside me still. And I cannot shake the sense that Nick is the one person capable of setting that terrible thing free.

~

By the time Jeff rises, I have a plan. A plan born of desperation, but surely even that is better than no plan at all. Jeff is the right choice, the good choice, and he deserves far better than what he's been getting from me of late. I need to do whatever I can to stick to the path I've been on for our six years together.

"You were up again?" he asks. "Stress?"

It's easy enough to nod in the affirmative. I've never been more stressed in my life. "Yeah," I say. "And I was thinking... maybe we should just go to Vegas. It seems like the wedding is triggering my seizures, and we don't even know if I'll be able to make it through the ceremony without having one. So maybe the solution is just to get it over with."

He laughs. "I'm marrying the most beautiful, brilliant woman I've ever known. I want everyone we love to see it happen. And people already have plane tickets. Think about the money your mom has spent."

"We can still do the big wedding," I say eagerly. "We'll just do Vegas first. It all feels so monumental. It's like we're wrapping the biggest moment of our lives up with the biggest performance of our lives, and it's too much."

"Honey—" he pleads. I hear apology, and thus refusal, in his tone. "I'm killing myself trying to get stuff squared away so we can go on our honeymoon."

Despair makes my voice hitch. "I know. But it could be a quick trip—"

"Hon, when would we even go? I've got the trip today and three more over the next month. Between that and my bachelor party and your bachelorette, we just don't have the time."

My shoulders drop. He's right. I'm not sure why I even suggested it. Jeff doesn't have a spontaneous bone in his body. "Ignore me. I'll be fine."

He kisses my forehead and moves away. He's relieved, but I am not. It feels like we're racing against time. I don't know the consequences of losing this race, exactly, but if these dreams continue until the wedding, I'm pretty sure I'll find out.

~

NICK CALLS AGAIN THAT AFTERNOON. I sit rigidly, swearing to myself that he'll be nothing more than my doctor from now on, yet from the moment he says *hi*, I'm rolling the sound of his voice over and over again in my mouth, like it's my last piece of chocolate. "I'm actually calling for a favor," he says.

Excitement and dread both seep into my blood until I can't tell them apart. "What kind of favor?" I ask.

"Darcy—you met her the other day—is having a birthday party tonight at six. It's actually her half-birthday, but...you know. And she's completely smitten with you. She told her mom you look like Starfire."

"Starfire?"

"I guess you don't watch a lot of *Teen Titans*. She's the hot one."

I find myself smiling despite my good intentions. "Do you rank the hotness of *all* female cartoon characters, or just on select shows?"

He laughs low, under his breath. "I keep an Excel spreadsheet. It's not as comprehensive as I'd like, but I have a demanding job. So yes or no?"

Every bone in my body screams *no*, but what am I supposed to say? It's a dying child's request. And as long as Nick isn't there, how much harm could it do? His days start early, so there's no way he's staying until six for a patient's birthday party. "Yes, I'd be happy to."

"Cool," he says softly. "I'll let her know. See you in a few hours."

Well, shit.

~

I WALK through the lobby of the hospital, trying to convince myself I'm not nervous, not excited. That the girl I see in the mirror as I wait for the elevator—the one with the bright eyes and flushed cheeks—is no different than the one I see each day.

I am here to see Darcy. I am doing a nice thing for a sick child. Nothing more.

I can repeat these words a thousand times, but it doesn't

change the fact that I am moving faster than I should, my feet skittering through the halls at twice their normal speed.

Darcy's door is open. Before I even set foot inside, I hear Nick's low, reluctant laugh. It flares deep in my stomach like a hundred votive candles lit at once. My mouth twitches toward a smile against my will and I pin it down by force.

I step into the room and for a moment, he is all I see. His grin, that dimple, the way something changes in his expression when his eyes lock on mine, like a predator who's spotted what he wants before even *he* realizes it. His smile doesn't lessen but simply morphs, becoming a private thing only for me. It's the smile he had before he flipped me on my back in Paris. I think of that mouth of his sliding over my skin and I can feel it, the way he tugged each nerve ending to the surface.

"Quinn!" shouts Darcy, breaking the spell. She's in bed, sitting with Nick and a woman I assume is her mother.

My smile for her is flustered and slightly panicked. Why the hell am I thinking rated-R thoughts about a stranger at a party for a dying child?

"Hello, Birthday Girl," I say, handing her the wrapped gift pressed to my chest.

Her eyes go round as dinner plates. "You didn't have to get me a present. It's not my real birthday."

I grin at her, and for just a moment—*thank God*—I'm able to forget the man sitting on the other side of her bed. "There's no reason whole birthdays should get all the fun," I reply, wondering what the odds are of her making it to age eight. She's obviously still getting chemo. That must mean there's some hope left, right?

Nick introduces me to Christy, Darcy's mom, as Darcy tears the wrapping paper. Acquiring this present in such a short period of time was no small feat, so I hope I chose well.

She inhales sharply as she pulls the purple satin from the box. "Raven's cape! And face mask!"

I smile wide at her enthusiasm, and as her mother helps her put on the mask, my eyes go to Nick. He is watching me again, neither smiling nor unsmiling. He doesn't look away when my gaze meets his.

"Thank you!" Darcy cries. She launches across the bed to give me a tight hug, tiny arms wrapping around my neck. The fierceness of the action has me swallowing down a lump in my throat. Have I ever thrown myself that wholeheartedly at anything in my life? I'm not sure I have.

"I don't know when the nurses are coming in," says Darcy's mom, "so maybe we should do cake."

I move to the chair next to Nick's while Christy places candles on the cake they've somehow procured. "How on earth did you find that cape on such short notice?" he asks quietly.

By calling twenty toy stores and taking a profoundly expensive Uber ride to Silver Spring during my lunch break. I shrug. "Just saw it."

His gaze is steady, his mouth ticking upward at the side. "Is that right?"

I can't seem to look away. What the hell is happening between the two of us tonight? I need to make it stop, whatever it is, but I don't *want* it to stop.

Christy begins singing "Happy Birthday" and I finally break the connection, joining the song just as the cake is placed on Darcy's bedside table.

"But that's eight and a half candles," says Darcy.

"Seven and a half, plus one to grow on," says her mom, blinking back tears.

Darcy falters before she gives us a too-wide smile, and I swallow hard. The sight of them, forcing themselves to be brave and cheerful for the other, makes me want to run a thousand miles away.

Christy cuts the cake into massive slices and passes plates to me and Nick. Grief weighs me down. It's a struggle to move the fork to my mouth.

"Hey," says Nick quietly, while Darcy and her mom talk to the nurse who's popped in the room. His hand clasps mine for a millisecond to get my attention, and I glance up at him. "Are you okay?"

I nod, staring at the cake that rests in my lap. "I don't know how you do this."

He hesitates. "I couldn't if it was always like this. But occasionally, instead, you get a woman in who tells you only the most boring details about your honeymoon in Paris."

I laugh. "Maybe if you'd been more interesting in Paris, I'd have better details to share."

"I refuse to believe the fault lies with me. I bet you're the type who wants to play *Words With Friends* on a date. Or insists on showing me one video after another of your cat jumping around in the snow."

It's a struggle to look stern. "My cat, if I had one, would be fascinating. You would love my cat videos if I chose to share them with you."

"Yeah?" His lashes lower and I get a glimpse of that secret smile of his again, the seductive one. I picture myself pulling the cake from his hands and climbing into his lap, but I realize as it plays out in my head, it isn't a fantasy, it's a *memory*. We were in our flat on his birthday, with the sun's dwindling rays streaming in through the kitchen windows, and I was in his lap. I remember kissing the corner of his jaw, shifting against him and relishing the tiny way he inhaled at the motion. His right hand slid into my hair, grasping a thick handful of it as he pulled my mouth to his.

My fork falls to the floor. Christy and Darcy don't seem to notice, but Nick's eyes flicker to my mouth, as if he knows exactly what was going on in my head. I'm so grateful he doesn't. While this would all be easier if he remembered things in the same detail I do, it would also be ten times more awkward.

I focus on Christy and Darcy, trying to pull my mind out of the gutter. I ask Christy about the candle business she runs out of her home, solely to think about something—*anything*—else, and then tell them I need to head to the Metro before it gets dark.

"I'll walk with you," Nick says.

I still. Spending time with him outside the walls of this hospital is a terrible idea. I should tell him no. But I've got no idea how to do it gracefully, and—more importantly—I don't want to. The idea of more time with Nick thrills me as much as it terrifies me.

15

NICK

I live nowhere near the Metro, but I assure myself there's nothing inappropriate in what I'm doing. She did a nice thing for my patient. Seeing her safely to her destination is just common courtesy.

But there's been nothing appropriate about my reaction to her tonight. Not from the first moment she appeared at the door, all flushed cheeks and bright eyes and uncertainty.

We walk quietly, in step, down Reservoir to 34th Street. Even though school is out, the sidewalks are clogged. My hand reaches out to the small of her back to keep us side by side.

"I had another dream last night," she says.

"More torrid memories from our honeymoon?"

Her laugh is throaty. God, I'd give *anything* to know what she remembers of this supposed trip to Paris. "The opposite of torrid," she replies, her smile fading. "I dreamed we were in the hospital."

"I apparently really knew how to show you a good time in my past life."

Her mouth twitches into a grin. "Yes. I'm sure it was a high point in our relationship."

It's so damn comfortable with her. It's comfortable with Meg too, but this is easier somehow, which is a really unfair comparison. *Of course* it's going to be easier with Quinn—she has no expectations of me. I might not even see her again after tonight. "So, what happened in this dream of yours?"

She swallows. Whatever she saw, it bothers her even now. "We were in the hospital and it seemed like I was dying or really sick, I'm not sure. And then this woman came into the room, and I knew she was going to take me away from you. It's the same dream I had as a kid."

We reach a crowd of people waiting to cross M Street and stop. "But *I* wasn't in that dream when you were a kid."

"Yeah," she says slowly. "You were."

I blink, wondering if this is a joke. The crowd moves forward and I remain standing here, stupefied. "*That* is completely impossible."

"Even when I was small, I told my parents about you. That your name was Nick and you were my husband. I'm sure it must have freaked them out."

"That—"

She laughs, the sound weary. *"Is completely impossible?* Yes, I know. But my parents sent me to therapy because of those nightmares. It's all documented. You could argue it wasn't the *same* you, but I swear to God it was."

I rub my temples. I believe her. And yet, it is wholly unbelievable. "I don't even know what to say."

She sighs. "Yeah. Me neither. It seemed so real too. My blood pressure started dropping and you shouted at the doctor to give me something. Levo...Levophed? Is that a thing?"

I can only stare at her. It's the exact medicine I'd have used to treat her blood pressure in an emergency, something she's highly unlikely to know. "This just gets weirder and weirder," I reply, starting to move across the street just before we miss the light. "I know you don't want to have these dreams, but don't you think maybe there's a *reason* you're having them? The next dream you have might be the one that helps you make sense of all this."

Her mouth purses. I wonder, fleetingly, what that mouth of hers would taste like—*the cake she couldn't bring herself to eat? Something better?*—and it grates inside my chest, the fact that I'm never going to know. "Maybe, but I doubt it."

I agree with her, but I'm still disappointed in her answer.

We reach the Metro far too soon. It had to be the fastest one-mile walk of my life.

"What line are you on?" she asks.

"I'm not," I tell her. "I live back near the hospital. I just didn't want you walking here alone since it's getting dark."

Something pained and wistful passes over her face. "Thank you," she says quietly, going up on her toes to press her lips to my cheek. She smells like oranges and sunshine.

I watch her step onto the escalator and remain there until she is out of sight, wondering if this is what it's like for my brother. If he's somewhere in the world cataloging all the experiences he'll never have too.

~

MEG IS WAITING in my apartment when I get back, which leaves me feeling guilty and irritated simultaneously. I hope some time away from Quinn will make my feelings for Meg return to what they were, but right now they are nowhere in sight. "Hey there. I didn't think you were coming over."

She shrugs. "I figured once I move in, we'll have to get used to working around each other's schedules, so I might as well stay here anyway. Have you eaten?"

I set my keys on the counter. "No, but I'm pretty beat," I tell her. "You want to rent a movie and order in?"

"We could," she says, crossing the room toward me. "Or we could do something *else*." She goes on her toes to kiss me, her fingers pulling at my tie. "We haven't been alone in forever."

I know what she wants and for literally the first time in my adult life, I can't. I know I'll be picturing Quinn, and that when it's done, I'll feel like I've cheated on Quinn *and* Meg, as insane as that is. My hand gently circles her wrist, staving her off. "I did something to my back swimming this morning," I lie.

"I could do all the work," she offers.

"I'm sorry," I tell her. "I really don't feel great."

I watch Meg walk away, the rigidity of her spine the only sign of her displeasure. I need to get my head straightened out fast, or I'm going to lose the good thing I have—*Meg*—for something that isn't even an option.

I SPEND the entire weekend trying not to think about Quinn. I spend Monday thinking of reasons I could call her, when I should never have called her last Thursday in the first place. My role as her doctor had basically ended at that point.

But there are no words for how pleased I am when she calls me instead.

"How's Darcy today?" she asks.

"I just saw her wandering around the hospital in her cape. It really cheered her up to have you there last week. Thanks for coming by. You're at work?"

"Yeah. My boss is out," she says, "probably buying Dalmatians for her next fur coat, so I'm able to actually place a personal call."

I like the idea of this being a personal call more than I should. "Dalmatian fur is way too hot for D.C. in the summer."

"You can never plan your fur coat purchases too far in advance." We both laugh and there it is again—this sense of ease in our conversation I don't have with other people, not even friends I've known all my life.

"So, I was thinking," she continues. "Both of my seizures, or whatever they were, seemed like they were triggered by that house at the lake, the one that might be your parents'. I was wondering if I could see a picture of it?"

"Sure, but why?"

She sighs. "I don't know. I'm just wondering if it'll help me remember something. Obviously, I can't stop the dreams, but maybe if I can figure out the significance of the house, or at least get used to seeing it, I can stop passing out every time I'm there."

Because of her wedding. It's funny how I keep forgetting it's happening, and how I flinch each time she reminds me. "Sure. Hang on." I quickly swipe through my pictures, send one and then wait while she pulls it up.

"Oh," she whispers.

"Is it the same house?"

"Yeah," she says. "That's it. But I'm fine."

I give a small laugh. "I've never heard someone so disappointed to not have a seizure."

"No," she muses, her voice distant and distracted. "It's good, obviously. At least I'll be able to make it upright through the wedding. I just thought...do you think I could see other pictures?"

"Of the house?"

"No," she says, hesitating. "Of you guys. You and Ryan, your parents. The treehouse, maybe. Do you have pictures of that?"

People always seem worried when they mention Ryan to me, as if I might have just forgotten that my twin is dead until their reminder. I hear the apology in her voice but it's unnecessary. A piece of me wants to share my past with her, wants to throw open the doors and let her be the one person I let inside. "Sure," I reply. "Give me a sec."

I go into a favorites file on my phone and hit several in a row. A picture of me and my parents when I graduated. My dad in front of our house, captured wearing a hat of my mom's to mow the lawn. Then me and Ryan—as teenagers out on the dock, both of us sun-burnished and way too full of ourselves. As kids, leaning out of the treehouse with big semi-toothless grins.

She laughs. "What is your dad wearing?"

"My mom's hat," I reply. "He has very little shame, obviously."

There's a moment of silence, and when she speaks again her voice is full of dread. "Oh."

I shoot forward in my seat. "What's the matter?"

"Nick?" she whispers, the sound distant and barely audible.

I hear a crash, and then nothing. I shout her name but hear only background noise. "Someone pick up the fucking phone!"

There is only silence in response.

16

QUINN

"How was the first day of school?" asks Nick, leaning against the locker beside mine, lanky and relaxed in the way only someone older and cooler than you can be. Despite that easy stance, concern darkens his blue eyes, furrows his brow. He's always been protective of me, although we're only a year apart, and he's even more so now that I'm in public school for the first time. But his protectiveness is big-brother-like, which I find highly annoying. I've seen the way he looks at me when he thinks I'm not paying attention, so who does he think he's fooling?

"Perfect," I reply.

"You found your classes okay?"

I feel a trickle of evil joy in my chest as I look up at him. "I did. And you'll never guess who just asked me out during Spanish."

Anything pleasant in his face bleeds away. "Who?"

"Colin Campbell." Nick and his twin brother are already stars at our school—both gorgeous, both straight-A students and star athletes—but they are juniors and Colin is a senior. A popular, hot senior. This is apparently a coup of some kind, but mostly I'm just relieved

there's a male somewhere in this high school who doesn't want to pretend I'm his sister. Who won't watch me like something he wants to devour and then rub my head like a favorite pet.

Nick's eyes narrow. "He's a senior. You cannot date a senior."

"I'm fairly certain I can, since I said yes," I reply, slamming my locker shut and heading for the front doors. It's still summer-hot outside, and I have to pick my way through lounging students to get to the path I take home. Nick is on my heels, his eyes the color of a summer storm.

"Where's he taking you?" he barks.

His distress is a balm to my soul. I've spent a solid two years trying to make him admit he likes me. I shrug, the very picture of ambivalence. "Some party."

"He's going to try something. He's at least going to try to kiss you."

He sounds pissed and it serves him right. We've just reached our cut-through in the woods, but I stop and turn toward him, shifting my backpack to my other shoulder. "Remember the time Ryan dared you to kiss me, and you did it, but acted like you were vomiting afterward? That is the grand sum of my experience. So, I hope Colin tries something, because that's a shitty memory to have as my only kiss."

He slaps a palm to his forehead. "For fuck's sake, Quinn. I was nine."

"Yeah," I reply. "And I'm 15. So I'm ready for something better." I turn to walk away and find myself spun back toward him before I've even had time to process it. His mouth lands on mine without hesitation or uncertainty, as if I'm a meal he's been waiting for years to consume.

And he consumes. With his lips, his tongue, his hands. He burns me alive, taking my oxygen and my common sense and leaving nothing but desire in its wake. Kissing is so much more than I realized. Not just mouths and fumbling, but something that turns my core into a pillar of fire and finds me arching against him, desperate for more.

When he finally breaks away, my back is against a tree, his hands are on my ass, and there's a bulge pressing into my abdomen—I suspect I know what it is, but this is all new to me, so I wouldn't swear to it. "Are you going to pretend to vomit now?" I ask.

"No, I'm not going to pretend to vomit." He sounds winded and gravelly. His hands move up, cradling my face the way they once did a robin's egg we found. I remember the awe in his eyes as he carried it. It's how he looks at me now too. "God, Quinn. You have no idea how badly I've wanted to do that."

He's older, and knows more, but this raw, wanting thing inside me surges and takes charge. I pull him down to me by the collar of his T-shirt. "Do it again," I command.

"Fuck," he hisses. "Yes." And then he's pushing me against the tree again and his mouth is right there, about to land on mine...except my name is being called. Somewhere far away, but it's coming from inside my head, and the voice is...Nick's. Older, different, yet still him. Another version of Nick, calling me home.

I want to ignore him. I want to stay right here against this tree and see what happens next. But that voice I hear has grown desperate and I can't stand it. I have to go.

I tumble through the darkness, but I am not actually falling, like I thought. I'm moving sideways, slipping through walls that press against me like the narrowest hallway, yet are made of absolutely nothing. And as I'm flying by, in the darkness across from me, I see a face. A girl—with long brown hair and gray eyes like nothing I've ever witnessed before—who looks as astonished to see me as I am to see her.

"Quinn," says Nick, stern in his panic. "Can you hear me?"

I'm on a stretcher, in an ambulance bouncing so hard over D.C.'s potholes that it feels like an amusement-park ride.

"Hi," I murmur. The pain is setting in, shearing my brain into pieces, jagged like glass. I want to raise my hands but I can't. "Head," I whisper.

"I have you," he says, pushing my hair back from my face. "It's going to be okay."

He looks at me the way I remember, from some other life: as if I mean absolutely everything to him and nothing else matters. On the other side of me, the paramedic is doing something. Wrong, apparently.

"Give me that," Nick demands, and seconds later, I feel the pain being pushed away, cleared, like he's taken a large broom to the whole area. As everything goes black, I wonder if I'm dying, and my biggest regret is that I won't have gotten to spend more time with Nick before it happens.

~

When I wake, it's dusk, and Nick is sitting in the chair beside me. My hand is clasped in his, and that's as it should be. It belongs there.

"Hi," I whisper.

His hand slides away. "Hey there. How do you feel?"

"Okay. A little achy, but that's it. What happened?"

"You passed out in your office while we were on the phone."

The entire morning is vague to me. I don't remember waking or getting dressed. But I do remember the dream, and the sound of him begging me to come back. "You came for me," I say quietly. "Thank you."

His mouth opens and closes, his hand reaches for mine and falls away. "The hospital called your fiancé," he says after a moment, his lip curling into a sneer at that last word. "He couldn't get a flight out until morning. Is there someone else you'd want me to call?"

I shake my head. "My mother, but she's two hours away and she'd just worry."

He stares at the blankets for a moment before raising bleak

eyes to mine. "We got another MRI while you were knocked out."

My hands clench reflexively, nails biting into the soft skin of my palms. His expression is so grim I barely have to ask if it was bad news. "Oh?"

"The tumor is growing," he says, his jaw shifting as he utters the words. "Quickly."

Everything inside me grows still and quiet. I take one deep breath. Another. "But you said it wasn't metabolically active," I whisper. "That it wouldn't grow."

"It shouldn't have. I have no explanation for this. None. I've never even heard of a tumor that could grow like yours without additional blood flow."

I bite my lip, willing myself not to cry. "And it's inoperable," I add.

He is silent for a moment. "Yes," he finally says. He squeezes my hand and I squeeze his back, not letting go as I turn my head away from him. A tear trickles over the bridge of my nose and onto the pillow. I was ready for this last week. Maybe not *ready,* but braced for it at least. Now I can only lie here feeling like I've been hit by a truck. "So how long do I have?"

He reaches out to touch my chin, forcing me to meet his eye. "It's not a death sentence, Quinn. Surgery isn't the only option. There's chemo and radiation. I need to refer you out to an oncologist."

I think of Darcy, tiny Darcy who is not going to be around for long. None of that worked for her, obviously. I think of my father. They told us he probably had five years. He was dead in six months. "And if those things aren't possible, or just don't work for me?"

He exhales. "If it were to stop growing...there are people who are okay. They just sit with it, and we monitor and hope for the best."

He's doing what all doctors do, pretending my one wispy

tendril of hope is something far more solid and stable than it is. Except I don't want the best-case scenario. I want the likely one. "But mine *is* growing. So how long if it continues at the current rate?"

He pinches the bridge of his nose. "Let's hold off on making predictions just yet. I've got a call in to the best oncologist in the city. He's on vacation but I should hear back by Monday." I just look at him, waiting, and he relents. "If it keeps growing at the current rate, you might have a few years."

A few years, and he's probably still giving me a best-case scenario. It's just as likely to mean one year.

My whole life, I wanted two things—to become an architect and to become a mother, and now neither of them will happen. I brush at the tears streaming down my face. It takes me a minute or two before I get it under control.

"You don't have to stay," I tell him once I've pulled myself together. "I'm sure you have things to do."

He squeezes my hand. "I'm not leaving unless you force me to."

We are silent for a moment. The truth is, no matter how badly I don't want to be dreaming about him, don't want to persuade myself I feel something for him...there is no one else in the world I want here in his place.

I glance out the window, at the dwindling light, and brace myself as I ask a question I've avoided all this time. "You don't have to be home to someone?"

"I made arrangements."

Ouch. "You're married?"

His eyes shift away. "No, but I have a girlfriend, Meg. She's a pulmonologist here, actually. I told her I was working late."

My heart sinks. He's got a girlfriend and she's a doctor too. It leaves an extremely bitter taste in my mouth, jealousy and also panic. In a few years I'll be gone and she'll still be here with him. "You should go home to her then," I tell him, the words grating in my throat on the way out. "I'll be fine."

"Quinn," he says quietly, staring between clasped hands at the floor, "I want to stay."

I hear need in his voice, and torment, and the sound of it opens this Pandora's box inside me. My eyes close. I want to soothe his torment and my own. I want to forget the entire world exists aside from him. But the world does exist, and in it I've made certain promises.

"I'll have to invite both of you to the wedding," I reply. "Two doctors would come in handy, given the odds the bride is going to pass out."

My forced cheerfulness fools no one. "Maybe—" he starts. "Never mind."

"No, come on. You started, so finish it."

His lashes lower, shuttering his expression. "Maybe you should postpone it," he says. "The stress of a wedding...I'm not sure it's what you need right now."

"People have already bought plane tickets. We'd lose all our deposits."

"You're not even sure you want to marry the guy," Nick says. His hands are clenched so tightly on the top railing of my bed that they are nearly bloodless. "A few lost deposits should be the least of your concerns."

I stiffen. "I never said I didn't want to marry him."

"You didn't have to say it," he replies, glaring at me. "I told you he couldn't get here until tomorrow and you didn't even blink. And every time you've mentioned him, it's like you're talking about a work friend, or a cousin. You don't feel the way you should about him."

"Oh, but you do with Meg?" I lash out and regret the words immediately. I don't sound like a patient, or even a friend—I sound like a very, *very* jealous girlfriend.

"No," he says, his eyes nearly translucent in the dim room.

"Because if I felt the right way about her, I probably wouldn't be in here with you."

Relief washes over me, sweeps beneath me and raises me high. I allow myself to float there, on its surface. It will all come to nothing, but just for this one night, I'm going to pretend he is mine.

17

NICK

I told the nursing staff I was staying late because Quinn was an old friend from college. This would probably have aroused less suspicion if she was a slightly less *attractive* old friend from college.

I order in dinner from an Italian place down on MacArthur. As I pull the containers from the bag, I realize this feels a bit like a first date, and a bit like a night with someone I've known all my life. Her eyes are smokier than normal, her face flushed. If this was even a first date I wouldn't be able to keep my hands off her.

I place the first container on her bedside table and she raises her surprised face to mine. "Penne alla vodka is my favorite."

I'm swept by an unsettling feeling I might have already known this. So many things with her seem to be automatic, so ingrained they've become a part of me—the same way I can drive home without paying attention to where I am or type without looking at the keys. "Sorry I couldn't get us any wine to go with it, but I'm already getting enough of a side-eye from the front desk staff without providing alcohol to a patient."

She takes her first bite of pasta and groans, a sound that has me reacting in completely inappropriate ways. Before I can stop myself, I'm imagining hearing that noise with her beneath me, on top of me, with my head between her thighs. Thank Christ the bed rail blocks her view of my crotch. I shut my eyes for a moment, scrambling to think of a topic that doesn't involve her mouth or my dick. Ideally, a topic that references no body parts whatsoever. Nothing comes to mind.

"I guess this is the point where I'm going to have to tell Jeff and my mother about the tumor."

I set my fork down. At least the erection is gone. "You didn't tell them about the tumor yet at *all*?"

Quinn exhales heavily, staring at her plate. "My mom would have worried, and...with Jeff, I was just being bratty, I guess."

"Bratty how?"

She shrugs. "After that last test I did, he kind of forgot to ask how it had gone. It wasn't a big deal but it made me feel...like an afterthought."

My hand flexes. She's got to be fucking kidding me. "How," I say, "could he not have asked?"

"I'm sure he just assumed things were fine."

Bullshit. If she were mine, I'd have been at the hospital when she was being discharged. I'd have tried to make her go home and rest. I'd have had a thousand fucking questions for her doctor about next steps. I'd have persuaded her to leave the job she hates. There are a million things I'd have done, and he hasn't done a goddamn one of them. "Do you want me to call them?"

She laughs. "Oh my God. If you called my mother, she'd go off the deep end."

"Why's that? My bedside manner isn't that terrible, is it?"

Her smoky-green eyes grow a little hazier. "Your bedside manner is just fine."

I find myself watching Quinn's mouth as she speaks, which was a really bad idea. My dick has a mind of its own and now strains hard against what *was* a roomy pair of pants. "Then what's the problem?"

"The problem is if she learns I've got a doctor named Nick after I spent my early childhood *dreaming* about a doctor named Nick, she's going to lose her mind. I think it was pretty unnerving to have your toddler talking about her husband from a past life." Her jaw tenses. "And my mother is easily spooked."

There's tension there, whenever she refers to her mother. I wish I knew why. "Those dreams...what made them stop?"

Her teeth pull at her lip. "I went to therapy but I don't think that had much to do with it. We had this...incident on the farm. And they became a lot less frequent after that."

I go on alert the moment she says *incident*. She's trying to minimize something I doubt was minimal. I'm guessing she does that a lot. "What incident?"

She stares at her lap, avoiding my eye. "A murder-suicide. My parents had these tenants on the property, this little two-bedroom house... They think the wife wanted to leave, so the husband killed her and their daughter while they were asleep."

"Their daughter? She was a child?"

She swallows. "Yeah. Jilly. She was nine, just two years older than me. She would tell me all about *Melrose Place* after school since I wasn't allowed to watch it. I still don't know if Michael and Jane ever got back together," Quinn says, with a raspy noise that is meant to be a laugh but comes out as something like a sob. She brushes at her face. "God, I haven't talked about this in ages. Anyway, it kind of messed me up a little."

I reach between the railings to squeeze her hand. "That

would mess up anyone. But I can't imagine how something like that would have made your nightmares stop."

Her eyes flicker to me and dart away again. "I guess I finally realized caring too much for any one thing...it just creates problems. I was better off letting it go."

Something about her answer doesn't add up. It's obvious she cares about things. She dropped out of school for her parents' sake, and she's getting married. Not the behaviors of someone who fears intimacy. "You don't mean that," I say. "If you really didn't want to be attached, you wouldn't be engaged right now."

"I didn't say I want *no* attachment. I said I don't want to get *too* attached. If Jeff cheats on me or leaves, he does. I'll be hurt, sure, but I won't be destroyed."

It seems like a fucked-up way to go through life. I've spent years waiting to feel *more* for another person, while she intentionally chose someone with whom that would never be possible.

She rolls toward me. "Which reminds me. I did a little research yesterday morning before I called you. There's a doctor in New Jersey who might be able to help me stop the dreams."

Right. The dreams that show her how much better her life should be. I wish I could convince her to pay attention to them, but instead I listen as she describes a study this guy published on repressed memories and sudden tumor onset, some case in which a teenage girl had a seizure and woke up speaking fluent Italian.

I've been combing medical journals since the day we met for something, *anything*, that could help, and have found absolutely nothing—which means any guy she's found online is probably a crackpot no respectable journal would publish. I lean back in my chair and rub my neck. "Quinn, I'm not trying to dissuade you, but there are a lot of people who try to profit off the misfortunes of others. For every single incurable disease, you'll find at least one charlatan offering some insane treatment that costs a fortune and makes no sense."

"He went to Harvard for medical school. That's got to be worth something."

"It's probably worth a lot less than you think. Guys like that...they either come up with a bizarre cure or a bizarre supernatural explanation for what they can't cure."

She smiles. "Are you ruling supernatural explanations out?"

"Look, even if I believed in ghosts, or reincarnation, you're remembering events that took place within the past few years. Besides, you seemed even more certain than me that there *was* no explanation."

"I know, but I was thinking something." She rolls on her back, her gaze on the ceiling. There are water spots there I've never seen before, but I don't think she even notices them. "I realize it sounds crazy, but the tumor gets bigger every time I black out, right? It was tiny, now it's not. So maybe if I can just figure out why it's happening, even just part of the reason, I can stop it from growing."

"Or maybe," I reply as gently as possible, "it's the progression of the tumor that's causing the incidents in the first place. And now you've got a tumor that needs treatment. We should be focused on getting you in with an oncologist, not some quack's insane theories."

She blinks rapidly, trying not to cry. "I need this to stop, Nick. I need someone to make it stop. Even if the tumor kills me, the way I find myself thinking and feeling...it has to end."

"Why?" I ask, harsher than I intended to sound. "Why does it have to end?"

Her eyes are so tortured as they turn toward me it's hard to meet her gaze. "Because I wake up feeling like everything in London actually happened, and I want it more than I want my real life. Except, my real life is what I have, and I need to be happy with that."

No, you don't. You could be with me.

I picture it: leaving here together. Starting over in a new city where no one knows us. Coming home to her every night and finding her beside me every morning. The thought of it makes me burn with want. What I'd like to do right now is hold her face in the palms of my hands and make a thousand promises I'd never be able to keep. Instead I jump to my feet and begin to pace. I'm angry and upset and being unprofessional and I really don't care. "I think these dreams are nature's way of telling you that you are settling for less. Way less."

"What I have with Jeff is exactly what I want," she replies, her voice breaking. "I don't want to feel more than that about someone. It causes too much pain."

I should let this go, because it's not like I have anything to offer in its place—even if every other obstacle was removed, it's never going to be okay for me to be with her. But I find myself arguing anyway. "The only other option is to go through your whole life never deeply loving anything at all."

"I'm okay with that," she replies. She looks at me for a long moment. "And you seem to be too."

18

QUINN

A nurse enters at six a.m., waking us both. We stayed up talking most of the night, and he fell asleep in the fold-out chair beside me. I have no idea how he explained his absence to his girlfriend.

"Oh," says the nurse, trying to master her surprise. "Dr. Reilly...I, uh, didn't realize you were...in here."

Guilt makes me flinch. I'm engaged and I shouldn't have had a man other than Jeff stay overnight in my room. "Nick's an old friend," I explain.

"From college," he adds, but he looks far too guilty to be believed. She raises a brow and, after giving him a look I can only interpret as scolding, leaves the room.

"I hope you don't get in trouble," I breathe when the door shuts behind her.

He gives me a small smile. "As far as I remember, nothing unprofessional occurred."

Just the suggestion that something *could* have happened is enough to have me squeezing my thighs together.

"But," he adds, "Jeff will be here soon, so I should go."

I dread him leaving. It's greedy of me to want more time with him, but I want it anyway. *And I absolutely need to stop wanting it.* "Thank you for staying over."

His fingers brush mine and his eyes shut. "If you're still planning to go see that doctor in New Jersey, I'll go with you."

I shake my head. "You don't need to do that."

"You cannot drive that far alone. Not when you're blacking out every other day. Unless you plan to ask *Jeff*." The disdain in his tone implies he already knows I won't. Or thinks Jeff isn't up to the job.

My hands twist together. The last thing I need are more hours alone with Nick. But he's taken anyway, so how dangerous could it be? And he's right—I shouldn't drive that far by myself, and asking Jeff means telling him about these dreams, which wouldn't go over well.

I tell myself I'm agreeing because it's my only option, but the truth is, as much as the idea of being alone with Nick scares me, it appeals to me even more.

So I guess we're going on a trip.

"QUINN!" my mother says excitedly when she answers the phone. "You must be psychic. I was just about to call. Nordstrom emailed to say they no longer have the heels I wanted you to get for the rehearsal dinner. So what do you think about getting the suede instead? I know you wanted patent leather, but I think they'd work and you'd probably get more use out of them."

Her words are like small, repetitive drips of water into an empty metal sink. So meaningless. It's shocking to me that a week ago I'd have been worried about patent leather versus suede. And now I'm so sad for her. I'm about to make her small worries seem as trivial as they are by dropping a big one in her lap.

"Mom," I say softly. "I've got some bad news."

By the time Jeff arrives, my tears have dried, but sadness weighs heavily in my stomach. My mother leaned on me so hard when my father died. Who will she have to lean on once I'm gone too? I gave her a best-case scenario instead of the worst, yet it was still the most difficult phone call I've ever made.

Jeff walks into the room with his carry-on in hand, looking weary and worse for wear. He presses a kiss to my forehead, drops into the chair that was Nick's during the night. "I'm sorry I couldn't get here sooner. There wasn't a single flight out and then we left late. So what happened?" he asks, gently pushing the hair back from my face. "I called again and again last night but you didn't answer."

Guilt delivers yet another tweak to my stomach. I begin to sweat and fling off the blankets. "I was sleeping a lot," I lie. "But they did another MRI and it's more serious than they thought."

He stills. "I assumed it was just another migraine," he says.

"Not exactly," I tell him, so quiet it's barely audible. "Jeff, I have a brain tumor."

He turns as white as bleached paper. "*What*? But that scan the other day—"

"It was tiny then and there was no blood flow around it, so they thought it wasn't growing. But it is growing. Quickly."

His jaw swings open. "They found a *tumor* and you didn't even mention it?"

I know he's just upset and looking for a scapegoat, but I'm in no mood to be one. "You didn't ask," I reply. "I had to even remind you I'd had a test done."

"I thought you'd tell me if there was a problem!" he shouts, jumping to his feet with his hands on the top of his head. "So, what? This guy missed it on the first MRI, so he had you take another and told you it was fine?"

"No," I begin. "He ran a test to check blood flow and—" He reaches over in the middle of my explanation and hits the call button. "What are you doing?"

"I'm telling them you need another neurologist. This guy obviously has no idea what he's doing."

Irritation claws at me. There are so many things I'm irate about in this moment that I don't know where to begin—the fact that he's making decisions on my behalf, that he's jumping to conclusions, that this moment has become about his distress instead of mine. For the last few years I've shielded him and carried the weight and made him feel like the center of the universe, but just once, I'd like to be the one who gets coddled. I lean forward and grab his arm. "Stop," I hiss. "I don't want another doctor. None of this is his fault."

My words are meaningless to him. They don't even seem to register. "I had a bad feeling about the guy from the moment we met him."

The nurse who saw me and Nick together this morning enters and Jeff rounds on her. "I want a new neurologist for my fiancée. Immediately."

I hate that he's demanding things of her like she's a servant. And I hate even more that he's acting like his opinion is the one that matters here. "No," I interject. "We *don't*."

Her gaze volleys between the two of us. *Great*. She probably thinks we're in some love triangle now. "I'll tell Dr. Reilly you need to see him."

She walks out and I tug on Jeff's hand. "Please stop this. *Now*. Nick hasn't done anything wrong."

"So he's *Nick* now, huh?" Jeff asks. "I didn't realize the two of you were suddenly pals."

I groan, so appalled by his behavior I'm struggling to form words. "This is not about you! *I'm* the one with the brain tumor, so *I'll* be the one who decides if I'm changing doctors. And you have no right to be making demands of the nurses on my behalf when I'm sitting right here, so don't do it again."

We are glaring at each other when Nick walks through the door, freshly showered. I have a memory of a time like this, a time when he came to my bedside and I pressed my lips to his neck, breathing him in. *Keep kissing me like that,* he said, *and I'm going to climb into bed with you.*

Except right now, there is nothing soft in his face. His sneer is barely restrained as he turns toward Jeff. "I understand you wanted to see me?"

"Yeah," says Jeff. "I want to know how the hell you managed to miss the fact that my fiancée had a serious brain tumor on her first scan."

"Jeff," I hiss. "I already told you that's not what happened."

But he's not listening to me. Neither of them are, really. They've already squared off, reminding me of gorillas in some nature documentary, on the cusp of battle. Jeff is not a small guy by any stretch of the imagination, but Nick is bigger, and the set of his shoulders right now seems threatening, intentionally so. "I *didn't* miss anything," he says between his teeth. "Her tumor is behaving in a way we haven't seen before."

"Well, I think a doctor with more experience might have noticed what you didn't."

Nick smirks. "If Quinn wants a second opinion, she's more than welcome to seek one out. But that's her decision, or that of her family. And if I recall correctly, *you're* not family." He's baiting Jeff, making a bad situation worse. I don't understand why he's doing it, but it's working: Jeff's temper is fraying. It's there in his clenched fists, in the way he steps forward.

"Then she must have failed to mention that we're getting married in four weeks," Jeff replies.

Nick's laugh is an angry bark. "I guess I keep forgetting because you're never around."

Jeff takes another step toward him and I'm on my feet. "Okay, I think this conversation has gone on long enough," I say, gripping the hospital gown as I step between them. "Thank you for coming in, Dr. Reilly."

Nick swallows, his whole body tense. He wants to refuse to leave, and for a moment, I really think he will. Finally, his jaw shifting in protest, he turns and walks from the room.

"You're fucking protecting him now?" Jeff demands.

I explode. "I have a brain tumor, dammit!" I shout. "And all you've done since you found out is yell at my doctor and make a scene. For once, how about if we let something just be about me and not you?!"

He gapes at me, shocked into silence for what is probably the first time ever. And then he sinks into the chair next to my bed, burying his head in his hands.

"I'm sorry," he says, his voice choked. "You're right. I'm just... it's a lot to take in."

I want to stay mad at him, but I can't. This is my fault. Each time I grow closer to Nick, I'm pushing him away. He senses it even if there's nothing specific he can point to. If he really understood the situation, he'd be a lot angrier than he's been and I'd deserve every ounce of it—because even now I'm wishing it was Nick here instead of him.

He drives me home once I'm discharged, attempting to malign Nick only once before I shut him down. He asks his mom to go keep mine company, and offers to stay home for the day, though I tell him it's not necessary. The truth is I *want* him to go, and I wish he'd stayed gone in the first place.

I keep my final dress fitting appointment that afternoon as scheduled. The gown is a sleeveless Monique Lhuillier with a plunging neckline and a sheer, hand embroidered overlay, so gorgeous even Caroline approved when she saw it. "Your fiancé will die when he sees you walk down the aisle," says the seamstress. But when I look in the mirror it's not Jeff's face I picture at the altar.

Which makes me wonder, for the first time, if I should be going through with this wedding at all.

WHEN I'M DONE I meet Trevor and Caroline out for a drink. I guess I'll have to tell them about the tumor eventually, but I'm going to put it off as long as I can. I don't want to be treated like someone who is dying. I want our nights out to continue involving margaritas and wince-inducing tales of Trevor's hookups, not chai latte at Starbucks and solemn conversations about my health.

By the time we arrive, the bar is loud and crowded, full of twenty-two-year-old Hill staffers in khakis, drunk off their asses and pushing each other off barstools. This, oddly enough, makes me smile. I'm still a part of things here. The land of the living hasn't written me off just yet.

Trevor, naturally, is hyper-focused on the events that took place in our office. "You should have seen her doctor," he tells Caroline breathlessly. "It was so hot. He flipped the fuck out—came in demanding to know where she was. And then he didn't even wait for the medic team. By the time they got in the door with that stretcher thingy, he'd already picked her up and was carrying her out, like a bride over the threshold."

Butterflies beat tiny wings inside my stomach, and I take a quick, sharp breath, waiting for them to settle. Nick *carried* me? I had no idea. But I shouldn't be thrilled by it, regardless. "I'm glad you've found a way to romanticize my collapse. I'm sure Nick's girlfriend would love it too."

"Wait," Caroline says, holding up her hand. "Isn't Nick the

name of the mystery guy you dreamed about in London? The one you'd never met?"

I groan, wishing I'd never mentioned it. "Yeah. I know it's bizarre."

"What mystery guy?" Trevor asks.

I slump in my chair while Caroline's eyes light up. "Quinn started having dreams about this guy in London...a doctor named Nick...*before* she met him."

Trevor gapes at us. "I can't believe you didn't tell me about the dream thing sooner. It's like a fucking Nicholas Sparks novel happening before my eyes! I'm going to look him up online."

I point a finger at him. "This is exactly why I didn't tell you sooner...because telling you anything like this is going to wind up with the three of us scaling his apartment complex drunk, and I'm too old for that shit."

"Do you know what apartment complex he's *in*?" asks Trevor, completely ignoring the important part of what I just said. "Because honestly, with just the bare minimum of upper body strength, you can..."

"Trevor, I love you, but we're not stalking him, and we're *definitely* not trying to climb up another balcony. You nearly fell to your death last time."

Trevor ignores me, holding out his phone. "I found him."

Caroline leans over his shoulder. "Oh my God, Quinn. He was a swimmer? You know that's my kryptonite."

Trevor looks her over. "Precious, anything with a package is your kryptonite. And believe me, this guy has a package. I could tell just by the way he carried himself."

I roll my eyes. "You could not *just tell*."

"I've seen a lot of dicks, honey, so yes, I can, but I'll prove it. Let me find a photo of him in a Speedo."

The two of them comb through photos while I pretend this

isn't happening. "That one," whispers Caroline, sounding like the lead detective on a police procedural. "Zoom in."

"Oh, Lord," says Trevor. "Quinn, you need to lock that down."

Caroline grins at me. "You really do."

I huff in exasperation. "I'm *engaged*, morons! And you're both in the wedding. I'm not sure why I need to keep reminding you."

"Just look at the photo," Caroline urges, snatching Trevor's phone from his hand and waving it in my face.

I fold my arms across my chest and close my eyes. "I'm absolutely not going to look at a picture of my doctor in a Speedo." In part, because I've already seen those photos.

"Mmm," Trevor says, licking his lips. "You know what I'd love? A photo of him in tighty-whities. Damp tighty-whities. My birthday falls right before Christmas. Get one for me. It could be a combination gift."

"I'm not sure how familiar you are with modern medicine, Trevor, but in *this* country, we don't routinely spend time with our physicians whilst dressed in wet tighty-whities."

He pouts. "I feel like you're not even trying."

19

QUINN

On Friday morning, I arrive at my office but don't go inside. Instead I scan the street for Nick, who's meeting me here for the trip to New Jersey. He offered to pick me up at home, but it seemed too intimate, somehow. I struggle to ignore the voice in my head insisting that the way we're meeting, on the surface, looks a lot like cheating.

I spy him in a Jeep, idling on the sidewalk with the top down, and my heart does this dorky little skip at the sight of him.

"Hi, stranger," I say, leaning my head in the window. "You wouldn't happen to feel like driving me to New Jersey, would you?"

He smiles at me just the way I remember from some other time, sheepish and cocky at once.

"Sure, pretty girl in a dress. Climb in, and I'll drive you anywhere you want."

I open the door and hoist myself in. "You'd make a terrible abductor."

"I am an *excellent* abductor, I'll have you know."

"You didn't even offer me candy. Candy is the lynchpin to a successful abduction."

He grins and reaches into the back, behind the passenger seat, and places a box of Hot Tamales in my lap. I stare at it. "This is my favorite candy."

His smile falters a little. "Lucky guess." Yes, a lucky guess... like knowing my favorite pasta and being so certain I was an architect when we first met. He doesn't see a past with me the way I do, but that knowledge exists somewhere inside him anyway.

"You're sure you want to do this?" he asks. "We could just play hooky instead."

For a single moment I allow myself to consider it. What would playing hooky with Nick consist of? A thousand possibilities occur to me and all of them appeal. I exhale. "As off-putting as I found Grosbaum's *excitement* about my inoperable tumor, I do feel like I have to check this out."

I plug the address into the GPS while he maneuvers through the crowded back streets of Georgetown to get us to Canal Road. I've felt vaguely guilty about the fact that I'm doing this without telling Jeff, but he's traveling again and it's a sunny day—not a cloud in the sky—so I decide I'm just going to give in to the experience. I may not even be around next summer, so if I want to have one perfect day with Nick—a day that actually *happened*—this is my shot.

"Does Jeff know you're doing this?" he asks.

I glance at him, wondering if it's an accusation. "No. Did you tell Meg?"

His eyes remain on the road. "She's at a conference."

I guess that's a no. "I hope it wasn't a big deal taking off work?"

He shakes his head. "I don't see patients on Fridays anyway, so I just got someone to cover my morning rounds. What about you?"

I shrug. "I hate my boss and she hates me, but it's hard to say too much when your employee tells you she has a brain tumor."

His jaw flexes. "Why the hell are you still there? How *exactly* is it too complicated for you to get your architecture degree? Because it seems kind of simple to me."

I let my head fall back against the seat and close my eyes. It's hard to argue on behalf of something I'm not certain of myself. "From a financial standpoint, it doesn't make sense. I'd be thirty or thirty-one when I finished, and to do what I actually want to do, I'd need a master's degree. Which means four or five years during which I'm not producing an income."

"I get it," he says. "It's intimidating enough to take money out for student loans without losing your income in addition to it, but long-term you'll earn it back."

I suck my lip in between my teeth. "Actually, I inherited some money from my dad. Enough to cover school, at least undergrad." I could explain why our living expenses are such a concern, but I don't want to throw Jeff under the bus. Nick already seems to think very little of him and telling him about Jeff's job history won't improve that. "But we have a mortgage that requires both our incomes. And Jeff really wants to use the inheritance on a down payment for a bigger place, which is probably the smarter thing to do."

His nostrils flare. "Do *you* want a bigger place? Or wait, let me rephrase that: do you want a bigger place more than you want the degree?"

No.

The answer reverberates in my chest. Would I *like* a bigger place, one with hardwood floors and a new kitchen and a bathroom big enough for both of us? Sure. But I don't hunger for it the way I do that degree. It doesn't make my heart beat hard at the thought. When I think of getting a new place, I feel more resigned than anything else. "Probably not," I say quietly. "But if I only have a few years to live, does it really matter whether I got the degree I wanted?"

"It's possible you'll have more than a few years, but that's really a question only you can answer: does it matter?"

My gaze turns toward the window, at the dense wall of trees outside, almost close enough to touch. Does it matter? The practical part of me says no. But there's another voice inside me, something wild and hopeful. And it says *fuck it. I want this. I want that life I've been dreaming about, even if it will amount to nothing. Even if it can't include Nick.*

"You were already at Georgetown and I assume you had good grades," he says, as if he can hear my internal argument. "Why not check and see if they won't let you just slide into classes this fall? And if that fails, I know a few people we could talk to."

I'm like a shaken bottle of seltzer, bubbling up inside but not quite stable. I can't believe we're discussing this—not as a hypothetical, not as a *someday it's possible*, but as something that really could happen. Jeff will not be pleased, but for the first time in my life, I sort of don't care. "I'll think about it."

"I know it's none of my business, but you're my best patient. I want you to be happy."

I laugh. "Best?"

His smile lifts high on one side. "Okay, the only patient who held my hand when we met and told me we were married."

Argh. I'm never going to live that down. I cover my face. "You weren't supposed to mention that! It's so humiliating."

His hand brushes mine, back to back, a quick but intentional sweep. "It's not humiliating. It's eerie, since you were so accurate. And cute. Maybe the only time eerie and cute have been combined together. But speaking of bizarre things you seem to know, did you have any more dreams last night? I'm still waiting to hear what retirement community we end up in."

I laugh. "That might be too *boring* for me to remember when I wake up. No, last night, it was just us walking around some campus I've never been to. And the bad dream...the one in the hospital. I had it again."

"I can't get my head around that one," Nick finally says. "That I'm in it. Maybe you saw something that's going to happen in the future."

It's occurred to me too, but it just doesn't add up. "You and I are *together* in that dream, but in real life, you're with someone and I'm about to get married, so it can't be the future."

"No one's married to anyone just yet," he replies quietly, and my heart begins that odd, fluttering rhythm. Half terror and half excitement. I shouldn't be in this car, I shouldn't even be entertaining the idea of cancelling the wedding. But I also can't deny that when Nick suggests it, I feel...set free. And I think maybe I haven't felt that way in a very long time.

~

WE PULL into Princeton just after eleven. Dr. Grosbaum's house, with its crooked shutters and the abundance of dying plants in the front yard, does not inspire optimism.

"You sure you want to do this?" Nick asks.

I square my shoulders. "Yeah."

He reaches out, his hand brushing my cheekbone, resting there for a single beat. "Hey," he says. "It's going to be okay."

I feel a sudden burst of love for him in this moment, warm as the sun. I love that he came here, even though he thinks this is a wild goose chase. I love that he's willing to support me, just *for me*, when it will cause him nothing but trouble. "Thank you for doing this."

His fingers trail away, a hair's breadth from my mouth—I

kind of wished they'd stayed—and he smiles. "Even if this doesn't amount to much, I'm glad I got this time with you."

We walk to the door together. I knock, and after a few breathless moments we hear shuffling coming from inside the house. The door opens and Dr. Grosbaum appears—looking far older than I'd have expected for a man of his age. Though he's probably in his early sixties, he could easily pass for seventy-five. It's less about age, I think, than that he's so grave and unkempt. His white hair is in desperate need of a trim, and he's wearing clothing that should have been donated long ago. This trip just became even less promising, if possible.

We introduce ourselves, but he is glancing past us and doesn't seem to be listening. "Come in," he says. "Come in."

We follow him into his office, Nick placing himself between us with his shoulders wide and his body tensed, like a lineman just before the snap. We sit patiently while he flips through a file on his desk. On the table behind him there's a wedding photo, and it takes me a moment to realize the groom is Dr. Grosbaum because he looks so young and so...normal. His bride's face is partially obscured, but it's obvious they're both radiantly happy. I wonder what went wrong, because I seriously doubt she's still living here—this place hasn't seen a woman's touch in a good long time. I look around and realize there are pictures of that same woman all over his office. In each, her face is slightly unclear, but I can tell she's young, and my initial disdain for him turns to pity. I assume she died, and it appears it wasn't far into their marriage.

"So, you're Quinn," he says. "And who is your friend?"

I knew he wasn't listening before. I introduce Nick again and Dr. Grosbaum's head cocks to the side, observing us both like pieces in a museum. "Interesting," he says, rubbing a pen against his mouth vigorously. "Very interesting."

Nick already looks irritated. "Your website said you're affiliated with Princeton?" he asks, his voice heavy with doubt.

"I was," says Dr. Grosbaum. "The university, in their infinite wisdom, no longer permits me on campus."

Great. I'm beginning to see all this through Nick's eyes, and it increasingly looks like a fool's journey. Nick's hand squeezes my thigh and I'm not sure if he's trying to comfort me or signal that we should leave, but either way I remain in my seat. We've come this far, and I have to at least try.

"Have you had a chance to look at the images I sent over?" I ask.

He nods. "Didn't need to, though. Based on your description of the events, I knew what was happening, and your MRI confirmed it." He flips on a light board, where my scans already hang. "Dr. Reilly, tell me something. Do you see anything unusual about Quinn's brain? Not the tumor. The brain itself."

Nick studies the images. "The amygdala. They're maybe a bit larger than normal. More oval in shape."

Dr. Grosbaum nods, a teacher rewarding an apt student. "What else do you see?"

Nick sighs heavily. Irritated, perhaps, or maybe he's just reluctant to answer. "You could argue that the frontal lobe has more density and nerve endings than is typical."

"Exactly," says Dr. Grosbaum, turning to me. "Quinn, the frontal lobe performs higher-order thinking. And yours, if I were to venture a guess, has about twice the capacity of a human's."

A small laugh escapes. "You say that as if I'm *not* human."

He shrugs. "Whether you are or are not is arguable. You're certainly a different variety of human than most. You are *thorax laneus tempore*."

I look from him to Nick, who is pinching the bridge of his nose. "Time jumper?" Nick asks. "Are you actually trying to say she jumps through time?"

"I am indeed," says Dr. Grosbaum.

For a single moment I'm speechless with shock. And then

common sense returns. "I'm not *jumping* anywhere. I'm dreaming. And this is the only time I know of."

"Except it's not really the only time you know of, Miss Stewart, since you appear to be remembering others, yes? Tell me something: these dreams of yours...are they particularly realistic? Do you emerge from them certain they happened and knowing things you couldn't possibly know?"

The accuracy of what he's said is unsettling, but just because he guessed something correctly doesn't mean his insane theory is right. "I suppose. But I'm remembering things that happened in the past few years, when I know for a fact they didn't. My passport very clearly shows that I've never been to London."

He leans back in his chair, the springs groaning beneath his weight. "If I were to venture a guess, I'd say there's been some foul play. Someone has gone back in time and done something to change the course of your life. I could jump back twenty-eight years ago, for instance, and give your father the job of his dreams somewhere in Germany. Suddenly, you are no longer here. You are Frau Stewart, dining on *wienerschnitzel* in Munich with your German best friend. One small tweak can alter everything."

Nick's lips press together, amused and irritated simultaneously. "So you're saying she's jumping between her life as it is and her life as it *could have been*?"

"No, I'm saying she's jumping between her life as it is and her life as it *was*," replies Dr. Grosbaum. He sighs. "Although I have no idea how. I've met many like Quinn but none who were able to go back and forth between different timelines the way she must be."

"Why would anyone reset my timeline in the first place?" I ask. "It seems like an awful lot of trouble for someone to go to, given that I lead a pretty uneventful life."

He gives me a small smile. "Maybe you do and maybe you

don't. You have no idea which of your actions *now* could have a lasting impact on someone else down the line. Maybe she's trying to stop you from doing something in the future. Maybe she wants something you have," he says, nodding at Nick.

It's a struggle not to roll my eyes. He's just like one of those palm readers who pulls tiny facts from what a customer is wearing or asks about to make predictions that *feel* real. He sees me here with a particularly attractive man and assumes jealousy is a motive I'd understand. I guess he's not entirely off base, but I resent it all the same. "And the culprit would need to be a female, and from the sound of it a jealous female, because...?"

"Because only females can jump. I'm not sure how, but it appears linked to the X chromosome. Men can carry the mutation, but that's it. So, your husband here might carry the markers for it to pass on to your children, though it would be incredibly unlikely, but nothing more."

"Dr. Reilly is not my husband," I remind him. Nick is tense beside me, ready to walk out the door. "Forgive me for my uncertainty, but this is a lot to swallow. How did you, um, come up with this theory about time-jumping?"

"It's not a theory. It's a fact," he replies. His eyes soften and he looks almost vulnerable. For the first time I see a bit of who he was in those wedding photos. "My wife...she was one of you."

"*Was?*" I ask.

"Time travel is far more dangerous than you can begin to imagine," he says, frowning at his desk. "She jumped back to check on something and never returned."

Ah. It's easy enough to see what happened and my heart aches a little for him. This poor guy was left by his wife—maybe he was already crazy, or maybe her leaving made him so—and he's created this whole myth to justify the fact that she's gone.

"I'm so sorry to hear that," I reply. I pick up my purse to signal the meeting's end. "Well, I guess that's about it. I appreciate you taking a look at the images and seeing us on such short notice."

Dr. Grosbaum shakes his head. "You don't believe me, but you should. Jumping into another timeline, inexperienced as you must be, must be deadly. It's shearing your brain as surely as I could with a pair of scissors."

I still don't believe him, but a part of me wishes I did. I want to think there's a way to stop what's happening in my head. And he seems so damn sure of himself when he says it.

"Okay," I reply, sinking back into my chair. "So how do I stop doing it then? I have no interest in these dreams, or *jumping* if you want to call it that. So tell me how to make it stop."

"You don't stop. You get better. You embrace your abilities instead of repressing them."

"Are you saying that would *heal* my tumor?" I ask.

"It could," he says. "I can't promise you that, obviously. But I can promise you that repressing them will only make things worse."

Nick's knee is bouncing and I can tell he's five seconds from calling this guy out for the quack he is. And I'd agree with that assessment. Despite the fact that there have been incidents in my life I can't explain, I don't think I truly have some kind of paranormal ability. Certainly nothing as extreme as the ability to travel through time.

I rise. "You've given us a lot to think about."

Grosbaum jumps up, blocking my path. "I'd love to run a quick DNA test before you go."

Nick, already standing close, steps slightly in front of me. "I don't think so."

"You're not doing her any favors, young man," Dr. Grosbaum says, his voice tight. "Whoever is resetting the timeline will continue to do so until she gets what she wants from your wife. If the resets don't kill her in the first place, that is."

"Quinn is not my wife."

Dr. Grosbaum throws his pen down in disgust. "And she never will be if the two of you refuse to listen."

WE CANNOT GET into the Jeep fast enough. Nick holds the door and I practically leap inside, feeling like the good Dr. Grosbaum could, at any moment, come running after us with a meat cleaver and a tranquilizer gun. And yet…as impossible as they are, Grosbaum's theories *would* explain everything. If only they'd been slightly less bizarre.

"I think I see why he's not permitted on the Princeton campus anymore," Nick says, backing out of the driveway.

I feel like an idiot for bringing him up here. If Grosbaum's theories were hard for me to buy, to Nick they must seem outrageous. "I'm so sorry I dragged you into this," I tell him.

His mouth stretches into a grin. "I forgive you, *wife*."

"Yeah, what was up with that?"

He laughs. "I have no fucking clue. So, are we safe to go eat lunch or do you think the crazy time-jumping lady, who wants to stop you from destroying the world, will interrupt?"

I grin. "I think we're safe. Besides, the impression I got from him is that this is about *you*, husband. Some woman wants to steal you away. Bitches be crazy and all that."

"You should explain to her what a dud I was on our honeymoon. Maybe that will dissuade her."

I curl up in my seat to face him. "I never said you were a dud. I said I don't remember."

The corner of his mouth turns upward, that dimple blinking into existence for just a moment. "That's kind of the same thing. All I can say in my own defense is that it'd be memorable now."

My stomach clenches with desire. I think of Trevor's question—*haven't you ever wanted someone so much you think you'll die if you don't get it?* I think I finally do.

~

WE GET BACK to D.C. just at the start of rush hour. I wish the drive had lasted longer. "Thank you for today," I tell him when he pulls up to my office.

"It was surprisingly fun," he says. His gaze brushes over my face, a muscle feathering in his jaw. "Will Jeff be home this weekend?"

The mention of Jeff's name replaces all my wistful infatuation with guilt. "Yeah. He wants to go look at houses. He's not going to be happy to hear I want to spend my inheritance on a degree instead."

His nostrils flare. "Only a selfish dick would try to tell you how to spend your money. Especially under the circumstances."

I shake my head. "Jeff's just looking out for our future. You probably make enough money that you've never had to worry about whether you'll be able to support a family. Jeff and I are not in that position."

I turn toward the door and his hand snakes out, framing my jaw. An intimate gesture, one neither his girlfriend nor my fiancé would appreciate, but I can't seem to pull away. "Please give it some thought, okay? Don't agree to anything with him just yet."

My pulse races. I get the feeling he's talking about more than just the house. I shouldn't agree, but with his palm pressed to my skin and the way he is looking at me, I'm unable to do anything else.

20

QUINN

The model home is cute but generic. To listen to Jeff, however, you'd think we were in Versailles. He fell in love the moment we pulled up. And once he saw the huge back yard, he was ready to put a ring on it.

"Think how awesome that yard would be for kids," he says. "It'll be just like how we grew up. Room to roam."

There's an unhappy little twist in my chest. Nick's question yesterday comes to my head—*do you want this more than a degree?* And the answer is still no, I absolutely do not. I'm not even sure I want it *without* the degree. I don't want what I grew up with. I want the city. I want to be able to order Thai food at midnight, walk places, be anonymous occasionally.

The agent gives us a tour and then suggests going to his office to look at pricing. Jeff is all in while I stand back. "Can we have a moment?" I ask the agent, who nods while Jeff's eyes dart impatiently between us.

"I think we need to discuss this," I say, after the agent walks away.

"It won't hurt to look at it," he argues. "We could write a check for the deposit today. We have forty-eight hours to change our minds."

I feel a tiny spark of anger. Has Jeff always pushed *this* hard for what he wants? Because I've made it pretty clear I'm not interested, and yet here he is using his hackneyed sales techniques on me, his future wife.

But maybe he's never needed to push this hard, because until now I've always just rolled over when he wanted something I did not. I'm not sure why it's taken me this long to see it.

"I've actually been thinking about going back to Georgetown," I venture quietly. My hands begin to sweat as I say these words aloud to him, far more directly than I have in years.

His face goes blank, uncomprehending. "As a *student*?"

I look up, rubbing my palms over my shorts. "Yes. I want to finish my degree."

"Quinn...Jesus. Are you serious? You...can't. Do you have any idea how much that will cost?"

Is he really asking me this, like I'm some naïve little girl who has no idea how much tuition would be? I'm the one who *went* there for Christ's sake. "Of course I do. But I've got that money from my dad, and I think that's how he'd have wanted me to use it."

"On some overpriced degree you're never going to use? Are you kidding me?" Jeff asks, rolling his eyes. "He'd roll over in his grave."

My jaw drops. "Are you actually trying to say you know better than I do what *my* father would have wanted for me?"

He digs his hands in his hair, then pulls me around the corner, away from the raised eyebrows of other people touring the model. "I don't understand what's going on. We've been talking about buying a house for years, and now, when we're finally about to pull the trigger, you think you want to go to school? I mean, is the brain tumor...I don't know, *influencing* you? Because it's coming out of nowhere."

Blood pounds in my ears so loud I can barely think. I can't believe he's trying to blame the brain tumor. I've been talking about school on and off since we first got together, and he just conveniently managed not to hear me. But before I can levy the accusation, he sinks into the stupid wing chair some designer has placed in the model home's mudroom and buries his head in his hands. "I shouldn't have said that. I'm sorry. I'm just under a lot of stress at work right now, so your timing isn't great."

I feel sympathy welling, and I resent it. I don't want to feel sympathy for him right now—it's an emotion that always ends with me giving something up. "What's going on at work?"

"They're laying people off. Our profits tanked last year and haven't come back...rumor is that they'll have cut forty percent of the sales force by the end of the year."

Forty percent? My eyes squeeze shut. I'm going to have to pay the mortgage alone again. And why the hell are we looking at houses if that's the case? "What will you do if that happens?" I realize, too late, that I didn't ask what *we* would do. Fortunately, he doesn't notice.

He stares at the ground, unable to meet my eye. "I have no idea. I can't go back to the farm."

Though I never, ever, wanted to live on his parents' farm, his words shock me a little. He loved that life and only gave it up to follow me here. I suppose I'd begun to think that maybe, if we didn't work out, if my doubts got the better of me, he would at least have that to fall back on.

"Why couldn't you go back to the farm?"

He doesn't look at me, and he doesn't respond.

Fear makes my voice sharpen. "Jeff, what happened to your share of the farm?"

"I sold it," he says. "That first job I took down here, when I followed you? It was a total pyramid scheme. I had no idea until it was too late. I was so desperate to make you happy, to impress you, that I just didn't see the signs, and I wound up so far in debt that I thought I'd never get out from under it. So I sold my share of the farm to my brother. I already knew for a fact you weren't ever going to want to live there, so it seemed like the best solution."

Shock knocks me backward. My mouth opens and for a moment no words emerge. The man in front of me is suddenly a stranger. How could he have gotten into that much debt and never mentioned it? "Why am I just learning this now?" I finally ask. I sound winded and I feel it too.

He buries his face in his hands. "I didn't want you to know. I was so fucking ashamed that I'd gotten played like that, and I just wanted you to be proud of me."

My hands clutch my throat. He loved that farm. He loved owning a piece of it, and I never wanted him to give it up. I just didn't want to be part of it with him. He brought all of this on himself and yet none of it would have happened if I hadn't insisted on moving to D.C.

He still won't look at me, so I sink to the floor and put my hand on his knee. This has been my role for a long time—soothing his wounds, holding him together. It comes naturally, but I'm a little tired of doing it. "We'll figure it out, okay? But if you're worried about your job, why are we out here looking at a house we can barely afford?"

"I just wanted us to have something," he says. "I'll get another job. Maybe not as good as where I am, but I figured if we had a home of our own, something solid and entirely ours, that it would be enough. We don't have to get this place. I got a little carried away when I saw the yard, but really I just want to know when push comes to shove that we have a place to raise a family. A place where we can get our life underway."

I squeeze my eyes shut, trying to temper my response

because the sheer stupidity of this plan is mind-boggling, and it's on the tip of my tongue to say it aloud. There's this canyon between me and Jeff, and I think it's always been there. We operate by shouting to each other over it, and it works, the shouting. It's been fine. But now I'm seeing what it's like to feel so close to another person I can barely tell where I end and he begins. And my God I want that. I *miss* it. "Committing to a mortgage we might not be able to cover won't make any house ours," I finally tell him. *Nick would know this,* I think before I can silence it. *Nick wouldn't need to be reminded about my desire to go back to school. Nick wouldn't discover I only have a few years to live and push me to give up a dream.*

"I just need to know that when we say for better or worse in a few weeks, that you mean it. That we're in this together," he says, his voice hitching on the last words. "Are we?"

He is so despondent, this man I love and have made a commitment to. And maybe there are other things I want now, things I want badly enough to weep and beg for them. Somehow, I'm just going to have to learn to let those things go.

"Of course we are," I reply.

~

On Monday afternoon, I return to Georgetown for the tests I need prior to my meeting with the oncologist at the end of the week. Nick walks into the waiting room with the sleeves of his Oxford rolled up, his tie loosened, the first hint of five o'clock shadow along his jaw. He draws eyes, and not just mine. The teenage girl and her mother sitting across from me nudge each other as they look him over. I'm tempted to tell them both to grow the fuck up, but I guess I'm no better.

I cross the room toward him and his smile is sudden, and stunning.

"Hi." I sound as breathless as a tween meeting her favorite boy band.

He looks around. "I assume Jeff's not coming?" I hear a hint of disdain in his voice.

"He left town this morning. He had a conference he really couldn't miss, but he'll be back for the meeting with Dr. Patel."

His hand presses against the small of my back as we head toward imaging. "And you didn't sign any contracts this weekend?"

I stiffen a little. "No." Though it's true, it's also kind of a lie. Because all I did, really, is put off the inevitable.

~

WHEN MY TEST IS COMPLETE, I head toward his office, with my brain flitting from Jeff to the house to Nick and back. I round a corner and collide with a teenage girl paying as little attention as I am. We look up at the same moment and for a millisecond she is a stranger. A breathtaking stranger with the most extraordinary gray eyes, going wide at the sight of me. It's her astonishment that jars my memory: she's the girl I saw as I floated back to consciousness during my last blackout, looking every bit as shocked to see me as I was to see her.

I stagger backward, still grasping her arm. "I saw you," I breathe. "I saw you in my dream." I know it sounds crazy, but I'm past caring about that right now, and something about the guilt in this girl's face tells me she already knows anyway. And knows she shouldn't have been there.

She swallows. "Yes, that happens sometimes."

"How?" I ask. "You're able to put yourself in someone's dream?"

"No. We were both just—" She grows still, suddenly, her eyes flashing to mine in alarm. "You don't know."

"I don't know what?"

She stares at her shoes, brown-and-white saddle shoes. The school uniform she's wearing could come from any time, really, but shoes like that haven't been popular for decades. It takes her a moment to reply. "You weren't dreaming," she says. "You were time traveling."

A chill slides up my spine. Four days ago, I laughed at the suggestion, but there's nothing about this girl that screams *mad scientist*. Her voice is matter-of-fact, reluctant even. And hearing the same information twice in four days is...unsettling. I lean back against the wall. "That can't be true," I whisper. "I'd know if I was doing it."

"Yeah?" she asks. "So if you hurt yourself—maybe got a tattoo in one of those dreams—would you be hurt when you woke?"

I think back to the hickey on my neck that day, the one that couldn't have come from Jeff. "That doesn't prove anything. Maybe it happens when I'm asleep."

Her mouth curves upward. "You're getting tattoos in your sleep?"

I close my eyes, struggling to make sense of this, create some logical argument. "Of course I'm not, but I think I'd know if I was time traveling."

"Apparently not," she says softly. She's probably 15 years younger than me, but right now she looks at me with sympathy, like a parent explaining death to a child. And as bizarre and difficult to believe as all of this is, I need answers and she might just have them.

"Can I ask you some questions?" I plead. "I'm trying to figure out why all this is happening, and—"

Her shoulders sag. "I need to go," she whispers, as she turns to walk away.

"Wait!" I cry. "Wait. Please!"

She turns around the corner and I lunge forward, my hand reaching out...and passing through thin air.

Only her clothes remain, in a pile on the floor.

I slide down the wall, staring blankly at the vacant space where she should be standing. Is it possible she really just did it? Is it possible I could do it too?

I think I'm starting to believe.

21

QUINN

When Nick finds me, I'm still on the floor, slumped against the wall. "Quinn," he says, dropping to his knees and gripping my shoulders. "What happened?"

"I just watched a teenage girl disappear in front of my eyes," I whisper. "She was there, and then she wasn't." I nod at the clothes in my lap. "These are hers."

I wait for him to smirk, to look at me the same way he did Dr. Grosbaum, but it doesn't happen. His eyes meet mine and in them I see faith. His belief in me makes my throat tighten. There's been too little of that in my life. "Do you have any idea who she was?"

I shake my head. "None. I can't believe I'm about to say this, but...I think it's possible Dr. Grosbaum wasn't quite as crazy as we thought."

"Did she say where she was going?" he asks. "What about her clothes? Did you check them?" He reaches for the clothes in my lap, digging into the skirt's deep pockets and pulling a handful of paper out. Candy wrappers, a few dollars, and something else. He holds it aloft after he's examined it. "It's a concert ticket for tonight. It's in Baltimore, but we could make it if we left right now."

"If she doesn't have her ticket, is she still going to go?"

A small smile cracks his face. "Are you really under the impression that a teenager capable of *vanishing in midair* is going to find a missing concert ticket an obstacle?"

I laugh, the sound slightly unhinged. I can't believe we're discussing this, and I can't believe it really may be true. "I guess not."

He pulls me to my feet. "Then let's go to a concert."

~

By the time we've made it through the tangle of traffic and construction on 95, found the club, and bought our tickets, the opening band—who I've never heard of—is done, and the crowd is chanting for the headliner, who I've also never heard of. Fortunately, the show is pretty loosely attended so we are able to push all the way to the front of the stage with ease. We get there and then walk all the way back, but she is nowhere to be found. She was probably my only chance to understand this and it just slipped through my fingers. My shoulders drop. "She's not here."

"We could wait..." Nick urges. "Maybe..."

"It's over," I tell him.

His jaw shifts. "I feel like you're giving up."

"There's nothing to give up. You can't possibly believe that —" I come to such a quick halt that he walks right into me. "She's here," I whisper.

She's ditched the sweatshirt in favor of a half-shirt and is wearing a plaid school skirt just like earlier...only now she's got it rolled up well above mid-thigh. And she's sitting at the bar surrounded by men I recognize from the posters and T-shirts being sold at a table near the entrance. The opening act, I assume. Each of them at least a decade older than her.

"*That's* our lead?" he asks with obvious skepticism.

"Does she look any less reliable than Dr. Grosbaum?" I counter.

"You have a point," he says, placing his hand at the small of my back. "After you."

I hustle through the crowd more easily than Nick because of my size. When I arrive, I lean against the corner so I can make eye contact with one time-traveling teenager and the four losers currently focused on her—one of whom is now holding a shot glass to her glossy lips.

"You guys know she's in high school, right?" I demand. Five faces turn to me, and the girl narrows her eyes. It's perhaps not the greatest idea to make an enemy of the only person who can help me, but so be it. "And I don't know where you're from, but statutory rape is kind of frowned upon around here."

The one beside her sets the shot glass down. "She said she was eighteen."

I roll my eyes. *For fuck's sake.* The girl barely looks like she's out of middle school. "Look at her. She's fourteen, if that."

The girl scowls at me. "I'm not *fourteen.* And you're being a total buzzkill."

"We'd be happy to drink with you instead," the guy closest to me says, his tongue sweeping his upper lip as his eyes slide over me. His hand shoots out to pull me by the belt of my dress, and suddenly Nick is between us, gripping the guy's wrist.

"Remove your hand," he growls.

I blink in surprise. Nick sounds *pissed.* And possessive. It's a new side of him. I can't claim to dislike it.

The guy takes one look at Nick and releases my belt. "Sorry, mate. Didn't know she was with you."

"Well, now you know," Nick snaps, "so keep your fucking hands to yourself."

The girl jumps off her barstool, but before I can lunge forward to grab her, one of the band members does it for me. "Let's at least get a picture," he says, wrapping an arm around her waist and raising his phone.

For a second, panic flashes across her face, and then she actually ducks her head to avoid being in the shot. "I don't like having my picture taken," she says, darting away.

I step around them and cut her off, grabbing her arm, not that it will do any good if she decides to disappear in midair. Her eyes raise to mine. "I can't help you," she whispers. "I'm sorry. I really can't."

"Please," I plead. "You don't have to do anything. We just need someone to explain this."

Nick comes up behind me, pulling me to his chest and wrapping his hand around my hip. Proprietary, the way I remember from so many of those dreams. The gesture would have shocked me a few days ago, but now it just feels *right*. All the more reason to figure this out as soon as humanly possible. "Please," he says. "We're desperate."

Her face softens when she looks up at him, in a way it did not for me. She sighs heavily. "I'll tell you what I can."

~

THE BAR IS no place for a delinquent teenager, but neither is the back of Nick's Jeep, so we walk to a diner across the street, where, under the bright lights, she suddenly looks painfully young, and fragile.

We slide into a red vinyl booth and Nick hands her a menu. "Order something," he says. "If you've been drinking, you need food."

She asks the waitress for a cheeseburger and a Coke.

Despite the outfit and the fact that we just caught her doing shots with a rock band in the back of a seedy bar, she is polite as she gives her order, and there's an air of privilege about her somehow. I'm guessing she's a trust-fund kid, the kind with wealthy parents who've handed over the child-rearing to their staff.

"What's your name?" I ask.

There's a split-second of hesitation. "Rose."

She's lying, but it hardly matters. "And how old are you really?"

"Sixteen."

Another lie, but I'm not sure that really matters either. "What on earth were you thinking tonight?" I ask. I know I shouldn't be wasting precious seconds lecturing this girl, but I can't stand the idea of her putting herself in a situation like tonight's. "Do you have any idea how poorly things could have gone if you'd left with those guys?"

She smirks. "You watched me disappear. An entire army of rock stars couldn't do anything I didn't want them to do."

Nick flinches at the suggestion that she might be a *willing* party to whatever an army of rock stars want to do. "Do your parents know where you are?" he demands.

She laughs to herself, but the sound is not a happy one. "Sort of."

"What does *sort of* mean?"

She looks away. "It means my father knows he can't do anything to stop me and my mother is dead, so if there's a heaven, she's watching my antics from there."

"Dead?" I whisper, my stomach dropping. "But you're so...young."

"A lot of us die," she replies, carefully aligning her flatware and avoiding my gaze. "There are so many ways a human can die, but for a time traveler, there are twice as many."

I think, fleetingly, of Dr. Grosbaum. I assumed he was lying to himself about his wife's disappearance, but what if he wasn't? How awful would it be to have the love of your life disappear somewhere, leaving you behind, wondering what happened?

"So you're in this alone," I say. "With the time traveling."

"My younger sister can do it, but she was born early and has some...problems. It's too great a risk."

"So how do you do it?" I ask.

She laughs. "Why are you asking me? You do it too. I saw you that day."

I sink back into the booth. "That wasn't time travel. It was just a dream."

"Right," she says, smirking again. "You just chose to go somewhere, then tumbled through darkness to get there, seeing me on the way, but you want to call it a dream."

I cross my arms, my voice hard. "I'm not *choosing* to go anywhere."

"Of course you are," she says. "You just don't know you're choosing it. You're attaching to a memory that exists. But maybe it's not one you consciously remember."

Nick buries his head in his hands. "I'm sorry, but I'm really struggling to believe this. I know Quinn saw you disappear, but it must have been some kind of trick."

She sighs, appearing exasperated by us both. "Look, I could go back a year and meet you, and you'd suddenly remember me now, but I don't really have time to prove it to you because it would take too much planning. But"—she turns to me—"in about twenty seconds, I'll need you to bring my clothes to the bathroom."

"Wha—" I haven't even completed the word before she slides under the table. And seconds later, she is gone, leaving only a pile of clothes behind.

Nick looks like he's seen a ghost. "What the fuck?" He pinches the bridge of his nose. "It's a trick. It's just a very, very good trick. We've apparently met the next David Blaine."

I laugh weakly. "*How?* Did she build a tunnel beneath the restaurant? Her clothes are under the table, and I'm fairly certain we'd have seen a naked kid running across the room. Everyone would have."

He rubs a hand over his eyes. "This isn't happening."

"Keep telling yourself that," I reply, giving him a small smile as I grab her clothes. "I'm going to find our naked friend."

~

I GLIMPSE bare feet under the closed door of a stall and hand her clothes over the top of it.

"Told you," she sings.

"The whole losing-your-clothes part must make all this jumping pretty difficult."

"You just have to plan."

She makes it all sound so easy, and so controllable, when I doubt it can be. "So the uniform you were wearing today...was that even yours?"

"My grandma lives near the school. I went to her house first, but she intentionally keeps the worst clothes to discourage us from jumping here, like housecoats and orange jumpsuits. So, I *borrow* from the school's lost and found."

She emerges from the stall with a wide smile and walks back to the table, where her Coke and cheeseburger now wait. "The one thing about jumping is that you're starving when you get back, and sleepy if you've gone far. You'll see."

She digs into her food and Nick watches, looking deeply unsettled. In a different world, I'd lay my head on his shoulder and pull his hand into mine. It feels like the action I'm supposed to take. I twist my engagement ring on my finger again and again instead.

"Okay, how does this whole thing work, theoretically?" he asks. "How are you able to do it?"

She takes a polite sip of her drink and looks up at him. "Every time traveler has this thing we call the spark. Time traveling's just part of it. Like, once we reach adulthood, the aging process slows for us as well. But, anyway, it's a genetic mutation, I guess. The only reason I have it is because both of my parents carry it. So both of Quinn's parents must have carried it too."

I laugh. I can believe in many things, but not this. "My mother thinks going to Philly for the day is a major trip. She is *not* a time traveler."

"You can be a carrier and never realize it. Or sometimes, for whatever reason, people refuse to use it," she says, glancing at me. "Like you. You obviously can, but you've chosen not to."

Nick rubs the back of his neck. "If Quinn is doing what you are, in *theory*, how come her body doesn't disappear like yours just did? She's not waking up naked anywhere."

"Because she's jumping into herself. It's sort of a baby step. But it sucks because you have no control over your actions that way, so you're just living something again. And it's dangerous too, because you're under the sway of the brain you had at that time. If you're happy there, you might not come back. You might not even realize you *want* to come back."

It's easy enough to picture. I remember Nick kissing me against that tree outside the high school. If any voice but his had been calling me, I'm not sure I'd have returned.

"These aren't memories, though," I argue. "These are things that never happened. Like, I see myself living in London with Nick, or growing up with him in another state."

She shakes her head. "All those things *must* have happened. You can't travel to something that has never or will never exist. All I can think is that maybe someone changed your timeline."

It's exactly what Grosbaum said. And it would mean that my dreams about London, about Nick as a child and our high school romance...aren't dreams at all. They actually occurred.

Nick blows out a breath, sinking backward into the booth.

"*If* this is all actually possible," he asks, "why would someone be messing with Quinn's timeline in the first place?"

"I don't know," she replies, raising a shoulder. "Maybe to make sure she doesn't do something in the future."

"I'm not Hitler," I argue. "I don't have a powerful job. I don't even fudge my taxes. There's *no* reason someone could ever be scared of what *I* might do."

"Maybe she wants something you have," Rose says. "Yeah, a time traveler can just take almost anything she wants but"—her eyes flicker from me to Nick—"some things you can't just *take*. Maybe it's him this person wants."

I can't believe I'm hearing *this* suggestion again too. "We, um...aren't together," I reply.

The girl raises one perfectly groomed brow and starts laughing. "Oh *really*?" She isn't merely dubious. She's acting like what I've said is so ridiculous that laughter is the only possible response.

"Yes. *Really*. I'm getting married next month." Nick's hand, resting at the edge of the table, clenches into a fist.

"Then I can only think of one other possibility," she says. "Someone's trying to kill you and keeps botching the job."

Nick's body leans forward, suddenly shot through with tension. "Why would anyone want to kill Quinn?"

She glances at me, hesitating. "I don't think I should say anymore."

I see her looking around as if she plans to disappear again and my pulse skitters. I *need* to know this.

"Please," I beg. "We've got to figure this out. If I can find a way to stop whatever it is I'm doing, or stop this person, maybe the brain tumor won't keep growing. You're my last hope."

She swallows, looking behind her before she turns back to us. "There's something called the Rule of Threes."

Goose bumps crawl up my arms. I recognize the phrase. It's something I talked about in therapy as a child. "I've heard of it,"

I say quietly to Nick. "I spoke about it in those dreams I had as a kid."

Beneath the table his fingers twine with mine as he looks at Rose. "What is it?"

"That spark I mentioned she has?" Rose says. "Imagine it's like a flame that can be shared but can't be spread too thin. It's limited to three females in a family. No one knows why it's this way, but it's what keeps the population small and ensures that no family has too much power."

I must be missing something. There's absolutely no way that can apply to my family. I have two living female relatives at most.

"So how do you choose who gets it?" Nick asks.

Rose yawns, covering her mouth with the back of her hand. I wonder where she's from and what time it is there. "That's like asking how you choose eye color," she says. "You're just born with the mutation, or you're not. And it would be unbelievably rare, but if four people were born with the mutation in one family, then that's one too many, and the weakest one just...dies. Usually the oldest, unless there's someone like Quinn, who's allowed her spark to fade out early."

"I don't see why that would lead someone to kill her," Nick argues.

She shrugs. "Think about me and my sister. It won't happen, but let's say my sister gave birth to two time-travelers. Then there'd be four of us, and one of us would die. Killing me would ensure that she and her kids were safe, right?"

Nick scrubs a hand over his face. "There's no...I don't know...penalty for that? I can't believe I'm even asking this question, but isn't there some authority who keeps you from doing that to each other?"

"There are penalties for a lot of things," Rose replies, aimlessly pushing the remaining fries around on her plate. "But not for that, if all the stories about it are true. In theory, if you do it in just the right way—stab a family member with the spark in the heart—it will strengthen yours. It might even heal Quinn's tumor. Or it could be some crazy old wives' tale. I've never done it, obviously, so I have no idea."

My fingers tap restlessly on the seat beside me. We are wasting precious time on a line of discussion that couldn't possibly be relevant. "Look, there's just no way this can apply to me," I interject. "I have no immediate family left other than my mom, and she obviously isn't time traveling. But this weird jumping thing I'm doing—why is it so limited? Every single memory is about Nick and things related to him. I don't remember my parents or my friends or my classes...it's like my entire life is a blank slate aside from him."

"*Limited?*" she asks with a sharp laugh. "Jumping between timelines the way you are—it's unheard of. I have no idea how you're doing it and how it hasn't completely fried your brain, but I guarantee you wouldn't be sitting here right now if you were letting in *more*. For you to be doing it at all... there must be something there you want super badly, is all I can say. Enough that you're willing to die for it."

I flush as Nick's eyes meet mine. I'm fairly certain we both know what it is I want so badly from those previous timelines. He leans in, his forearms on the table, hands clasped. "So is there any way you can help us?"

"Like what?" she asks warily.

"I don't know," he says, staring at his hands. "Maybe you could undo something. Or time travel forward and see if they've developed a way to bypass the amygdala so we can reach Quinn's tumor."

"I'm fifteen," she says. "You're really going to trust what I tell you so much that you'll cut into her brain based on it?"

His mouth twitches. "Probably not. Especially since you said you were sixteen a minute ago."

She grins. Her smile reminds me of someone, but I can't

place it. "I've jumped back and forth all day. Maybe it scrambled my math a little."

"Convenient," says Nick, restraining a smile of his own. "What about going backward to fix things? If someone died, and you knew how to cure it or change something, could you do that?"

I feel a lump in my throat. He's thinking of his brother, I'm sure, and I wonder once again how devastating it must have been for Nick to lose his twin. I've never even met Ryan in this lifetime, yet somehow the fact that he's dead is hard for even me.

"Like, could I go back and assassinate Hitler and stop all those deaths in World War II?" she asks. "No, for a variety of reasons, but most importantly, it wouldn't do any good. Once someone is gone"—she averts her eyes—"they can't come back. Otherwise, I'd have gone back to save my mom." For a moment, she looks young, and heartbreakingly fragile.

"Which reminds me," she says, throwing her napkin on her plate, "I have to get home to my sister."

I exchange a panicked glance with Nick. I'm not done. Rose is the key to solving this, I feel certain of it. "Is there any way for us to get ahold of you?" he asks.

She smirks. "Sure, if Quinn finally learns how to time travel." She thinks for a moment, rubbing a finger over her lower lip. "Look, I really have to go. But I can come here tomorrow morning, if you want. Early, though. Like, seven. Just bring my stuff."

With that, she slides under the table. And all that remains behind are her clothes.

22

QUINN

Nick and I sit alone, staring at each other in shock.

"Dammit," he says. "I just wish she'd stayed five minutes longer."

"Well, there's still tomorrow." I look at my watch. "It's already after midnight though. You should go home. I'll get a hotel up here somewhere and see what she has to say in the morning."

His jaw sets. "No way. We're in this together. We'll stay up here and come back tomorrow."

My heart flops in my chest like a dying fish. It's one thing to go get a second opinion with my gorgeous doctor in tow. Jeff wouldn't have liked it, but it felt justifiable. As did driving to Baltimore tonight. But staying here with him? There's no stretch of imagination by which that is okay. And yet here I am, nodding in agreement.

We get in Nick's Jeep. "I'll go on Expedia," I say, pulling out my phone. He's doing all this for me and I can't possibly let him pay for his own room, but my stomach sinks at the cost of one room, much less two.

He shakes his head, pulling onto the street. "That's okay. I know exactly where we can go."

A few minutes later we pull up to the valet stand in front of the Four Seasons.

I flinch. A room here will be a fortune. Six hundred? More? And I'll have to pay for two. I briefly think of all the things I could have paid for with that much money. It's half the mortgage. And how the hell am I going to explain this to Jeff? I can't. There's just no way.

"Nick," I breathe. "I think this place might be a little out of my price range."

He does a double take. "You actually thought I'd let you pay for this?"

"Of course I did," I tell him, frowning. "You've already done way too much. I'm sure we can find something more reasonable nearby."

He hands the valet his key and tucks his head, trying hard not to laugh. "Quinn, you're not paying. I think you remember the starving-resident version of me from London. That's no longer the case."

"But..."

"Stop," he says. "Consider it payback for the honeymoon in Paris during which I apparently never let you leave the room."

With that, he places his hand at the small of my back and leads me to the registration desk. He asks for two rooms and the bright smile on the clerk's face fades a little. "You don't have a reservation?" she asks. I'd have thought this was obvious, but apparently not. She goes on the computer and makes a sad face when she looks back at us. "We're pretty much sold out. There are three rooms available but two of them aren't cleaned yet. I can get you in a one-bedroom suite if that will work? It has a fold-out couch."

Nick and I exchange a glance. It's less than ideal for both of us. "Is that okay?" he asks quietly. "I can take the couch."

"I'll take the couch," I argue.

"No, you won't," he says, turning back to the clerk and handing her a credit card. She begins ringing us up. "I promise it'll be every bit as boring as our honeymoon apparently was," he adds under his breath.

The clerk hands Nick our key cards. "Can we assist you with any bags this evening?"

I feel my cheeks turning pink—even though we asked for two rooms, showing up here with no luggage has *cheaters* written all over it. "No bags," Nick says casually. "We got out of a show and decided we'd rather not drive back to D.C. this late."

We head toward the elevators. "You sound like you check into hotels with strangers all the time," I mutter.

He raises a brow. "And you sound jealous."

"You wish," I reply, though he's absolutely correct. I am painfully jealous of any woman who has ever checked into a hotel with Nick Reilly. I wasn't the first and I won't be the last, and that fact bothers me more than I care to admit.

~

THE SUITE HAS two double beds with plush white duvets and a mountain of pillows. I eye them longingly as I help him open the sofa bed, which is pretty much the opposite of plush. It also has loose Cheerios inside it, which makes my stomach turn a bit.

"We need to ask housekeeping for sheets," I say. "Go to bed. I'll call down there and wait out here for them."

He laughs wearily. "Quinn, you're not sleeping in this shitty bed."

I pull my hair back into a ponytail with my hands and let it fall again. "You can't sleep out here. This bed isn't as long as you are, even if you sleep diagonally."

His arms fold across his chest. "You are absolutely not sleeping on this thing. I spent many nights as a resident napping in a supply closet. This is luxurious by contrast."

"And you came home afterward totally wiped out and miserable," I counter, before I realize I don't *actually* know this. I sigh heavily. "Look, this is stupid. There are two beds. You take one and I'll take the other, unless this is some kind of ethics thing."

He flinches. "I'm pretty sure I fucked that up the minute I agreed we could stay in the same suite."

Shit. My life is a disaster but am I making his one too? He'll probably need to lie to his girlfriend about this. And what are the consequences if it gets back to his boss? "Are you going to get in trouble for this?"

"It's fine," he says. "Don't start feeling guilty. This was my idea, remember? Look, you were right. There are two beds. And I was a perfect gentleman the night I stayed in your room at the hospital, right?"

I have a sudden vision of him stretched out on a bed—naked from the waist up, only a sheet covering the rest—asking me to admit he'd been a gentleman the night before. I also remember how badly I wanted to suggest he stop being one. My breath comes in a single shallow burst. "Yes," I whisper. "You were a perfect gentleman."

"Do you want to take a shower?" he asks. My eyes widen and he bites down on a grin. "*Alone*, I mean. Do you want to go shower *alone*, behind a locked door?"

I laugh. "Yeah."

I rinse off and emerge a few minutes later in a hotel robe. His eyes drift over me before he looks away. I guess what I'll be sleeping in here once I remove the robe isn't exactly lost on him, but it's not like I can sleep in the dress I wore to work.

"You're all done in there?" he asks.

I nod, hiding a yawn behind the back of my hand. "I'm so tired, I may be sound asleep by the time you're out."

His grin lifts high on one side. "Maybe *you're* at fault for our unmemorable honeymoon."

The truth is that I have no specific memory of sleeping with him. Just the build up to it, the heaviness of anticipation in the base of my stomach, a small beating heart between my legs. And it's probably for the best that I can't remember more than that—the last thing I need is one more way in which real life is unsatisfactory. "No, I feel certain it was you," I reply, perching on the edge of the bed. "Maybe you were impotent."

"If you remember *that*," he says, with a look that makes my whole core clench tight, "you are definitely not remembering *me*."

BY THE TIME he gets done in the bathroom, I'm in bed with the lights off. There's just enough moonlight in the room to reveal that he is all muscle, and he's filling out those boxer briefs in a way that would make Trevor salivate.

"I just saw your underwear."

I see a flash of teeth. "They're boxers. It's like seeing me in shorts."

"Hmmm. Interesting you think so. Expect my friend Trevor to be stopping by the hospital on casual Fridays from now on."

He climbs into bed, the sheets pulled haphazardly to the bottom of his rib cage. I can make out the definition of his arms, even in the dim light. I'm torn equally between guilt and a desire to look some more.

He rolls toward me. "We have somehow avoided talking about the most glaringly obvious subject," he says.

"The fact that we are currently sharing a hotel room?" I ask. "I thought we'd be better off pretending that wasn't the case."

"Since it could get me fired, you're probably right. But I was referring to the fact that two different, unrelated people have told us over the past few days that you can time travel."

It hasn't been far from my head either. "I'm finding it all a little hard to believe," I reply. "I'm 28. It seems like any magical powers I have should've kicked in by now."

"Rose said you might not even realize you're doing it, though," he counters.

I wave my hand at his words, shooing them away. "How could anyone *not realize* they were time traveling?"

He pushes up a bit, his elbow bent, his head supported by his forearm. I wonder if he has any idea just how good he looks like that. "You've been thinking you were dreaming all these times when you go back to see me, right?" he asks. "Have you ever dreamed something else and had it wind up coming true?"

I hesitate. Swallow down the crazy impulse to tell him things I swore as a child I'd keep to myself. "Yes, but everyone does. That's just coincidence."

"Okay, what about this Rule of Threes thing? There must be something there."

"How could there be?" I ask. "I mean, I have an aunt I've never met on my dad's side, but as far as I know, she never had kids, and I have an uncle on my mom's side, but he's gay. And even if my aunt did have kids, and it kicked this whole thing into play, why would she mess with my timeline? Why not just kill me?"

He laughs. "Good to know how *you'd* handle the situation."

I smile at him in the darkness. "I'm not saying I would. But you know I'm right. If she needs me out of the picture and wants to take my spark or whatever, she could do so pretty damn easily. What good would changing my timeline do anyway?"

His voice is soft when he finally replies. "It might keep you from meeting me."

We both fall silent, and the sudden absence of sound underscores something I'm increasingly certain is true—I was meant to meet him. To remain with him. It's happened before, it may be happening now...and someone is going out of her way to prevent it.

"I wish Rose had been able to change things," he says quietly.

I wish she was too. When it all comes down to it, time traveling seems to have way more negatives than positives. You can't keep anyone from dying, but you're way more likely to wind up dead yourself. "I'm sorry she couldn't help you...with your brother."

"That isn't why I was asking her about going back to save someone," he says. Our gaze holds, locks, for half a second, my pulse racing. I wish for so many things right now. I want to live, I want to solve this. But mostly I want to cross over and slide into bed beside him, if only to press my head against his bare chest, feel his legs tangle with mine.

I close my eyes, desperate to stop my thoughts, and when I open them, he's rolled to his back and is gazing at the ceiling. "It's so weird that you know about Ryan. I don't talk about him to anyone. Even my parents don't talk about it anymore."

For some reason, the topic of his brother opens up this chasm inside me. *Fear*. I don't want to ask about him, don't want to know, yet it feels like the monster under the bed: I'm never going to rest easy until I've seen what's there. "How did he die?" I ask.

"He got in a car with this drunk idiot. I still have no idea why he did it. He knew better. But if I'd gone to the party, it never would have happened." His voice is heavy, quiet with guilt.

"You can't blame yourself for that," I say softly.

"We were bickering about everything back then—competing," he says. "I don't even know what the hell we were competing *about*. It's like adolescence kicked in and suddenly we were at each other's throats. But anyway, I knew he was making bad decisions, but I was sick of his shit. That's why I didn't offer to be designated driver."

A memory of some past conversation with him pushes inside my brain. From London, right after we met. His hands on my face, his eyes so earnest. *How can I possibly deserve this,* he said, *when Ryan got nothing*?

A puzzle piece snaps into place somewhere in my brain. I can almost hear it click. "That's why you're with Meg," I whisper. The words surprise me. I'm not even sure I meant to say them aloud.

His eyes flicker toward me, luminous in the moonlight. "What do you mean?"

I barrel on, saying things I have no right to say but in the dark it feels safer for some reason. "I've been trying to figure out why you're with her when you're obviously not in love with her. And I think it's because you feel like you don't deserve more, you don't deserve to be happy when Ryan can't be."

He's silent just long enough to leave me wondering if I've pissed him off. "Maybe," he finally says. "So that's my excuse, but what's yours? Why don't you think you deserve more than Jeff? And please don't bother trying to tell me he's everything you ever dreamed of. He obviously isn't."

I guess I brought the question on myself, as much as I dislike it. "Jeff isn't perfect," I reply firmly, "but I'm not either. I love him for who he is, and I forgive him for what he's not."

"And what is he?" Nick asks. The words echo with scorn, but they shouldn't, because there's plenty to love about Jeff. Qualities I've given short shrift to ever since Nick came into the picture, which is so unfair.

"He's a good person. He's kind to children. He stops to greet every single dog he passes. And he's tried harder than any person I know to make D.C. work for him no matter how many times it knocks him down." I could keep going, but I get the feeling there's nothing I could say that would leave Nick convinced. "I know the two of you were at odds the other day and you seem to think less of him for being at work so much, but you've seen him at his worst. We wouldn't have gotten through my father's death as well as we did without him."

"My boy scout leader was a good person too," he growls. "Doesn't mean I need to marry him. And it's great if he helped your family but that was what—seven or eight years ago? What's he done for you since then? Because he seems pretty fucking self-centered from where I stand."

"He's not. He gave up what he loved most to follow me to D.C. And he's stuck it out no matter how hard it's been, all for me."

"Give me a break. He followed you because he *wanted* to. He didn't give up what he loved most...you're what he loves most. He did that for himself. Tell him you're going back to school. Let's see how selfless he is then."

I flip on my back and pull the covers up to my neck. "You're making all this sound so terrible, but it's easy to take one aspect of a relationship and make it seem defective. All couples argue and all couples want different things. I'm not going to fault him for having opinions of his own."

He presses his eyes shut and when they open, I see an apology there. "You're right. I'm sorry. I just feel like you should have more than that."

No, I think. *I have exactly what I want*. Even though I now remember something better. Even though I can feel in my chest what it was like to be in love with Nick, the kind of love that expands inside you until you're so full it almost hurts. Because a sort of terror consumes me when I imagine having that now. I can't begin to explain what it is, but as I lie here I know that it's related, somehow, to Ryan. The mere thought of him makes dread seep into my bones.

"I'm sorry about your brother," I finally whisper, as I drift off to sleep.

"It was a long time ago," he replies.

Except I wasn't apologizing for his loss. I was apologizing because I think it might have been my fault.

The Homecoming Committee has done their best with the whole "Midnight in Paris" theme, but the truth is, a bunch of balloons and drawings of the Eiffel Tower aren't enough to transform our gymnasium into anything other than...a gymnasium with balloons and handmade drawings.

"So, this is what I've been missing being homeschooled," I say, taking it all in. Nick and I exchange a smile. "I feel like I don't even need to go to Europe now."

Nick laughs and brushes a lock of hair back from my face, his eyes flickering over my mouth with a longing I feel down to my core. "So I don't need to worry about you taking off for London and leaving me behind anymore," he says. "Mission accomplished."

"You could always come with me," I suggest. I don't know why my heart beats so hard as I say the words. We're talking about something that's years and years from now. "You could do your residency there."

He moves closer, close enough that his mouth is nearly on mine. "We could get an apartment together. But I should probably marry you before any of that."

He has only the ghost of a smile on his face. I have one on mine as well. But our eyes are serious. We phrase these things as jokes, but we mean every word. "Yes, you should probably marry me."

He releases a tiny huff of air, as if desire is displacing the oxygen in his chest. "God, I want to kiss you right now."

All he has to do is use that low voice on me and I'm weak-kneed. I blow him a kiss and back away an inch. "This is my first homecoming. I'm not spending it being mauled in the back seat of your parents' Volvo."

He closes the distance between us again. "You love being mauled in the back seat of my parents' Volvo."

I do. I like it way, way too much. But it's too early in the evening for me to be thinking about how badly I want him to do it again. "Come on," I say, pulling him by the hand, forcing him to mingle and pour me a glass of punch, just because it's so ridiculously old-fashioned. He's a good sport about the whole thing, but after an hour he is itching to leave.

"We have to at least wait to see if you're Homecoming King," I chide.

He glances away. "I won't be. I told them to throw out any votes for me." His eyes remain on the floor between us. "I just... Things are tense enough without that."

What he means is that they are tense with Ryan. Because of me.

"Let's dance," he says, trying to distract me—something he accomplishes with ease, because no one alive is more distracting than Nick, whether we're standing in the middle of a crowded gym or alone in the treehouse, though my mother's now forbidden that last bit.

He twines his fingers through mine and leads me onto the dance floor. Some sappy ballad is playing. "I don't think we can swing dance to this one."

Our eyes meet. He tried to teach me to swing dance once, in the treehouse. It was one of the rare times we found ourselves alone, without any adults around. Needless to say, the lesson devolved quickly into something else entirely.

"I'm not sure I got enough of a lesson to do it right," I reply, wrapping my arms around his neck. Even in my heels, he towers over me. His face is boyish, but there's nothing boyish about the rest of him. All his hours of training in the pool have left him with the

ripped body of a grown man. I feel heat at the base of my spine, just picturing him climbing out of the water. I made a promise to my mother that I intend to keep, but it's getting harder by the day for us both. Every time he kisses me, I want to climb him like scaffolding.

He leans toward my ear. "Remind me to give you another lesson sometime."

I'm about to reply when he turns me, and I find myself looking directly at Ryan, who is watching us with that look on his face, the one he wears far too often of late. He's here with Lisette Durand, a French exchange student almost every guy in the school wants to date, yet our eyes meet and his expression—already grim—turns into a scowl. Why can't he just let this go?

"You okay?" Nick asks as I stiffen.

"Yeah," I reply. "But I'm ready to leave whenever you are."

"I'm ready now," he says, pulling my hand. I've promised my mother we'll wait until we're out of high school to have sex, but when we are alone, it's a struggle to remember that. And the look in his eyes right now says it'll be extra hard to remember tonight.

We head toward the auditorium's exit, but Ryan has beaten us there. He stands hand in hand with an irritated Lisette, blocking the door, legs spread like he's ready for a fight.

"Where are you going?" he asks Nick, never glancing at me once, because I no longer exist to him. Not the way I used to.

Nick straightens and his chin goes up. "I don't answer to you."

"No, but you answer to Mom and Dad," Ryan says, his eyes shifting to me, "and you made them a promise."

"I know that," Nick growls. "And I don't need a reminder from you."

"Well, since we now know that keeping agreements is a struggle for you, I thought I'd better mention it." Their mother told them they couldn't ask me out until I turned sixteen, an agreement Nick broke when he kissed me that day in the woods. I was always going to choose Nick. But Ryan doesn't seem to believe it.

"Get out of my way, Ry," Nick says. He has a slow temper, but

there's steel in his voice when he's on the cusp of losing it, and even Ryan knows not to mess with him when it's present.

"Don't fucking forget," Ryan says, as Lisette pulls him away.

We go out to his car, but guilt weighs me down the entire way. I hate that I'm the reason things have gone wrong. I stand still by the passenger door, staring at the gym.

"Come on," Nick whispers, the words coming so close I can feel them against my lips. "Let's go before one of the teachers comes out here." He smiles, leaning closer. Anticipation crests in my stomach, making me breathless.

I am not normally the aggressor, but tonight, I am. I ignore his words and pull his mouth to mine, letting the slow sweep of my lips and my tongue do the work for me. I will make us both forget how much Ryan hates us now.

23

NICK

I am certain I won't be able to fall asleep. Not with Quinn a few feet from me, presumably wearing next to nothing. I try to focus on anything other than her, lest she wake up to find me dry humping the mattress in my sleep, but I can't seem to stop. I'm remembering her face after we left Grosbaum's office, relaxed and happier than I've ever seen it. Remembering the moment she walked into the room for Darcy's birthday party, looking so fucking ethereal she hardly seemed real.

And then I'm thinking of the lake, and when I fall asleep that's where I go. Quinn is in that red bikini, floating away on the Sunfish, shouting at me to come help her, panicked and laughing at the same time. I swim to her, pulling myself up, and her body presses to mine. She is taut and sun-warmed, and as our mouths join, I want to groan with the relief of it—decades, centuries of separation finally behind us. I pull her on top of me and she comes willingly, sliding against my skin. Her top is gone, though I don't remember undressing her. My palms go to her breasts—how could I have forgotten how perfect they are? —and then to her nipples, pressing pebble-hard against my chest. She gasps then, and I lose that last ounce of restraint I was clinging to.

I roll her under me, my hands gripping her hips, my mouth hungry for every inch of skin. I'm hard as nails and just the friction, being pressed to her stomach, has me close to coming. I slide her bottoms off to the side. She's drenched, ready.

Except…there's something wrong here. I want to plunge inside her more than I've ever wanted anything, but how did we get here? How is it that her bikini is gone and beneath us it is soft, nothing at all like the Sunfish's fiberglass bottom?

I open my eyes.

I'm not in a boat. I'm no longer in high school. And Quinn is beneath me, in the hotel room we rented. I have no idea how she wound up in my bed, but she is quite obviously sound asleep, despite the fact that she's arching against me and my hand is…fuck…between her legs. I'm so hard my dick has pushed through the slit in my boxers. With a suppressed, reluctant groan, I remove my hand and go the bathroom to take care of an issue I probably should have dealt with earlier. The obsession with her has to end… It was one thing to have a painful crush, but this has gone too far. I could lose my fucking medical license over what just happened.

I stand beneath the hot spray, one hand pressed to the wall to support myself. I think about the feel of her beneath me and the way her body arched toward mine, begging for more. I think about what would have come next, how I would have thrust into her and fucked her hard and fast, with the kind of desperation that comes from years of denial.

I come in five seconds flat.

24

QUINN

I open my eyes to daylight streaming in and sit straight up with a gasp. I went to sleep in the bed next to the window. I *know* I went to sleep in the bed next to the window.

I am no longer in that bed. I clutch the top sheet to my chest and turn toward Nick, who is slowly blinking awake. "Good morning, roomie," he says with a yawn.

"Why am I in your bed?" I grit out.

"Maybe you time traveled there."

His smile is teasing, but I barely even register it. My heart feels like it's going to explode. *I knew we shouldn't have shared a room.* Practicality and sleep deprivation made the decision for me, but I knew better. "I seriously need to know why the fuck I'm in your bed."

"I think you must have been sleepwalking," he says. "I woke up and you were there, so I just switched over to your bed."

My stomach takes a nosedive. He's making light of it, but the fact remains that I climbed into bed with him, wearing nothing but a thong. Even if nothing more happened, that's sort of enough, right there. "Oh my God."

"Quinn," he says, pausing long enough that I'm forced to look over at him. "It's not a big deal."

"I'm pretty sure Jeff wouldn't agree with that," I whisper.

He lifts himself up on one arm. The sheet is down at his waist, so I get to watch a thousand muscles blink into life at the movement. For a moment I'm so spellbound I forget what I just said. "Please tell me you're not going to feel guilty about something that minor, especially given that it happened when you were asleep."

"I guess," I say with a sigh. "It's still..." *Awful, wrong, humiliating, inappropriate.* There are so many ways to end that sentence. "Bad."

"Hey, come on," he says with a grin, "you and I are apparently married in some alternate universe, remember? Technically, I think that means you're cheating on *me* when you're with Jeff."

I laugh reluctantly. "Is that how it works?"

He looks over at me from where he lies, his smile fading. There are words there, right on the tip of the tongue, but they never emerge. He pushes the sheet away and walks to the bathroom instead, and I remain behind, drinking in the sight of him —that swimmer's back, boxers clinging to his tight, perfect ass. As horrified as I am by what might have happened last night, I sort of wish I could remember every single second of it, whatever it was.

WE ARRIVE at the diner far earlier than necessary, the two of us rumpled and walk-of-shame-esque in yesterday's clothes. He's in no rush since someone is covering his morning rounds, so we order breakfast and nurse cups of coffee while we wait. There's nothing magical about it. The diner isn't particularly clean and the coffee isn't especially good. But I'm *happy*. Not that lukewarm, milquetoast version of happy I normally am, but something so much better. For the first time, my soul is full. All I want in the world right now is more of him. More time, more knowledge. "What's your favorite color?" I ask.

He looks at me for a long moment. "Green," he says. "Favorite movie?"

I shrug. "I don't think I have one. What's yours?"

A small smile warms his face. "*Inception*. Have you seen it?"

I shake my head. I've always meant to, but when you're part of a couple things tend to get decided based on who cares the most, and it's never me.

"You should," he says. "Favorite song?"

"It's an old Foo Fighters song," I reply. "*Everlong*."

His smile grows slightly wistful. He rubs a hand along the back of his neck. "Mine too."

The waitress refills our coffee, and he stirs cream in his until it's the lightest beige. Almost the color of his skin right now, with that tan of his. Before I can stop myself I think about that skin, which I saw a great deal of this morning. His smooth back, his broad shoulders. *Stop, Quinn. Those thoughts can only cause trouble*. I focus on my own coffee instead. "Do you think Rose could help with Darcy if she really can do what she says she can? Like go back in time and change something?"

He sets his spoon on the saucer and looks at me, thinking. "Darcy had headaches for months last summer, and her pediatrician blew it off. I suppose she could warn Christy about the tumor somehow, but what would compel her to believe a teenage girl's advice instead of a pediatrician's?"

I laugh. "Rose is a lot more duplicitous than either of us. She can probably figure something out."

"That kid," groans Nick. "The only thing worse than having

an out-of-control delinquent teenage daughter would be having one who is capable of time travel."

"And lands everywhere naked."

"*And* aspires to party with an army of rock stars," he adds, shaking his head. "Anyway, speaking of our troubled new friend, I was trying to come up with questions for her since we might not have much time."

I nod. "We should ask if there's someone else we can talk to," I tell him. "Maybe her grandmother or someone who's been at it longer would have ideas for us."

He leans back in the booth. "I think we should also ask if there's a way she can go back and reset things somehow. If she could keep you away from the lake, maybe you'd never have had these flashbacks at all."

I feel a sudden urge to smile and cry at the same time. "If I didn't have these flashbacks, I wouldn't have met you."

He glances away. "I thought that's what you wanted."

"No, I..." Heat creeps into my face. It would be better if we hadn't met. I just can't bring myself to wish for it. "It's almost seven. I'd better get in there with the clothes."

I slide from the booth, before he can see my face, and head to the bathroom, my mind a whirlwind of things that aren't related in any way to my brain tumor, or the fact that time traveling exists, much less that I might be capable of it. With everything that has happened in the last twelve hours, the most terrifying revelation of all is this: I wouldn't want to change anything that's happened if it meant never meeting Nick.

In the bathroom, I lean against the sink and wait for a pair of bare feet to materialize at the bottom of the bathroom stall. How does she do this? How does she land in a bathroom stall without discovering it's occupied? What does she do when there's not someone waiting outside with clothes in her size? If I was capable of time travel, I think I'd avoid it just because it seems so fraught with difficulty.

At 7:00, I watch expectantly. At 7:01, I shrug—just because she can time travel doesn't mean she's punctual. At 7:05, I start to worry. That's when I finally open the bathroom door and find her note.

I'm so sorry. I really can't help you anymore. Good luck—Rose

25

NICK

Quinn and I are both quiet on the way home. She gazes out the window with unseeing eyes. Her hopelessness destroys me.

"Hey," I say, reaching out to grab her hand, "don't give up, okay?"

She forces a smile. "It seems unlikely to me that we will meet a *second* time traveler to answer all our questions."

"There are lots of other possibilities. You're seeing Dr. Patel on Friday. Don't give up on regular medicine just yet."

She sighs. "This is obviously not a standard tumor. Can an oncologist even help?"

I've tried to avoid thinking about it, because I can't stand where my head goes. Right now, I just need to believe in something, and so does she. "We have no idea until we try."

She's quiet for a moment, staring out the window. "Why did you decide to do your residency in London?" she asks suddenly.

The question surprises me, mostly because I really have no

answer to it. "I have no idea, to be honest. It just hit me when I was in high school, and I never seriously considered anything else. Why?"

She runs her thumb over her lower lip. "I had a dream about it last night. We were teenagers, and in my dream, I was the one who wanted London, not you. It's just strange you wound up there anyway."

She points to a street and I turn, pulling up in front of a small house that's seen better days. In a neighborhood that's seen better days as well. I hate the idea of leaving her here alone.

"How much longer is Jeff out of town?" I ask.

Her lips press together. "Just until Thursday night."

I shouldn't have asked and I also shouldn't ask the question I'm about to, but it seems like a very lonely life out here by herself, in this depressing box of a house. "What do you do at night, when he's gone?"

She shrugs. "Usually, I just go home. Sometimes I go out with my friends or walk down to the harbor for a while. People swing dance there when the weather's good."

My spine tingles. It's one of my two recurring dreams—me with a girl I assume is her, dancing in the grass. I never gave it too much thought until now, but I'm pretty sure we were swing dancing, that I was teaching her how. Did it happen before? Is it supposed to happen now? "And you just watch?"

She smiles sheepishly. "I'm too uncoordinated to dance, and I'd look pretty damn silly out there alone, even if I did know how."

"Anyone can swing dance."

Her mouth opens to speak, and then closes again. Whatever she was going to say, she's decided against it. "Not me."

"Maybe I'll come down there sometime and prove you wrong," I say softly.

A hundred emotions flicker over her face. Love and hunger

and desire and, finally, grief. I'd give anything to heal that grief, except I think I'm the source of it.

I GO TO WORK, but the thought of Quinn and everything we've just learned is never far from my mind. I stare at the images from a recent scan of one my Alzheimer's patients, studying the tangle of amyloid plaques that indicate its progression. There will be nothing happy about the conversation I'm about to have with his children. I don't regret my decision to enter neurology, as depressing as it often is, but for the first time, I truly consider what led to it.

If Quinn's life changed, mine must have too. Was there a part of me that somehow *knew* she'd have problems this time around? Knew my best shot at finding her again was by entering a specialty she'd be likely to seek out? Or did some piece of me just long for her and attach to the discipline that led me to her in the first place?

There's a tap on the door and Meg walks in. She's been at a conference for the last week and I didn't expect her back until later today, but based on her presence here now and how deeply unhappy she appears, I assume she came home last night instead...and wants to know why I wasn't there.

Guilt kicks sharply in my stomach. Even if I can cut myself some slack for what I did with Quinn, unknowingly, the bigger issue is this: discovering just how much I feel for her has proven I *don't* feel enough for anyone else. What Quinn said last night was correct—I let things get this far with Meg because it didn't seem fair to ask for more when Ryan wound up with nothing. But Meg deserves to be more than the penance I pay for what I did to my brother.

"I thought you weren't coming back until tonight," I say, at a momentary loss for words.

She sinks into the seat across from mine, her arms folded over her chest. "Yes, that became pretty obvious to me when you didn't come home last night."

I rock back in my chair. "I went to a show in Baltimore, and it was late so I just crashed there."

Her eyes narrow while she looks for the cracks in my response. Thank God it's actually true. "Alone?" she asks. "You went to Baltimore *alone*?"

"Yeah," I say. A small lie, more for her protection than my own. "But I think we need to talk."

She freezes. I suppose the phrase *we need to talk* never leads anywhere good. "Talk about what?"

I place my hands flat to the desk and force myself to say words I know will hurt her, no matter how gently I deliver them. "Meg...you're amazing, but I don't think this is what I want."

Nothing in her face changes. She was unhappy before and she's still unhappy. "I knew you'd do this," she finally says, eyes narrowed. "I've never seen a man more scared of commitment in my entire life."

I rub the bridge of my nose. I should have anticipated an argument. She's not the type to just let things go. "I don't think that's what this is."

"Of course it is!" she cries, throwing her hands in the air. "And *why*? I'm the one who's a child of divorce while *your* parents are still happily married! If either of us should be freaked out, it's me. You don't have a single reason to be scared. But you are. And that's all this is...you're scared."

If she knew how I felt about Quinn she'd realize how off-base she is, but God knows that wouldn't improve this situation. "I'm so sorry. There's just a certain way I want to feel before I get serious with someone, and it's not there with us. We have a nice time together, but you deserve more than I can give you."

Her eyes bulge. "Are you fucking serious right now?" she

demands. "We have a *nice* time? We've been together for a *year*! We've practically lived together for three quarters of that, and all you can say is that it was *nice*?"

I close my eyes. I've never dated anyone as long as Meg, but I've been through some version of this situation a thousand times. "I wanted this to work, but it isn't fair to keep going down this path, when it isn't right."

"Nick," she pleads, her voice catching, "if no one is ever right, it means you want something that doesn't exist. We've had this conversation before, remember? This is just how you are."

I thought she was right at the time. I'd dated more beautiful, intelligent women than I could count, and it never worked —because I was waiting for one specific person without ever realizing it. "I think it exists, Meg."

It's the wrong thing to say. Her eyes dart to mine, reminding me of a lioness zeroing in on her prey. "There's someone else."

"No, not really."

"Not really isn't *no,*" she hisses.

I lean forward, clasping my hands on top of my desk. "I'm not seeing anyone, if that's what you're asking."

She brushes the tears from her face. "My landlord already rented my apartment. I have to be out in a week."

Guilt hits hard. I can't break up with her and force her to crash with friends for weeks while trying to find a new place. "You can take mine. I'll find something else."

She buries her face in her hands. "So this is just *it*? Just like this?"

I clear my throat. "Yes. I'm sorry."

She jumps to her feet and marches out. I watch her go, knowing I've made the right decision and wondering, at the same time, if I'll come to regret it. What we had was nice, and it was easy, and I'm not sure what I've opened myself up to, aside from a lifetime of wanting a woman who is about to marry someone else—a woman I couldn't be with even if she were free.

It's never going to be fair to anyone I date, to any woman I end up with. Because I will always be wishing I was with Quinn instead.

26

QUINN

Dee spent most of Tuesday pissed off that I came in late. Since I took sick leave, she couldn't really reprimand me, but she spent the day punishing me for it, and Wednesday appears to be no better. "I need a mock-up of the D.C. housing supplement on my desk by four," she barks.

I blow out a weary breath. I expected her reaction, but it exhausts me nonetheless. Maybe it's just that losing my last shot at talking to Rose has left me depleted. "That isn't due for two weeks."

"And now it's due today," she replies with a brittle smile. "If you'd been around more this week, it wouldn't be an issue."

She walks away, and I think of my conversation with Nick on the trip to New Jersey. About architecture, about why I'm shuffling along in this job I hate. I guess it's selfish to consider blowing that money on a degree I may never use when Jeff could start a new life with it after I'm gone. But there's a tiny seed of resistance inside me that says *No, it's not selfish. You've given up enough for him, gone along with what he wants, what's best for him, long enough. No.*

I go online and look up the information for Georgetown's admissions department. And then, with shaking hands, I send them an email asking if I might be able to come back.

~

JEFF CALLS THAT NIGHT, miserable. He hates traveling, which makes each of these trips, for him, an endless series of small irritations—the long rental car line in Albany, the hotel room that reeks of smoke, fast food for days on end, running out of toothpaste in a town that closed an hour ago. We both knew at the outset this job would be a bad fit in many ways. But he was desperate to find work after his last layoff, and I was desperate too. I probably should have encouraged him to hold out for something better.

"I'm sorry," I sigh. "Maybe you should look for something else when you get back."

"The hell with D.C.," he says. "We should just move home." It's not the first time I've heard it. In his bones, Jeff will always be a country boy. He wants quiet and wide-open spaces, but I don't. I never have. "Coach has suggested a thousand times he wants me back as an assistant, and he's got to retire soon. Up there we could live decently on a teacher's salary."

A warning note chimes in my head, a chill between my shoulder blades. I've held all the cards during our relationship. I'm the one who left for D.C., ready to end it. He's the one who followed, who gave things up to be with me. But once we're married, will I still hold the cards? He knows I don't want to live up there, but he also knows I'm not much of one for fighting about anything. If he insists, I'll end up agreeing to go. And my inheritance will no longer be *my* money, it will be *ours*, and he'll have just as many rights to it as I do, most likely.

"I emailed Georgetown today," I blurt out. I meant to introduce the topic slowly. *Alas*. "Admissions. To see about coming back."

He's silent for so long I begin to wonder if he even heard me. "Honey," he finally says weakly, "you're not really considering this?"

He makes getting a degree in architecture sound like some outlandish pipe dream. As if I just told him I want to be an Olympic gymnast or star in *Hamilton*. It's one of many ways he and my mother are similar—the things they want in life have never required a degree, so to them it's mostly a useless accessory. A *second* degree, therefore, is completely frivolous. "Obviously I am, or I wouldn't have emailed them."

"Jesus, Quinn," he groans. "I tell you I might lose my job and you think it's a good time to quit?"

Will there ever be a good time to quit, Jeff? Will there ever be a time when you aren't about to lose a job? Irritation blossoms into anger as I hold in all the things I want to say. "Why was it okay for me to blow my inheritance on that house I didn't even want in Manassas, but it's not okay for me to use it on a degree I've wanted my entire life?"

He sighs. "Because a house moves our lives forward. Our neighborhood isn't a good place for kids. You know that. But think about how long your degree will take. Four years? Five years? And all that time you're accruing debt and not working. Which means we're not having a kid until well after you're done. I'm 32. I don't want to wait until I'm in my 40s to start a family, and that's basically what you're asking of me."

"I may only have a few years to live," I reply. "I don't think kids are even in the picture for me anymore."

"Stop saying things like that!" he demands. "You have no idea how long you're going to live! We haven't even met with the oncologist yet."

"Whether I have a year or a century, I'm going to want the degree more than a house."

He's quiet again, recalibrating. "Look, hon," he finally says. "I know I'm not reacting the way you want me to, but you're kind of springing this on me. If the degree is that important to you, we can discuss it, okay? Just wait until I'm home."

I agree, but as I hang up there's only one thought in my head: *that money is mine*. And it suddenly feels very important that I spend it the way I want before it becomes *ours*.

27

NICK

It's been forty-eight hours since I've spoken to Quinn.

Too long.

I need to hear her raspy laugh and see that surprised smile of hers, the pleasure in her face over the smallest things.

God knows I shouldn't, but I find myself dialing her number on Thursday morning. I could pretend this is a professional call, but I'm not fooling anyone at this point.

"I was just checking to see how many vanishing teenagers you've run into since I saw you last," I say.

She laughs. "My yogurt appears to have vanished from our break room, if that counts. Hey, guess what I did?"

I settle into my chair, leaning my head against the wall behind me. "Learned how to time travel?"

"Think slightly smaller. I talked to Georgetown about coming back."

There's something new in her voice. A certain charge, an excitement, that I've never heard before. "What did they say?"

She sighs. "I, of course, had some ridiculous hope that they might fit me in for the coming school year. I'm too late for that, but they said next fall for certain, and possibly January."

I might be able to help, but I don't want to get her hopes up. "The important thing is it's happening."

"Yeah," she agrees. The excitement has left her voice. "Probably."

"What do you mean by *probably*?" I demand. "This is what you want. There's no *probably* about it. It's happening."

She hesitates. I can picture her there, pressing fingers to her temple or twisting her ring. "I don't know. If I put it toward a house, Jeff would be able to enjoy it...or he could sell it and move back to Pennsylvania and start over. It's what he wants to do anyway. Is it selfish to spend that money on a degree I might never use?"

Anger, sharp and all-consuming, pierces me. She has a fucking brain tumor. He should be turning over the world to make every one of her dreams come true. "No," I hiss. "It's not. What's selfish is him asking you to do anything else with it."

"Well, once we're married it's our money, isn't it? It won't even be my decision anymore."

Jesus Christ. The idea of her really going through with this wedding kills me. The idea of Jeff keeping her from that degree bothers me almost as much. "Can you meet me at the harbor tonight? Around six?" I ask. "There may be something I can do. I need to make a few calls first."

She hesitates. "Sure," she finally says, her voice soft and a little uncertain.

And I begin to count the minutes until I see a woman I can never have.

~

THE LIGHT IS ALREADY WANING when I finally get out of the hospital. I walk fast, weaving through the throngs of students and tourists, a pulse of people entering Dean & Deluca, and another pulse trying to escape it. The sun is at half-mast by the time I reach the waterfront, and I scan the crowd with a sinking heart, wondering if I've missed her.

She is sitting on a bench in a blue dress, the sheer fabric floating around her knees. The expression on her face is wistful as she watches the dancers. When our eyes meet, the wistful look disappears, and she gives me a smile that is pure sunshine.

I take the seat beside her, trying to focus on my reasons for being here and not her proximity, her smooth skin, the smell of her shampoo. It's harder than it sounds. "I placed a call today. A buddy of mine works in the admissions office. You're in this fall, if you want to be. Most of the classes you'll need will already be full. He said he can find a way to get you into the majority of them. He'll email you in the morning."

Her mouth is open, her eyes wide and uncertain. "Wha... what? You got me into the fall class? Just like that?"

I nod. "If you want to be. I don't want you to feel like I'm pressuring you. I just thought—"

She springs forward and throws her arms around me tight, laughing and crying at the same time. "Pressuring me? You just saved me!" she cries. "Oh my God, I love you so much!"

Jesus, what I wouldn't give to hear her say it for real.

She releases me, pressing palms to rosy cheeks. "This is unbelievable! I'm starting school!" she squeals. "I'm really starting school!"

She's beaming, and it's impossible not to smile back, but I still need to discuss something else with her and it's slightly more sensitive. "I also talked to a friend who practices family law about protecting your money. He said a prenup would be best, but as long as you've signed the contract with Georgetown prior to the date of your wedding, the money from your father will be considered legally committed to your education and should precede any claim Jeff might have to it."

She gives a small nod. "Thank you," she says quietly. "So much. I don't even know what to say."

"You don't have to say anything. I just want to make sure you're happy."

She bites her lip as her eyes flicker to mine. Maybe she hears the finality in those words, the way I'm trying to convince myself this is goodbye. And it *does* have to be goodbye. As much as I don't want to walk away tonight, leaving her in Jeff's incompetent hands, I also don't have a choice. It'll have to be enough for me to know she's going back to school. Whether she marries Jeff or not, at least she's getting something she wanted.

I rise. "I think maybe you owe me a dance before we leave."

She looks up with cautious eyes, then slowly stands. "I really have no idea what I'm doing," she says.

I take her left hand and place it on my shoulder, before taking her free hand in mine. "Okay, just step," I tell her. "One, two. One, two. Now rock step."

That dream I always have of us dancing—was it something in the past or was I dreaming about this, right now? What I mostly remember is how badly I wanted her. How badly I wanted to keep her with me forever. I feel it now, every bit as much.

"Are you okay?" she asks, frowning.

"I guess you won't be too weirded out if I tell you I think I've dreamed about this?"

Her gaze shifts away from me. "I have too. You used to...I mean, I've *dreamed* you used to come meet me outside of this evening class I took to walk me home. And one night we danced in the grass."

Her words settle, fill the blank spaces in my mind. I pull her closer. "Is that why you come here to watch?" Because if I'd known this existed, I think I would have come here too.

Her smile flickers out for a moment as she looks around us.

"I think so. And now it reminds me of—" She flushes, letting her words trail off.

My hand presses to her hip. "What does it remind you of?"

She focuses on the ground rather than me. "The night you proposed."

I stop dancing for just a moment, surprised by what she's said, but even more surprised that I already sort of knew this. I can't detail our past the way she can, but I know the color of it, the feeling behind it. I know I *wanted* to marry her, even if I can't remember asking the question. "I feel like I knew that," I tell her. She's still embarrassed by the admission, so I pick up our steps again. "And now we do a little spin."

"I can't sp—" she begins, but she is already twirling away from me, unfurling effortlessly like a spinning top before momentum pulls her back. She lands against my chest, and when I glance down, I find our mouths are inches apart. My eyes focus there a moment longer than they should. We've been here before too. Exactly here. I wonder if I wanted her as badly then as I do right now.

She swallows and steps away. "It's getting dark," she says. There's a breathless quality to her voice that would give me a semi if I didn't already have one. "I should probably head to the Metro."

I want her to stay. I want this goodbye to never end, but it isn't my choice. We head to the path along the water, though it's the longer way to go. The sun is in its last gasp, coloring the sky in swaths of charcoal and pink. The crickets seem to begin chirping all at once, although it's probably just that there's finally enough silence to hear them.

"I had another dream," she says quietly. "The night we were in Baltimore."

I freeze. She'd be better off remaining unaware of some of what happened that night. "Yeah?"

"About your brother."

My brother has been dead for over a decade, but the idea that she climbed into my bed seeking Ryan makes me want to throw my fist through a wall. "Please tell me you don't remember anything sexual with my brother when you were apparently *married* to me but remember nothing."

She laughs. "No. It wasn't like that. I was at homecoming with you, and he was there with...what was her name? Lisette Durand. She was French."

Jesus fucking Christ. She remembers things even I don't remember. "So, I took you to homecoming and what you remember about it is my brother. You are singlehandedly destroying what remains of my self-esteem."

Her laugh is throaty, and the sound goes straight to my cock. "Are you jealous?"

"Weirdly, yes."

"Don't be," she says, smiling. "We wound up in the back of *your* car."

I groan. This is not what I need to hear in a public place, but I can't stop myself from asking for more. "And I guess that, just like our honeymoon, you mysteriously don't remember what happened there either?"

She flushes, her tongue tapping once against her upper lip. "Actually..." she says, "I do." We've reached the Metro at the worst possible moment.

"But you're not going to tell me any of it, are you?"

She shakes her head, blushing furiously. "Nope." And, pressing her lips to the corner of my jaw, she turns and walks away.

28

QUINN

Getting home from Foggy Bottom is never *not* a pain in the ass. It involves taking the orange line back to Metro Center, then catching the yellow line to my stop. I'm bumped and jostled, pushed forward as I climb onto the train, pushed backward when others join us. My toes are stepped on. I inevitably give up my seat for an old person or a child, while some douchebag sits with his legs spread, taking up two seats instead of one.

Tonight is no different, yet I smile the whole ride home.

Going back to school is a part of it, a *big* part of it— it means taking the classes I've been dreaming about for so long and telling Dee to kiss my ass sometime in the near future—but I'd be lying to myself if I gave it full credit. Because what really has me smiling right now, closing my eyes to remember the last hour more fully, is Nick. It's dancing with him, having him walk me to the Metro, the call he placed that singlehandedly made something I've wanted for years happen in an instant.

When the long ride finally ends, I walk home, preparing

myself for less happy things—like the discussion with Jeff that's coming. He's in the yard when I arrive, playing football with Isaac, and I stay where I am for a moment to watch them.

"Go long!" Jeff shouts and Isaac runs hard, catching the pass with his fingertips before he turns back to grin at Jeff, waiting for the praise he knows is coming.

Jeff gives him a thumbs-up, beaming like a proud father. The sight makes me happy and sad at the same time, because this is who Jeff was meant to be. A dad and a football coach in some small town. But instead, he's been trying to fit into my world, trying to constrict himself to my parameters, attempting one thing after another that doesn't interest him or come naturally. He did all of that for me. Have I considered him once while I fantasize about someone else and make plans to quit my job?

There's a brick in my stomach as Jeff sees me walking toward him and smiles wide, clutching the football to his chest. His love for me is so pure and uncomplicated, but I can no longer say the same. "Hey babe," he says, kissing my forehead. He throws the ball back to Isaac and waves to him as he wraps an arm around me and walks me inside.

He opens the refrigerator door. "I was going to start dinner, but I wasn't sure when you'd be home."

His goodness makes me feel petty and small. "I thought you weren't getting in until later."

"I caught an early flight," he says, squeezing my shoulder. "I just needed to see you after our talk last night. I know it's been a pretty stressful couple of weeks, between your tumor and losing our reception hall. And maybe I've been pushing too hard on the house. I just really want—"

"Georgetown is letting me start in the fall," I say, all in a rush.

His jaw swings open. "*What*? We said we'd talk about it."

"No," I reply. "*You* said we'd talk about it. I want to finish my architecture degree, and I have the money to do it. I'll give Dee notice sometime in the next few weeks."

"What the hell, Quinn?" he cries. "We discuss these things. You can't just go off and do whatever you want."

I meet his eye, and I feel…different. Like there's another version of myself eager to be brought into the light, one who's tired of sacrificing. I'm giving up everything I could have with Nick, but I'm done pulling my punches. I'm done acting like his happiness and my mother's matter more than mine. "*Do* we discuss these things?" I ask. "Because I don't remember you saying a word before *you* quit your job. Twice."

"You know I've been trying," he says, almost mute with shock. What he's really saying is *how can you throw this in my face right now?* And maybe he's right. I'm no longer sure of anything. "And what you're talking about is so different. I tell you I might lose my job and you just decide to *quit* yours. Even if I keep my job, do you realize how tight things will be on one income?"

My hand grips the counter. *Did he really just ask me that question?* We've been living on one income—*mine*—on and off for the past six years. I'm not sure I realized, until this moment, how much I resent him for it. "Of course I fucking realize how tight things will be," I reply, and I march into the bedroom and shut the door behind me before I can say anything worse.

I hear the roar of his truck, and instead of being worried that we're fighting, I'm just really glad he's gone.

I want Nick right now. Instead I turn on Netflix and find *Inception*. Even watching it feels like a small act of rebellion. I'm two minutes in when Nick texts, and it doesn't even surprise me. I needed him, and here he is.

Nick: I'm listening to *Everlong* on repeat.

Me: I'm watching *Inception*. It's just starting.

Nick: With Jeff?

I hesitate. The impulse to whine to Nick about the fight we just had is an unworthy one.

Me: No, he went out.

Seconds later the phone rings. "I'll watch it with you," Nick says. "Where are you at?"

I tell him, wondering if his girlfriend isn't there or if he's just been slightly more open with her than I've been with Jeff about all this. Somehow, I doubt he has.

We watch, mostly in silence, aside from my occasional pleas for spoilers. "Is his wife going to be okay?" I whisper.

His laughter is low. I can almost feel it against my ear, can almost feel his warmth against my side, smell his chlorine and shampoo. "I can't tell you that."

"Just tell me if—"

He cuts me off. "Watch the movie, baby."

It's a quiet thrill, that word. I wonder if he realizes he said it.

At the movie's end, I am weeping. Not pretty crying, but hysterical sobbing. "I'm so glad you can't see me," I say with some combination of laugh and sob. "I look like an idiot right now."

"No, you don't," he says quietly, certainty in his voice. "Did you like it?"

I swallow. I am full and heartbroken at the same time. "It was the most gorgeous movie I've ever seen. But do you think he got home? I guess we're not supposed to know." My voice breaks. I can't believe I'm crying this hard over a movie. "I think he got home."

"I think he did too," Nick says. We sit in silence for a moment, and I let myself picture an entire life like this, one in which all the beautiful and painful things in the world are shared with someone else, someone who feels them and sees them like I do. My eyes squeeze tight. I wish I could have that. I wish he was mine.

29

QUINN

The next morning, Dee barks at me from her office and I walk to her slowly, teeth grinding. I'm never in the mood for her bullshit, but that is especially true today with so many other things stressing me out. I still have not exchanged a single word with Jeff since our fight last night.

Dee regards me with even more hatred than normal when I walk in her door, but I expected it. Today when I got ready I didn't downplay anything. I put on my favorite pale gray sheath, red strappy heels, careful makeup. I knew I risked a day of her ire by coming in pink-cheeked and shiny. It was *freeing* that I no longer had to care. It's freeing even now. I can't believe I've spent so many years at this job I hate, cowering as if the fate of the world rested on remaining here.

I haven't decided when I will quit—it would make sense to wait until just before school starts, especially since Jeff could lose his job any second now—but I expect it'll be the moment she pushes me too far. Which could be anytime, really. Maybe today.

She has a litany of complaints, of course. She hates the layout, hates the cover, she even hates the design elements she herself insisted on. Funnily enough, it bothers me less than it normally would, because at last there's a finish line, a light at the end of the tunnel. Her time to use me as her whipping boy is running out quickly.

I'm at my desk making yet another set of unnecessary changes when Trevor pulls up a chair beside me.

"You look gorgeous today," he says. "And way too happy."

I grin at him. "The times they are a-changin'."

"And now you're quoting Bob Dylan," he says. "So, you're either morphing into a seventy-year-old or you finally got laid."

My phone chimes. Jeff's name flashes across the screen and my smile fades. He was in bed beside me when I woke this morning. I took in his face, dredging up every good memory I had of us in order to feel the way I'm supposed to feel—but it didn't work. "No one's getting laid, I assure you. But I'm leaving early today, which is almost as good."

"To see Dr. Hottie?" he asks eagerly.

I swallow. "We're meeting with another doctor but he'll be there, I think."

"Jeff and Nick in the same room?" he asks, eyes lighting up. "Can I come today? I'll be your plus one. There's bound to be punches thrown."

I laugh begrudgingly. "I'm not sure you bring a plus one to a doctor's appointment. And there will be no fight. I plan to tell Jeff he has to be civil."

Trevor grins. "From what I saw the other day, I doubt it's *Jeff* you need to worry about."

I HAND Trevor the proofs for Dee on my way to lunch. When I return, Dee is waiting in reception, clicking those nails of hers on the desk in a failed attempt at self-control.

"This is entirely wrong," she says, handing me the pages I gave Trevor earlier.

My teeth scrape against each other. "That's exactly what you asked for."

"Just start over," she says. "Start from scratch. It's all wrong."

I gape at her. She expects me to throw two weeks of work in the garbage and re-do it all five days before we go to print. "That's not possible," I say flatly. "We go to print on Tuesday. There's just not time."

She gives me a short, bitter smile. "Then it looks like you know how you'll be spending the weekend, doesn't it?"

There's nothing wrong with the layout. She's just punishing me. Maybe for the dress, maybe because of my infuriating insouciance all day. Jeff would ask me why I antagonized her in the first place, but Nick would ask me why I'm still here, and why the hell I ever let someone treat me so poorly. Questions I'm asking myself now.

I slide the layout back to her. "I'm not redoing this."

Her eyebrows go to her forehead. "You seem to be forgetting who signs your paychecks."

I wanted to go out in a blaze of glory, but instead the end will be simple and absent any drama. "Then don't sign them anymore," I reply without emotion. "I quit."

I've never seen Dee shocked into silence. I head toward my desk and she follows me. "You can't do that," she sputters. "We go to print next week."

I grab my belongings, grateful that almost everyone is at lunch so I don't have an audience. "Well, I've noticed that you've been playing around with the layout when I'm not in the office," I reply, "so maybe you'll be able to figure it out."

With that, I head straight out the door. Late July in D.C. is miserable—air so thick it's a struggle to breathe and heat that has your clothes stuck to you the moment you step outside—but right now, to me, it's perfect. Right now I'm not Quinn, the twenty-eight-year-old who might die. I'm eighteen again. A girl with dreams, about to escape the farm and go to the city, with her whole future ahead of her. My father encouraged me back then. I'm not sure what changed when he got sick, what made him so desperate to keep me safe and small with Jeff. But I like this version of me better, and I think he would too.

I pull out my phone and make a call before I can change my mind. Nick answers on the first ring. "Quinn? Is everything okay?"

He sounds slightly panicked. I like, far too much, that he worries about me. "Yes, it's fine, I just... Is this a bad time?"

"No, not at all," he says. "Hang on." I hear background noise, then a door shuts and there is silence. "Okay. I'm in my office. What's up?"

My mouth curves into a smile. "Guess who just quit her job?"

"Are you serious?" he asks. I love him for sounding thrilled rather than concerned. "That's fantastic. Was your boss pissed?"

"*So* pissed."

He laughs. "God, I wish I'd been there."

I lean against the wall, under the shade of an awning. "It was pretty sweet. I'd say it almost made it worth staying there as long as I did, but that would obviously be a lie."

"I'm proud of you," he says. "I just wish you'd done it years ago."

"Yeah, me too." Why didn't I? Why the hell did I let Jeff decide what I'd do about school? My only answer is that I trusted my father's opinion about things more than I trusted my own and allowed Jeff to assume that position once he was gone. "Anyway, I guess I'll be seeing you in a while at the meeting with Dr. Patel."

"Is Jeff actually attending this one?" he asks. There's no mistaking the hostility in his tone.

"Yeah." I sigh, brushing a hand through my hair. "But speaking of Jeff, I, um, haven't told him I quit. So, if you could maybe not mention that, I'd appreciate it."

There is a beat of silence. "You told me before you told your fiancé?" he asks. "Interesting."

I groan. "No, it's not. I just..." I really have no excuse. The truth is that, in just a few weeks, Nick's become my person. It's him, not Jeff, that I want to turn to with all my good and all my bad. I want to hand him my problems in a tidy package and have him help me carry the weight. I want him to hand me his. "I'll see you later," I say, ending the call abruptly.

I close my eyes, wishing I could just push a pause button on my life for a week. Long enough to get things straight in my head. Nick's taken, I'm taken. Even though we're arguing, I love Jeff. I picture how devastated he'd be if I were to suggest cancelling the wedding and feel this unbearable lurch in my stomach. He's loved me and trusted me for most of our adult lives, and I can't just throw it all in his face now, weeks before the ceremony. I just can't be that person.

I WANDER through the city and arrive at the hospital an hour later. Jeff is in the waiting room when I walk in. He rises and wraps his arms around me. "I'm sorry about last night," he says. "I shouldn't have taken off like that."

My eyes close and the air slides from my chest. "I'm sorry too." I've always hated any kind of friction between us, so I'm not sure why I merely feel resigned rather than relieved.

A nurse takes us back to Dr. Patel's office, and as we are

introduced, a joke I heard somewhere long ago comes to mind: *Why do they have to nail coffins shut? To keep out the oncologists.* In other words, if you're faced with an oncologist who doesn't seem optimistic, who doesn't have a long list of options for someone who is obviously beyond hope, you are really screwed.

And Dr. Patel does not seem optimistic.

His smile is muted, rather than encouraging. There's a lack of urgency to his movements, as if he already knows he won't really be doing anything today. "We're a little early," he says. "So we should give Dr. Reilly a moment to get here."

"I think we can start without him," Jeff says, a flicker of irritation in his voice.

"Let's wait," I say. Fortunately, Nick appears at the door just then, with the look of someone who ran to get here—loosened tie and tousled hair. His eyes go immediately to me, his gaze drifting over each inch of my skin so intensely it feels palpable. There is a connection between us, something physical I can't put my finger on. It's as if my nerve endings wake from a long rest whenever he's near.

The two doctors shake hands. Jeff and Nick merely nod to each other, the movement so small and so hostile on both sides that even Dr. Patel seems to notice. Nick pulls up a chair alongside mine.

"So, I've looked at your scans," Dr. Patel begins, facing me, "and the reports from Dr. Reilly. I think he explained that this tumor is an area we can't reach?"

I nod, holding my breath. I want him to lay out options and tell me there's a good chance. A seventy percent chance, but I'd settle for thirty. I'd settle for twenty.

"Unfortunately," he continues, "a tumor like this is unlikely to respond well to available treatments."

My breath releases and my spine bows. I was held upright by hope, and he just took it away from me. Nick's hand clenches into a fist. He knew, just like I did, that the situation wasn't optimistic. We were both hoping for a miracle, when neither of us believes in them.

"*Unlikely* doesn't mean it won't," says Jeff.

Dr. Patel nods. "Right, it doesn't mean it won't. But I think our best-case scenario is that chemo might give Quinn a little more time."

My hands shake, but inside I feel absolutely empty, depleted. *Zero percent* is what he's saying. I have a zero percent chance of surviving this. I look out the window. There are students in the distance, backpacks slung over shoulders, talking and texting and thinking about evening plans. This is the moment I officially separate myself from them, from all the people in the world who've forgotten the value of time. And Patel is offering me more of it, but I've seen firsthand how that goes. We begged my father to fight. We convinced him to try experimental treatments when the regular ones failed. He got an extra three months out of it, but it was three months during which he was bedridden and nauseous. He turned into a dry, wizened old man before our eyes. "More time during which I am very, very sick," I finally say, still looking out the window.

The doctor frowns. "Under normal circumstances, a tumor of this size would be having significant side effects, and I'm not quite sure how yours isn't. But given how well you're doing, I can see where you might not want to commit to a course of treatment, knowing it will make you feel worse."

I think about that. I think about the fact that I'm finally going back to school. I have a chance of making it long enough to get my degree. *And more time with Nick*, I think before I can stop myself. If I start on chemo, will I enjoy any of it? Will I even be well enough to go to school? No. I'll be sick and frail and miserable.

"I'm not interested in that," I reply.

"Quinn," hisses Jeff. "You can't just dismiss what he's saying.

You haven't even considered it." He turns to Dr. Patel. "What are the options? Because the tumor might not be making her sick, but it's definitely affecting her personality."

Nick's head jerks toward Jeff's. He looks like a volcano on the cusp of exploding. "What's that supposed to mean?" he snaps.

Jeff narrows one eye at him and offers his reply to me rather than Nick. "You're making decisions that aren't...that might not be rational. I'm worried it's a sign there's worse to come."

My jaw clenches. Is he really trying to imply that the decision to get this degree is irrational? A product of my tumor rather than the thing I've wanted, without cease, for a decade? I have many, many things to say about that, but not with an audience. "We can discuss this at home," I say tightly. "But I'm not interested in treatment."

"I know you don't want to hear this," he says softly, "but brain tumors do cause personality changes—and irritability and impaired judgment are two of those changes. I read about it earlier. You need to at least hear what the options are." He turns back to Dr. Patel. "So there's chemo and radiation, right? Which of those might help?"

Nick's voice emerges, a low growl. "You seem to be struggling to hear what Quinn's saying," he seethes, "so allow me to repeat it: she doesn't want treatment."

Jeff snaps his gaze toward Nick, the thin veneer of civility discarded. "And you seem to be forgetting you're not a part of this decision."

Nick's eyes have this gleam to them that doesn't bode well. "I haven't forgotten anything. It's just unclear to me why you think it's okay to ignore what she wants and talk over her."

Jeff stands, pushing back his chair, and in seconds, Nick is on his feet too. Their hatred for each other is a force, the fifth member of our little gathering, and someone is about to get hit.

Fear propels me from my seat. "Jeff, you stay here and finish the conversation," I say breathlessly. "Find out the options. I have some questions to ask Dr. Reilly outside."

Without waiting to hear Jeff's protests, I place my hand against Nick's chest and push. He doesn't move a muscle, even with all my force behind it, but I glance up at him, a silent plea, and he gives in, slowly leaving the room with me in his wake.

Nick is rigid as we walk to his office. I suspect it's taking every ounce of self-restraint not to turn on his heel and pull Jeff back out of his seat.

He opens his door and ushers me in. The last time I was here I refused to look at his photos because I was so terrified I'd see a wife and kids. I'm still terrified by what I'll see, but this time I look anyway. There's one of him with his parents, one with him and a bunch of guys in suits...and one of a very pretty woman in scrubs who must be his girlfriend. I wish I hadn't looked.

He shuts the door, but instead of taking his seat at the desk, he turns to me, standing closer than is safe for either of us. "Are you okay?"

I nod, my shoulders dropping. What Dr. Patel just told us was a shock only briefly. The truth is, I'd never hoped for much in the first place. "I got the feeling from you a long time ago it wasn't likely to work out. I knew what to expect."

His eyes close and he leans his shoulder against the wall. "I'm not giving up. I still think there are people who can help us."

"Maybe," I sigh. It's a long shot, but I'll cling to whatever hope I can find at the moment. "I should probably get back in there."

Nick moves, closing me in. "So, did you actually have something to discuss with me, or were you just trying to keep me from kicking his ass?"

He's so damn cocky, and it only makes him more attractive to me. I just learned I'm definitely going to die, but here I stand with *lust* my primary emotion. "You say that like you know you'd have won."

He steps toward me—far, far too close. My breath comes in tiny sips. His hand rises, the tips of his fingers grazing my cheekbone as he pushes my hair back, but instead of pulling away, his hand hovers there—cupped, ready to descend at any moment to cradle my jaw. "I'd have won."

God, I want to lean into the warmth of his palm. "I—"

"Tell me what to do," he says hoarsely. "I refuse to give up on this. There's got to be a way to find Rose or someone else and go back to fix things. I will do any fucking thing you name if it will help us figure this out."

There's a desperation on his face that I remember. I saw it when he kissed me for the first time in high school. When I was in the hospital and my blood pressure dropped. When I walked out of the diner's bathroom on Tuesday and told him Rose was gone. His eyes flicker to my mouth, and the pull toward him is so strong it takes all my willpower not to close the distance between us. "I...I can't think of anything."

He swallows. "I'm going to the lake tomorrow. You could come with me. See the house, the dock. Maybe it would jar something."

For a single moment I allow myself to imagine it: the two of us, the way I remember. Him swimming out to me, lifting himself into the boat without effort. The breeze in my hair, the sun beating down on us. His slick hands on my skin.

I want it so badly. And it terrifies me at the same time. "I can't."

"I'm not asking you to do anything wrong. You'd have your own room. You don't even have to stay. Just come out for a few hours."

I shake my head even as some distant part of my brain tries to rationalize agreement. I want to tell myself it's an *investigation*, altruistic in some way. It's not. "Imagine if the situation were reversed," I say softly. "Imagine that I'm engaged to you, and while you're out of town, I go stay at the lake with another guy. Would you think that was okay?"

He is silent, the answer written in the throb of his jawline. "I wouldn't be leaving you this weekend in the first place."

I go on my toes to press my mouth to his cheek. "I know," I reply.

My chest aches as I walk out the door.

30

QUINN

Jeff emerges from Dr. Patel's office to find me sitting in the waiting room. We walk out to the car in silence and the crowd shifts away from us, fearful our unhappiness might prove contagious.

We get to the car. He puts the key in the ignition, but doesn't turn it, shifting in his seat to face me instead. He seems less angry than he does incredulous. "Why are you being like this? Why are you just giving up?"

"There's nothing to give up," I say softly. "You heard the doctor yourself. There is no chance of survival. None."

"But he can give you time!" Jeff cries. "And you have no idea how much time he could give you because you wouldn't even let him speak. You just accepted the first thing he said like we were discussing a car repair. You didn't even seem surprised."

"I wasn't. I'd already spoken to Nick and I—"

"Nick," he sneers. "Since when are you and *Nick* best fucking friends?"

My stomach drops. Were we so obvious in that meeting

today? I tried to make things seem professional, but I doubt I succeeded. Admitting to any of this will get me nowhere however, so I go on the offense. "And since when do you nearly start a fistfight with the doctor who's been trying to save my life? If you really want to help, maybe you shouldn't be going out of your way to make him the enemy."

"I don't like the way he looks at you."

My heart thumps in my chest. "I have no idea what you're talking about."

"He walked into the damn room today and only looked at you, like me and Dr. Patel weren't even there. Like he was your husband and I was just some lowlife harassing you."

I glance away from him, knowing he's right and that I'll never be able to admit it. "I think you're reading too much into it. And let's not move away from the point, which is that you were ignoring my wishes, just like he said. And implying that me pursuing a degree I've wanted my entire life is some kind of symptom of this tumor, when really it's just me refusing to put everything I want in life on the backburner in lieu of what you want."

His mouth falls open. "I'm trying to move our lives forward. It isn't about what I want or what you want. It's about logic."

Wrong choice of words, Jeff. Resentment, held back for so long, floods me. "It's funny, then, how your logic always leads to *me* giving things up," I snap. "Do you realize I'd be done with grad school by now if you hadn't convinced me to wait? But you did. And then you convinced me we should buy a place, just before you quit your job. Yes, I can see how it's plenty logical for *you*—you get to flit from one job to the next, knowing I'll pick up the slack, but how was any of that logical for *me*?"

He stares at me for a long moment, shaking his head like he can't believe what he's hearing. "My God, Quinn. Have you felt like this all along? I thought you agreed. I thought you wanted the house."

"I didn't *not* want it," I admit. "I just didn't know that it was going to mean giving up everything I wanted more."

"You should have told me," he says. His shoulders are rounded. Every last bit of confidence he's regained these past few months seems stripped away from him. "I had no idea."

My inclination is to take it back, to apologize, but I don't. "And I had no idea you thought me going back to Georgetown was a sign that my brain was *malfunctioning*. You might have said that in private instead of announcing it to my doctors first."

He's silent, and then he leans over and pulls me in for a hug. As much as I want to resist, I don't. "I'm sorry," he says. His voice is choked. "I want to be what you need, but this whole situation brings out the worst in me. Everything's changing, and I hate it. I don't know what's going on with us, but I feel like I can't do anything right with you now."

I let my head drop to his shoulder. This situation has gone too far and it's entirely my fault. I've been pushing him aside ever since that first day at the inn, before I even knew Nick existed. I've been telling myself I was protecting him, but when Nick spent the night in my hospital room, when he went with me to meet Grosbaum, when we wound up staying together in Baltimore…I didn't keep those things to myself because of Jeff's tender feelings. I did it because I knew they shouldn't have happened. Each step has been slightly less justifiable than the one before it.

I swallow, forcing myself to make a suggestion I probably should have made long before. "Should we call off the wedding?"

His head jerks back. "Call it off? Why?"

I was hoping it would be obvious to him. "Because we aren't getting along. I mean, are you even sure you still want to get married?"

"Of course I do! What kind of question is that?"

His astonishment leaves me flustered. *Surely* the thought

has occurred to him at least once? "It's just...I'm just being realistic." I press my lips together, staring out at the dense summer foliage just beyond the parking garage. These are the last few days of July, and I don't even know if I'll have another one. "We don't want the same kind of life. You want to move home and live on a farm, which is my idea of hell. I'm keeping you from all the things you want in the world, aside from me, and the truth is that neither of us knows how long I'm even going to be around."

His eyes well. "But you're the part that matters, Quinn. You. Not living back home. Not the farm. Okay? So, we are still getting married. If you want to cancel the big wedding, we'll do that. People will get it, under the circumstances. I'll talk to the church down the street and see if they can open something up next weekend."

I freeze. The dread I've been feeling—about the future, about staying with Jeff—it sinks into my very bones at his words. "Next weekend?" I repeat, my voice too breathy. "I don't know if we can pull it together that fast."

"Just family and close friends," he says. "You've already got the dress. Instead of a reception, maybe we just go to dinner somewhere."

An anchor sinks deep in my stomach. I made a commitment—to Jeff, to my father—and it's not as if Nick's an option anyway. I look at the tears in Jeff's eyes and my shoulders sag. I'm not sure a year or two of independence would be worth the number of people I'd have to hurt to gain it.

~

THAT NIGHT, I try to persuade Jeff to leave town as planned for his bachelor/camping weekend, but he insists on staying. "I'll leave in the morning instead," he says. "Let's just have a nice night in. It's been too long."

It's probably what we need. A night where we're enjoying something together instead of a night where I'm thinking about all the things he's not. I could have watched *Inception* with him last night. There's this ugly assumption inside me that Jeff can't quite fill Nick's shoes in any given situation, but I'm not even giving him the chance to try.

"*South Park*?" he asks after dinner, turning on the TV.

"Let's watch *Inception*," I tell him, ignoring the strain on his face when I say it. Just because he prefers to watch comedies doesn't mean he's incapable of feeling something as deeply as Nick does.

It starts. I'm every bit as riveted as I was the last time, perhaps even more since I know just how badly it's all going to go. Jeff doesn't look particularly intrigued, but he's not complaining either. *Give it a chance, Quinn. Give him a chance.*

At the forty-minute mark, he sighs and hits pause. "I'm sorry, hon," he says. "This movie doesn't make a damn bit of sense. You keep watching. I'm going to bed."

I want to argue. For some reason it seems like my entire future, the fate of our relationship, rests on just getting him to the end of the movie. And that's insane. He doesn't have to like what I like. I don't like to watch football and that's not a deal-breaker for him.

But as soon as he's gone the next day, I do what I absolutely should not. I pick up the phone and call Nick.

31

NICK

Ever since Quinn left my office yesterday, I've been hunting for a solution that doesn't exist. There's a very good reason doctors can't date their patients, especially in a situation like ours. It's possible we could tell the right lies and hide it enough to get away with it, but that still wouldn't make it ethical.

Yet the minute I get her call, I know I'd be willing to do it anyway.

She insists on driving herself. We arrange to meet at a market near the lake, since my parents' place is off a series of unmarked roads.

"And pack the red bikini," I add, only half-joking.

"Nick," she says softly. "I'm still engaged. This is just one last effort to figure things out."

But whether she's admitting it or not, it's also one last chance for her to figure out she would rather be with me.

The air is warm and moist, the buzz of insects rising toward the clouds. I stand for a moment outside the car just before I leave to meet Quinn, feeling something that's been absent so long I'd forgotten there was a time when I expected it—hope.

All I *should* want from today is that Quinn remembers enough that we solve this, or remembers enough of who she was that she decides to end it with Jeff. The hope I feel is a warning sign, a reminder that my desire to get her away from Jeff is not wholly altruistic. There are things I want from today for myself as well as for her, whether I'm supposed to have them or not.

She arrives at the market not long after I do. I watch her climb out of an old Jetta, wearing a gauzy sleeveless dress with a slit up the side. I'm trying hard to pretend I don't see a flash of tan thigh as she walks toward me. Today is about convincing her to give this a shot, convincing her that she has no reason to fear me. Thoughts about those thighs straddling me in a hotel bed a few nights ago will have to wait.

"There's a deli here," I say, pulling the door handle. "I thought we could grab some lunch and eat it out on the dock."

She walks in ahead of me and makes it five feet before she comes to a sudden stop, pressing her fingers to her temples.

My hands are on her arms in an instant. "Are you okay?"

She nods, slumping against the glass door of a drink refrigerator. "I've been here before," she whispers. "With you. We were buying food for the weekend, because the grocery store wasn't done yet."

There's a chill up my spine. "Yeah," I say casually, pretending it's not completely bizarre she knows this. "The grocery store opened just before I got out of college."

She looks off into the distance, like she's watching our past on a movie screen only she can see. "We bought a bunch of food here, enough to last the weekend, but we ended up coming back…" She trails off, looking so embarrassed I have to ask.

"What?"

She shakes her head and turns toward the deli. "Nothing. So, what's good?"

"That's not fair," I tell her, gently cupping her elbow to turn her back toward me. "You can't keep starting a memory and not finishing it."

The color rises in her face. "We ran out of condoms," she whispers, not meeting my eye. "So you came here for more. Twice. The cashier gave you a hard time about it."

It's a gut punch, but the good kind. The idea of running through multiple boxes of condoms with Quinn…*Jesus*. I want to pin her against the refrigerator case and make what happened in Baltimore look like child's play.

Pull it together, Nick. I clear my throat. "I could buy some now, only in the interest of a by-the-book investigation?"

She laughs, as if I was entirely joking. I definitely was not.

MY PARENTS' white, two-story colonial sits at the end of a long gravel road that is dappled with sunlight beneath a canopy of trees. By mutual agreement she rode with me instead of following behind. It still doesn't seem possible that the sight of the house itself is causing her seizures, but a few weeks ago I didn't think time travel was possible either. As the house comes into view, I find her hand in mine. I'm not even sure which of us is responsible.

"Still okay?" I ask.

"Yes," she breathes. "I've been here too. Your and Ryan's room was up there." I stiffen as she points to the room I once shared with my twin.

"That's probably the first time anyone's spoken his name

here in a decade," I tell her. "My mom—I guess we all try to protect her."

Her face falls. She couldn't look guiltier if she tried. "I'm sorry."

"It's fine. Seriously." I open her door and get another flash of her legs as she climbs out of the Jeep. It's probably for the best that she refused to bring the bikini. I'm having enough trouble as it is.

We walk into the house and I watch her face, hoping, *praying*, for a reaction. Some memory that will provide an answer we need.

Her mouth curves downward. "It's just like walking into the home of your favorite childhood friend as an adult. Familiar, but meaningless. Why the hell did I ever think seeing it might heal a brain tumor? I was expecting miracles."

I return and find my hands wrapping around her arms, forcing her to meet my eye. "Who says it would have to be a miracle?" I ask. "We can't explain *anything* that's happening. But there was a time when people couldn't explain the change in seasons, or sunlight, or gravity. It doesn't mean there wasn't an explanation. It just meant it hadn't been discovered. Why should this be any different?"

She looks away, pressing her lips together. "But the tumor—you don't actually believe we can stop it."

I tip her chin up, feeling a little desperate. She can't start losing hope now. I need her to keep fighting until we find a solution. "Do I think it's unlikely this can fix the tumor? Yeah. But your tumor is also unlike anything I've ever seen. And how could I say it was impossible anyway? Every day, you and I are witnessing the impossible. We're having the same dreams, for God's sake. You know things you couldn't possibly know, and from the moment I met you, it felt like you were..."

"It felt like I was what?"

"Mine," I reply.

The awkwardness of that word washes over us both. I've never called anyone *mine* in my life, and she is with someone else. But I also know what I said was right. She is meant to be mine, and somehow today I need to convince her of that.

~

SHE SITS on the dock and keeps me company while I prepare to pull the jet ski out of the water. I throw my shirt in the grass and I'm just about to pull the trailer up the hill when I glance up and catch it—Quinn's eyes on me, cheeks flushed, her full lips slightly ajar. I've never seen a female watch me with such blatant, unconscious lust. Probably the way I'm looking at her every time we're together. God, what I wouldn't give to act on it.

I catch her eye. "Remembering our honeymoon?"

"Our honeymoon was in December," she says primly. "No one was wearing a bathing suit."

I grin. "If it was a *good* honeymoon, I imagine we were wearing a lot less."

"Yeah," she breathes, her lids fluttering closed for a second. She's fucking remembering it, right here in front of me. Today is going to be a test of my self-restraint, as it is, without having to watch Quinn when she's thinking about sex.

"Jesus, don't do that," I plead, giving the waistband of my shorts a quick, desperate tug.

"Don't do what?"

"Don't say *yeah* like that, as if you're remembering it all while you sit there."

Her cheeks turn pink. "Sorry," she begins. "I wasn't remembering our honeymoon, I promise."

My teeth grind. I haven't gotten laid in weeks and the only girl I actually want has her dress hiked around her thighs and is swinging her bare legs a couple feet from my face. "Well, you were sure as shit remembering *something*. It was written all over your face."

"I had this dream about you," she begins. "We were in high school, right after homecoming, and we were in the back seat of your car. In the parking lot. And—"

Her voice has gone low and breathy again, full of longing. She's been with her idiot boyfriend for so long, she's forgotten what a turn-on she is, even when she's *not* talking. Add in that rasp to her voice while she describes a memory of something that was clearly sexual—with *me*, no less—and I'm a goner. She may not know she's doing it, but my dick certainly does.

"Don't do that either," I tell her, and I turn away, pulling the trailer up the hill. I feel like an asshole almost immediately, but I just don't know how to do this—how to balance being what she needs and restraining what I want all at the same time. I get the jet ski into the shed and return.

She watches me, her face solemn. "What did I do wrong?" she asks.

I push my hair off my forehead, racking my brain for any excuse I can make, before I give up entirely. "Nothing. But you were describing the two of us, together, in the throatiest, sexiest voice imaginable. Let's just say I walked away for a reason."

"Oh." Then her eyes widen. "Ohhhhh."

There's something so innocent about her at times. I love that innocence and want to preserve it, but at the same time, I want to destroy it into a million pieces. The jury's still out on which way I'll go.

32

QUINN

Nick goes to the house and returns with our sandwiches and drinks in his hands. He hasn't bothered to put his shirt back on, though I wish he would. I find my eyes going south far too often, resting on that trail of light brown hair below his belly button, imagining where it might lead if I flicked the button of his shorts to follow it.

I don't want to be having these thoughts about him, thoughts I've never in my life had for anyone else. But how do you make yourself stop thinking the wrong thing, and wanting it? He swings the bag down behind us, sitting too close. The distance he might sit if I were his and he were mine.

I think of the way he said that word earlier—*mine*—and how it sent a visceral thrill through my chest. The way something inside me—that hard seed that began to flower the moment I met him—took another leap, came into full bloom.

While he pulls food from the bag, I look over at the paddleboards on the beach, the Sunfish bobbing nearby. "Is this what we'd have done if we came here in high school?" I ask.

He gives me a sheepish grin, handing me my sandwich on a paper plate. "Well, I'm guessing, based on your memory of condom purchases, it's not *all* we'd have done."

I feel myself blushing as I remember that moment of intense déjà vu at the deli. It was our first time together. Something we'd waited years for. Different than London, where we must *barely* have waited, given how fast we got married. I don't know how many lives I've lived with him, but it feels a little unfair that I can't live this one with him too.

He's watching my face in a way I can't pretend is just *friendly*. "I like having you here," he says.

I twist my ring, letting my feet swing over the dock, inches from the water. "It's been the best Saturday I've had in a long time." A disloyal thing to say, but not as disloyal as what I'm actually thinking, which is that it's been the best Saturday I ever remember.

I catch a flash of his dimple. "Even if it's no Paris."

"You say that as if I routinely go to Paris. I've never even been out of the country."

"Why not?" he asks.

I smile. "Spoken like a kid who grew up with everything. I was dirt poor in a town so small you'd miss it if you blinked."

He leans back a little, a casual gesture, but there's nothing relaxed about the way he's watching me now. "I guess that's how you wound up with Jeff."

I bristle at his phrasing. He makes it sound like I'm *saddled* with Jeff, as if I chose him by default. "What do you mean?"

"You're just...ill-suited. He doesn't seem like someone you'd have chosen unless you were someplace where there weren't a lot of options."

He hasn't seen the best side of Jeff since this thing started, but it's not like I chose him out of desperation. I had plenty of options back home. "Going through a tragedy with someone shows you pieces of them you wouldn't have seen otherwise. And when my father died, I realized what a good person Jeff was."

His mouth twists as if he's just eaten a piece of fruit gone bad. "Right. Your dad dies, and Jeff, who'd probably been after you for years, suddenly comes to the rescue."

I place my sandwich carefully on the plate and turn toward him. "He did, yes. Why are you trying to make that sound like a devious thing?"

"I just suspect he had an ulterior motive."

I run my tongue over my teeth, feeling flustered and angry, though I don't know why. While it's true Jeff was interested in me well before I moved home, he didn't act on it for a long time. He just remained quietly in the wings, helping us where he could. "He's not a bad person, no matter what you think."

His eyes are as stormy as the clouds that now gather in the distance. "He's also not quite as good a person as you seem to want to believe. He left you alone at the hospital after you had a very serious episode," he says, his voice low and gritty. "He should have been there. He should have been home every fucking night since it started happening."

I want to cover my ears like a child, or simply walk away. "Well, we can't all be doctors, Nick. He was trying to keep his job. And it's how we were raised. Men wake up at 5 a.m. and work until dark, and they do it until they're in the grave. That's how Jeff shows he cares."

His jaw shifts. "That doesn't mean you have to accept it."

This is a fruitless topic to explore. Nick was raised with different values. He will put whomever he ends up with first, always, the rest of the world be damned. There's a piece of me that cries out for that kind of care, but it's not reasonable to hope for it from Jeff. "Why are we discussing this?"

He stares hard at the water. “Because I think you should cancel the wedding.”

I glance at him quickly and away. I long to ask if he’s saying it as my doctor, or as something...more, but I doubt he’d tell me the truth.

“Jeff is suggesting moving the date up,” I reply. “He wants to do something small and private next weekend instead.”

His head jerks toward mine. “I wasn’t saying you should skip the big wedding. I was saying you should skip *any* wedding. You can’t seriously be thinking about marrying him next weekend.”

My spine goes straight. “I’ve been with him for years. Why wouldn’t I consider it?”

“Because you’re not in *love* with him,” he says, standing, fists clenched.

“Ah,” I challenge, gathering our stuff as I climb to my feet, “but you and Meg are? It must be a real love story for the ages, what with you spending all your free time with me.”

“I’m not *marrying* her.”

My throat tightens, and I feel the start of tears...*angry* tears. “But you will,” I rasp. “Or someone just like her.”

He steps toward me, pulling the bag from my hand and throwing it behind him before he cups the back of my neck and pulls my mouth to his. Without hesitation or gentleness, he kisses me, and the moment his mouth touches mine, all thought seems to stop. I am only a mass of nerve endings and sensation and want. There is heat and pressure and his hands sliding over my skin, leaving a trail of fire in their wake.

I moan against his mouth and he pulls me harder against him. *I’ve missed this. My God, I’ve missed this.* For years, for decades. I am molten, nothing but a collection of burning atoms, so weightless I could be floating in midair, for all I know. My hands are on his chest, but itch to lower, to pull at his shorts, to slide my dress around my waist.

Sex for me has always been precise and careful, led by thought rather than impulse. This is the opposite of that. I'm driven entirely by instinct, some ancient part of me rising up and taking over. I want everything from him, right here on this splintery dock. I don't care who sees. His hands are on my thighs and my greedy fingers are already sliding into his waistband before I come to a sudden, shocked halt.

Jeff.

I gasp for air, pushing away from him so fast that I stumble backward, steadied only by his hands on my hips. "Oh my God. What are we doing?"

His hands soften, but he doesn't let me go. "I must be ridiculously bad at this if that wasn't clear."

"You're about to move in with someone, and I'm engaged," I reply, pressing a palm to my forehead. Yes, my actions around Nick haven't been completely pure, and my dreams decidedly less so, but this crosses a line I can't begin to rationalize.

"I broke up with Meg the morning we came back from Baltimore," he says, closing the distance I've placed between us. "Because I want to feel the way I do around you, and I'm not willing to settle for less than that. And you shouldn't be settling for less either."

The world seems to stop. The birds are silent, the air grows still. Nothing exists but Nick in front of me, and this thing in my chest—terror and desire, twisting until I can't tell one from the other. He's offering me everything I want in the world, and yet something inside me panics at the thought of taking it. I hate the idea of disappointing Jeff and my mother, but that's not what this is about.

"Say something," he urges. My hands are pressed to his chest, and I can feel, beneath them, his heart beating away at a pace that can't be normal, his body taut with what could be desire, or could be impatience. I think of his hands tugging at my dress, the heat of his mouth on my neck.

"I can't think when you're so close," I whisper. "I need to leave."

He stiffens. "Quinn—" he starts, but I cut him off because he is too compelling, and already a big part of me is hoping he refuses to let this go, refuses to let *me* go.

"I'm not a cheater," I say quietly, focusing on his chest. "I... just need to think. And I can't make a reasonable decision when we're standing here like this."

Slowly, he releases me, running a frustrated hand through his hair. "I know what I'm asking of you is huge, and I'll take you back to your car. Just please promise me you'll consider it."

I tell him I will, but I suspect it's a lie. Because I don't really need to think, and it has nothing to do with the size of what he's asked. What keeps me here, refusing to take what I want most in the world, is a truth it seems I've always known, one proven to me as a child: something dangerous lurks inside me, and it would only take loving someone too much to set it free.

And if I allowed myself to, I would definitely love Nick like that.

I'd love him far more than Jeff. In fact, I'm scared I already do.

THE RIDE BACK IS QUIET. He drives slowly, but we arrive at the market much too soon. I've never been so reluctant to step out of someone's car. If only his words didn't make as much sense as they did. I may not have a lot of time left. Would it be so wrong to make myself happy while I can?

I just don't know.

My eyes flicker to his mouth, remembering our kiss earlier. I want to lean over and bury my nose in his skin, consume that lingering hint of soap from his morning shower. I want to bite that lower lip of his and climb him like a ropes course. "Thank you for today," I say instead.

I reach for the door handle, and he tugs me back toward him, his hands grasping my jaw as he presses his mouth to mine for one long moment. I breathe, memorizing all of it—the smell of his skin, the softness of his lips, the pressure of his calloused hands. "Please come back to me, Quinn."

My ribs squeeze tight. I want to promise him something, but terror and desire...they're equally weighted right now. Can I really abandon Jeff after he gave up everything for me? Can I move past this nameless fear and give in to that desperate, wholehearted kind of love I've felt for Nick in my memories of other lives?

I don't know. So instead of replying, I press my lips to his cheek, and then I slide from the car, refusing to look back as I walk away.

33

QUINN

"I'm outside your building," I whisper. My voice is raspy from crying most of the way back to D.C. "Can you let me up?"

Caroline has known me long enough that she asks no questions. She merely says 'of course' and moments later her head is peeking out the door, looking one way and then the next for my car.

We get up to her apartment. Even now, in my despair, it calls to mind the home of some Arabic princess in a Disney tale —a jewel box of rugs and artwork and furniture, all of it vivid and alive.

I sit on her purple velvet couch and she takes the chair across from me, hugging a fur pillow to her chest. "Based on your current level of blotchiness, I estimate you've been crying for at least a full hour."

My laugh is shaky. It threatens to turn into a sob, but I pull it back just in time. "Good guess. You should have a show."

"Like the kid who talks to the dead, but I guess how long

people have been crying?" she asks. "I can't see how it could fail."

I smile, but I don't attempt a laugh this time. Too risky.

"So, what's up?" she asks softly. "You and Jeff never fight."

"He left this morning for his camping trip," I reply, flinching a little. He went away for his bachelor party and I *cheated* on him. I can't believe I did it, but I can't quite regret it either. "We aren't fighting."

She tips her head, thinking, and then her mouth opens into a perfect circle. "Oh. My. God. You slept with that doctor."

She's not accurate, of course, but she's not that far off from it either, which is pretty impressive. "I didn't sleep with him."

She leans forward, her whole face alight, more excited than she is concerned. "Tell me everything."

So I do. Jeff's inability to sit through the movie. The trip to the lake. Nick asking me to call off the wedding. The kiss.

That's when her face falls. "That's *it*? He only kissed you?"

I manage another smile. Only Caroline would be disappointed that I didn't cheat *enough*. "I kissed him back, and...I don't know." My voice catches. "I have no idea what I'm even doing anymore."

"Quinn," she groans, "do I need to get a flashing neon sign? Or maybe have God descend from Heaven and speak to you directly? It's so freaking obvious you shouldn't be marrying Jeff to everyone alive but you and your mom."

I sink low into the cushions behind me. I want her to convince me she's right. It's probably why I came here in the first place. And, at the same time, I need to convince her she's wrong—except the objections I can actually say *aloud* are weak ones. "I love Jeff."

"You may love him, but not in the right way," she argues. "He's familiar and you care about him, but there's no spark. I've never once seen you light up about him the way you do when you're discussing Nick."

"Even if that's true, Jeff gave up everything to come down here. And my dad...he *begged* me at the end to choose him. It's like he knew something I didn't."

She leans forward. "He was a dying man high on painkillers, and you were his baby. He just wanted to leave the world knowing you were taken care of. And that's sweet, but that doesn't mean he was psychic."

It's so tempting to let her sway me, but my fears remain. And I can't imagine breaking up with Jeff this late in the game, especially when the rest of his life isn't going so well.

"At least tell me how the kiss was," she urges. "Because if he's the guy who uses too much tongue or whatever, you need to say so upfront, so I know whether or not to encourage your fling or discourage it. You know my opinions on tongue usage."

I laugh through my tears. "Yes, you prefer it sparingly. I know."

"And?"

I can still feel the imprint of him on my mouth. The heat, the pressure. The smell of his soap, the needy way his fingertips pressed to my skin. I want to groan at the memory. "It was good," I admit. *Such an understatement. It was perfect.*

"Well, then I feel like there's only one foolproof way to decide if you should go through with your wedding," she says. "You have to sleep with Nick."

I glance at her to make sure she's joking. I'm not entirely sure she is. "I'm not *sleeping* with him. I'm not a cheater."

"Fine. I'll make the ultimate sacrifice and sleep with him myself and report back to you."

I know she's joking, but it doesn't stop jealousy from tearing through me like a white-hot needle. I bury my head in my hands. He broke up with Meg, but there will be someone to replace her eventually. Even if I choose him, there will be someone else eventually anyway, thanks to the tumor. And that thought makes me want to run from all this now, before it hurts even more.

~

Eventually I return to my empty home, despite Caroline's entreaties to join her for enough margaritas that I "forget about Jeff entirely". I move woodenly through all the normal things I'd do on a night at home. I shower, put on pajamas, and stick a frozen pizza in the oven. There is nothing different about my life. It just makes me feel numb. I think perhaps I've been numb for a very long time, and meeting Nick is what's made me realize it.

I watch hour after hour of a stupid sitcom that doesn't elicit a single laugh. It's after ten, and I'm preparing to go to bed when lights turn in the driveway. My heart leaps despite itself.

Jeff's deep in the Pennsylvania mountains right now. And there's only one other person who'd show up at this hour.

I know I should make him leave. Maybe I shouldn't answer at all. But that eager, desperate part of me throws the door open anyway…to find Jeff climbing out of his truck.

He carries his gear into the house and I hold the door, while disappointment continues to carve itself wide through my stomach. I'm not even capable of a fake smile, much less a real one. "What happened to your bachelor party?"

He dumps the last of his gear in the foyer and points at the lightning off to the west. "It's supposed to storm all night. Wasn't really ideal for a camping trip."

There's something forced in the words which makes me suspect I'm not getting the whole truth. "But…you didn't want to go to a bar or something at least?"

He raises a brow. "I thought you'd be happy to see me."

I *should* be. And maybe I actually would be if I hadn't expected Nick in his place. If I buckle down, if I avoid Nick from now on and focus, could I be happy with what we have again? That's the problem though. I'm not sure how you stop craving joy, and fullness, once you realize they exist. "I just hate that your bachelor party was ruined."

He steps close, backing me to the door. "I had an idea anyway, and it inspired me to come straight home," he says. His mouth fastens on mine. His lips are dry and thin, the kiss perfunctory. Has it always been like this? I feel panicked, unable to respond, and my reluctance only makes him try harder.

I slide away. "What was your idea?"

"I was thinking about Vegas, like you said a while back—you were right. I booked us on the first flight out in the morning," he says, pulling me back to him. "By this time tomorrow, you'll be my wife and it will all be over with, just like you wanted."

I freeze. I'm...I'm just not ready. That other version of me, the one from London, says *stop this. Tell him you can't go*. But I just stand here with a blank stare on my face and the words trapped in my throat.

He laughs at my reaction. "Thought I was incapable of spontaneity, didn't you?" he asks, wrapping an arm around my waist.

I did. And I fall asleep wishing I'd been right.

~

Nick and I are in the master bedroom of the house at the lake. I hear the crinkle of a condom wrapper being torn. The mattress dips as he climbs in behind me, his hand grasping the curve of my hip.

"You can still change your mind," he says against my ear. "At any point. Okay?"

I roll toward him. "I'm not going to change my mind."

Everything I want in life is a distant second next to him. Even the promise I made my mom. I think I've known this for a while, but when he pulled himself into the boat today and said those words —"I'd never just let you float away"—I felt it. And I knew it was time.

My bikini is untied, and the bottoms are tugged down. His hand slips between my legs. "Jesus," he whispers, pressing his face into my hair and breathing deep. "You're already wet."

My hand slides between us, but he stops me. "Just the idea of it has me close. This will be over before it starts if you do that."

He moves down the bed. His breath skates over my inner thigh, closer and closer until he reaches my center. His tongue flicks—once, twice, again—and he slides a finger inside me the moment my back arches. He continues and after a moment he adds a second finger, glancing up at me to make sure I'm okay.

It hurts but it's oddly pleasant at the same time. His fingers move and it becomes less like pain, and more like a small fire that burns and warms simultaneously. I'm floating, anchored only by the pressure of his hand. And I want more.

"Come up," I plead and I feel a pulse of breath against me, his low laugh.

"Not yet." He adds a third finger and my objections die on my lips. It burns, but his tongue is moving faster and without even a second to warn him I shatter, squeezing those fingers of his so hard I'm surprised nothing breaks.

I just came but it's not enough. I lean up just enough to rest my hands on his shoulders and pull him down to me. "Now," I demand.

There's a small, ragged noise in his chest at the words, need and capitulation and relief. He shifts until he's right there. I feel that first hint of pressure, of the fullness that's coming. "I'm not going to last long," he groans.

Lightning strikes outside and I jolt awake, my entire body rigid, seconds from coming. Jeff is snoring quietly beside me and all I want in the entire world is to go back where I was. Because being with Nick just now felt so different, so much better, than anything I've ever known that I can't stand not having it.

I sit, curling my knees to my chest and pressing my face against them. In a few hours Jeff and I will be heading to the airport and it'll be over. I'm never going to risk anything and I'm never going to know what it's like to hand myself over to another person, to love someone so deeply and want him so much I'd give up anything on his behalf.

Outside, the storm is upon us, and the thunder hammers overhead, making our house shake like a terrified small thing. I slip out of bed and stand by the window, watching the trees sway. My father told me a story once, during a storm just like this, about the good wind and the bad wind. He said they came one day to visit a little girl just like me, because all of his stories were about a little girl just like me. The girl had waited a long time for the good wind to come along and blow all kinds of wonderful things inside, but when it finally came knocking, the bad wind was right there alongside it, which meant she couldn't let in one without letting in the other. "All the wonderful gifts the good wind would bestow could only come alongside the bad wind's chaos and disaster," he said.

"Couldn't she tell the good wind to come back later?" I asked, and he shook his head.

"They're a package deal. So nothing bad ever came into the house, but nothing good did either. And that's when the girl discovered there was something far worse than the bad wind."

I frowned at him. "What?"

He picked me up and set me in his lap, and I think it's only because his voice was so grave and serious when he replied that I remember the story at all. "What's worse than the bad wind is the emptiness of letting nothing in at all," he said.

It puzzles me now, that story. I'd almost forgotten there was a time when he wanted me to eschew safety, to soar to greater heights. But when the end came he wanted the very opposite for me. What changed? Is it possible my father knew about Nick somehow? Because it seems obvious that finding Nick is the point at which my life seems to end, again and again, and pushing me toward another man might have seemed like the only foolproof solution left.

I glance over my shoulder at Jeff and, though I couldn't begin to justify my behavior if he were to wake, I open our window to the storm. Just a crack. Because, at the moment, even a bad wind would be welcome. Anything would be better than the emptiness I feel right now.

~

It's still storming outside when I wake. Jeff is up and dressed, standing at the end of the bed. "I'm glad you're up. I figure we might want to get to the airport early because of the weather. I don't want to get bumped off our flight."

I swallow as I look at the empty duffel he's left on the end of the bed. "Okay," I whisper, taking the bag into the closet.

I just need to *think*. I need time.

And there isn't any.

I unzip the bag and begin filling it. My wedding dress is still at the bridal boutique, so I shove another dress in the bag instead, ambivalent about the fact that it will be crushed when we arrive. I can't believe this is really happening. With each passing moment I get closer to a Vegas wedding while some voice in my head screams *Stop! Stop!* with increasing distress.

"Don't forget your swimsuit," Jeff calls.

Am I really doing this? Will we be at some hotel pool tomorrow as newlyweds? I open the drawer where I keep my bathing suits, but my hand climbs past the ones I wore all summer to an older one. Red, tiny.

It makes me think of Nick. For that very reason, I should not pack it, but I do. If I could, I'd clutch it to me like a blanket throughout the whole ordeal to come.

~

THE CAR ARRIVES, and I take my purse and carry-on to the tiny Honda idling by the curb, the wind whipping my hair around my face. The car smells like something fake and floral, barely covering the odor of dirt beneath. Like our wedding will be—me saying all the right words to cover the ugly ones. *I don't want this. I think I'm in love with someone else. You don't make me happy.*

"I'm not sure we can take off in this weather," I suggest.

"It'll be fine. They take off in worse weather than this all the time." His fingers wind through mine. "How weird is it that the next time you're back here, you'll be Quinn Walker?"

A chill climbs up my spine. I catch my reflection in the driver's rearview mirror—pale beneath my tan, eyes wide and scared—just as a burst of wind brings the trees to swaying, terrifying life. Inside the car, we are sheltered from it, breathing in only the dirt and its fake floral overlay. And I am so absolutely still, and empty.

I am suffocating here. I need to let the wind in, both the bad and the good. My father gave me two different messages. I don't know what changed, but the version of him that wasn't dying and drugged would never want this for me. He'd want me to embrace the unknown, even if it was dangerous.

Yes, Nick could break my heart, could hurt me in ways that make the tumor's damage seem minimal by contrast. But maybe even that is better than this stillness, than being so empty inside I'm not sure I care if the plane goes down. There are worse things than chaos and disaster. There is death.

This, with Jeff, feels a lot like death.

The cab turns into the airport's entrance and pulls up to ticketing. Jeff jumps out first, grabbing his bag and setting mine on the curb. "Wait," I tell the driver as I slide out. Jeff is halfway to the doors before he realizes I'm still by the car.

"I can't do this." The sound of the words shocks me.

He comes back and reaches for my hand. "Quinn, it'll be fine. They aren't going to put the plane up in the air if it isn't safe."

I shake my head. "I'm not talking about the plane. I'm talking about the wedding." I slide the ring off my finger. "I can't marry you. I'm so sorry."

He steps close, wrapping his hands around my arms. Just like Nick did the other day, only his grip is hard, bruising. "Stop this," he hisses. "We made a plan and we're seeing it through."

My heart stutters, trips over itself. "No." I try to pull back, but his hands tighten. "Let me go."

"Let's just get on the plane," he says, struggling to control his voice. "We've already got tickets. If you really don't want to go through with it when we get there, we won't. We'll just have a fun night in Vegas and come home."

I'm tempted to go along with it, to not make a fuss, because that's who I am. That's who I've been with him, always. Except I don't want to give him another day, or another hour, of my life. He's had far too many of them as it is. "I'm sorry, Jeff. I'm so sorry. But our life just doesn't make me happy."

A vein in his neck throbs. "I can't believe this shit. Since when does our life suddenly not make you happy?" he demands. "Since you met *Nick*?"

No, I think. *Our life always made me unhappy. I just didn't realize it until I saw something better.* "You're not hearing me," I tell him. "I probably only have a year or two to live. I'm not sure how I want to spend it. But I know this isn't it."

I pull out of his grip and step into the Uber before he can find a way to stop me. He's banging on the window and trying to open the door, even as we pull away.

34

QUINN

It should only take an hour to get to the lake, but between the weather and the beach traffic, the trip takes twice as long. It would feel long anyway. Now that I've made my choice, I'm desperate to see Nick, and every minute I'm stuck behind the wheel seems to occur in slow-motion.

Yes, maybe there's something evil inside me. And maybe Nick is what will set it free. I'm going to risk it because the reward—*him*—is too great to miss out on.

Jeff is calling, again and again. I don't answer, but just before I can turn it off, my mother calls too… and ignoring my mom when she's upset is never a good idea.

I answer to find her crying uncontrollably, already drinking though it's not even noon. My mother isn't an alcoholic, but when she has a drink or two she flies off the rails. Soon she'll be buying stuff she doesn't need off QVC and telling anyone who will listen that she's heartbroken and her life isn't worth living. Abby's been the one monitoring her mood of late, but I'm guessing, thanks to what I've done, she won't be willing to comfort my mom anytime soon.

I've probably just ruined the relationship she has with her best friend *and* the man she considers a son. *She'll be completely alone when I'm gone.* It's a thought that brings all my misgivings to the surface. If it were for anything less than Nick, I'd probably have called Jeff and taken it all back by now.

I tell her I'm coming up there, make her promise to stop drinking, and turn off my phone entirely. She and Jeff are the two people I've carried, in one way or another, for most of the last decade. It's a relief to know that for a brief period of time, I won't have to carry anyone but myself.

THE DRIVE IS UNEVENTFUL, despite the weather. It's only when I reach Nick's exit that the nerves hit. I have no idea how it will work. From what he's implied, I doubt he's allowed to date a patient. Right now, I don't really care. I'd live quietly in his basement, hidden from sight, if it meant we could be together. But what if he isn't so willing? I know what he said yesterday, but people say all kinds of things in intense moments, before they've thought them through. At heart, Nick—like me—is logical. And potentially risking your job for a girl who may not even be around in a year is hardly that.

I pull into the parking lot of the market where Nick and I met yesterday and walk inside. Behind the counter is the same old guy who teased us about condoms in another life. "Hope you've got an umbrella," he says, glancing from me to the windows outside. The sky has turned ominously dark all of a sudden. "There's a flood warning."

I smile without teeth and head to the bathroom, where I wash my hands just for something to do and look at myself in the mirror. There, I see clearly the girl Nick married at least once, and chose more than once. I think of what Caroline asked yesterday—if the situation were reversed, would I want to be with him in spite of everything? And my answer is the same. Yes, I would. And he would too.

I walk out the bathroom door, waving to the woman we ordered sandwiches from yesterday, and then come to a shocked, stumbling halt. Up ahead, at the front of the store, is someone I recognize. Not from some past life, but from this one. From the photo in Nick's office.

Meg.

It cannot be a coincidence that she's in a market a mile or two from Nick's parents' house. It *can't* be.

It takes me a second to move my frozen limbs. I step into an aisle, letting a display of chips block me from her view but not blocking her from mine. She's even prettier in real life than she was in the photo, and she's obviously put forth a level of effort I never have. Her hair is curled and her makeup is done. The guy at the counter is asking about her car. I peek into the parking lot, and there, beside my fifteen-year-old clunker with its rusting paint, is a sleek, silver BMW.

"Lot of dirt roads around here," the guy says. "Gonna be a mess with all this rain. Hope you've got a four-wheel drive as a backup."

Yes, Meg, the roads are bad. Maybe you should go home.

"It's okay," she replies with a too-wide smile. "My boyfriend has a Jeep."

The potato chips rattle as my body sags against the display. Even as my brain scrambles to create any explanation for why she would be here, I already know the most obvious answer is usually the correct one. Nick called her to reconcile after I left, if he ever really broke up with her at all.

I wait until her car pulls away before I walk out of the store. My shoulders are back and my is head up, but I'm made of twigs right now, skeletal and frail, ready to collapse—which I do, the moment I get in the car, leaning my face against the steering wheel and weeping like a child.

Why did it take me so long to leave Jeff? And Nick...did he even wait until I was back on the road yesterday before he called Meg and invited her out here? It takes all my self-control not to turn on the phone and rage at him, blame him for my disappointment, ask him why he said any of those things when he clearly couldn't have meant them. Mostly I'm just so...blindsided. I wouldn't fault him at all for deciding I wasn't worth the risk. But I never thought in a million years he'd change his mind so easily. And maybe if he knew I was here he'd change his mind about her, but if he did, he wouldn't be the person I know he is.

Or the person I thought he was, anyway.

I'm still crying as I turn my car on and head back to the highway, toward my mother's house. Time no longer drags for me. I'd like as many minutes as possible between now and the moment I have to stand in front of her defending my decision to leave Jeff—never mentioning that I did it for someone who decided he didn't want me back.

WHEN I GET up to Rocton, I don't go straight to my mom's. It's not a conscious decision, but when I find myself at the river I'm not surprised. It's where I came when I was young too, all those times when it seemed like I didn't belong.

I park on top of the hill, and go sit on a big rock since the ground is soaked, letting my legs dangle over the edge. This view—the lazy river winding endlessly in both directions—used to be one of my favorite things in the world, but today it doesn't touch me. I look at it, but all I'm seeing is Meg's face in the convenience store, vivid with excitement. I understand that feeling. It's exactly how I felt too, until the moment I saw her there.

Did he kiss her the way he kissed me on the dock yesterday? Did he tell her all the things he told me? I'm incapable of imagining it. The man I thought I knew just wouldn't do this.

I dry my tears and take one last glance at the river. As a child, coming up here reminded me that the world was incomprehensibly large, and in it, somewhere, I was bound to find my place, and the one person who would accept me the way I am. Now it just reminds me that so many of the things I wanted as a child didn't come true.

I drive down to the far side of town, to the neighborhood my mom moved to after we sold the farm. It's only a few miles away, but it feels like a different world: shiny, hollow, artificial. All the trees are new and all the houses look the exact same.

God, I don't want to be here.

I don't want to hear everything she's about to say. As bad as I feel about what I've done, my mother will manage to make me feel worse, and I can't even blame her for it. I know how this town works: she'll never walk into the grocery store again without being the object of gossip. Without people discussing what her daughter did, how she and Abby are no longer friends. For the rest of my life, I'm going to be *the girl who broke poor Jeff Walker's heart*. And for the rest of her life she'll be the mother of that girl.

I tap once on the door and then—guessing correctly that it will be unlocked—I walk in. She's waiting for me in the kitchen with a thin smile and circles under her eyes.

"Have you eaten?" she asks, walking to the refrigerator. In two seconds, she's got a pan on the stove and is unloading the contents of the dairy drawer. I feel a sudden burst of affection for her. Even in a crisis, even when I've destroyed her, she still wants to make sure I'm fed. "I could make you a sandwich, but I only have mozzarella. Or if you can wait, maybe we could just go out to dinner. There's a cute little cafe now, where the barber shop used to be—"

"I'm okay, Mom," I reply. I give her a tentative smile. "So how much have you bought off QVC?"

Her hands grip the counter, her head sags, and I finally see what all her bustling around the kitchen has been hiding—intense disappointment, grief, shame. All caused by me. I should have known a joke wouldn't lighten the mood. We've never had that kind of relationship. "I just don't understand how you could have done this."

I lay my palms flat against the old oak table. It fit in the farmhouse, but it's too worn and heavy for this bright room with its thin walls. "I never meant for any of this to happen. But the tumor has put everything in perspective," I say, carefully skirting around how limited my time may be.

She frowns. "Jeff thinks it's the tumor making you behave this way."

The softness I felt just a moment ago, watching her move around the kitchen, is gone. In its place is something sharp-edged and cold. I know I'm not the daughter she wants. I never have been. She wanted a normal child who couldn't occasionally predict the future, who didn't wake knowing things she shouldn't. And maybe any parent would, but I'm still her child. Her *only* child. And that's where her loyalty should lie. "How long have you been having conversations with Jeff about me?"

"I'm just—" She stops, throwing up her hands. "I know you won't want to hear this, but you have to look at it from my perspective. Imagine if I had some disease. If I were schizophrenic, for instance, and suddenly decided to give away all my belongings and live on the streets—you'd intervene, wouldn't you?"

I'm more weary than I am angry. "I really hope you're not comparing my tumor to a severe mental illness."

"I don't know what to compare it to!" she cries desperately.

"You're making a lot of decisions that don't make sense. You and Jeff were really happy together, so I *have* to question it when you suddenly decide you want nothing to do with him."

I'm not sure why Caroline and Trevor figured out so easily that I wasn't entirely happy with Jeff, while my mom doesn't appear to have a clue, but I'm guessing it's my fault: ever since her breakdown after my father's death, I've been on a tight wire, trying to keep her safe from grief or disappointment. Just as I did with Jeff, I made it my mission to hold her together in the wake of tragedy—a role I never allowed myself to retire from. And part of that was convincing everyone I was thrilled to be dating her best friend's son.

"Mom, I don't know if we were ever all that happy together. Dad pushed this relationship, and then you and Abby did. I don't know what was real and what I was convincing myself of to make all of you happy."

Her lips go into a flat line. "Of course you were happy. Don't start telling yourself otherwise to justify your cold feet. You're throwing Jeff off to the side like garbage now, but I have no doubt that in a week or a month you'll realize what a mistake you've made, and I'd rather you figure it out now."

I know she's wrong. Maybe I'll be sad, and lonely, but Jeff would not make me happy now that I've seen how much is possible. If I got back together with him, I'd spend my remaining few years wanting something else, something more, and it wouldn't be fair to either of us. "It wasn't a mistake. And long-term, Jeff's better off this way too."

"Do you see how unlike you this is?" she asks. "Look at all the people you've hurt. Jeff's devastated. His parents are devastated. And these are people who were good to us, who supported us emotionally for years. Financially, too, when your father died. It's just such a slap in the face."

Ah, there it is...the spiraling guilt. I knew she'd find a way to bring it to the surface eventually. I feel sick, and she hasn't even gotten around to mentioning what a nightmare it will be to cancel the wedding at this late date. The flights people have paid for, the gifts to be returned, the deposits we won't get back. Or the fact that when I die in a few years she will have absolutely no one to lean on.

"Think about your uncle flying out here," she continues. "I bet he can't get his money back for the ticket. Abby's siblings are flying in too. Jeff's grandparents are driving up from Florida, and I think they've already left—they made a three-week trip out of this. It's not just about you."

Maybe she's right, I think. *Maybe I should just fix this and suck it up for the next year or two. Leave people thinking well of me, leave my mother's life somewhat intact*. The crying and the drive have exhausted me, have left me unable to think clearly, but when I hear those words in my head I feel a kind of sick resignation, a *familiar* resignation. It's exactly what I felt when she asked me to stay after my dad died, and when Jeff followed me to D.C. with his big romantic speech. Fear is what led me to walk away from Nick yesterday. And guilt is what's led me to make every other bad decision in my life. Maybe it's time I took a different path.

"I'm going to lie down for a while," I tell her.

"That's a good idea," she says tersely. It sounds an awful lot like what she *wants* to say—*go sit and think about what you've done*.

The room I think of as mine is really just a guest room, full of bland white furniture and muted pastels my mom found at some discount store. The quilt at the end of the bed is the only remnant of my past. I curl up, pulling it over me, and feel a fresh wave of tears coming. Was I blind, with Nick? If our situations were reversed I wouldn't have gone running back to my ex at the first sign of failure. I'd have waited. I'd have fought. It just feels as if there should be more to our story than this pathetic end.

Nick and I lie safely curled in bed, listening to the wind rattling the windows, blowing over the chairs out on the terrace. It's the biggest storm I've seen since I arrived in London so many months ago, and it serves as a reminder—even here, deep in the heart of a foreign city, we're still never entirely safe. Not that I really needed reminding. It's rarely out of my head for long these days.

"Mary downstairs stopped me this morning," I tell him.

He laughs, dragging the fluffy duvet up to my neck. "Did she accuse us of harboring pets again?"

I smile against his chest. "No. She wanted to show me these historic photos she found. Did you know our building was bombed during World War II? She had pictures of it. It was all practically rubble."

He pulls me closer. "Yeah. It's weird you're bringing it up. I've been thinking about that a lot lately."

"Our building being bombed?"

"Not that exactly. Just how terrifying it would be to live here during the Blitz. Especially if we were separated. If I were at work, or you were at school and I couldn't find you. I never gave it any thought before, and now, especially now," he says, placing a hand over my swollen belly, "I think about it constantly."

I think about us being separated constantly too. My reasons are probably different than his, but maybe not...maybe some residual memory tells him he has reason to worry because we've been separated before. I place my hand over his. "I'd come find you," I tell him.

"Yeah?"

"Unless you stopped being hot," I amend. "In that case, the jury is out."

His hand slides over my hip, down my bare thigh. "Hot, huh? You'll have to warn me when I'm in danger of slipping."

"You're in no danger," I say, but the words end on a gasp as his fingers slide between my thighs.

"I wasn't too worried." He laughs low in my ear. "If you don't come find me, there will never be a time when I won't come find you."

He rolls me on my back and for a brief time, I forget my fears, but later, when he's sound asleep, his breathing deep and even, they all reemerge. I look at his face in the moonlight—the boyishness of those long lashes and full lips offset by the sharp jaw, already in need of a shave.

Should I tell him everything? I can't. It will sound insane, and he'll never believe me. I figured out the truth months ago and I hardly believe it myself. But I can't lose him again.

"I'm not going to let her separate us," I promise him quietly. "Not this time."

~

MY MOTHER KNOCKS on the door, waking me. I'm so stunned by the dream I don't even respond the first time she calls my name. I was *pregnant.*

"Quinn," she says, more urgently. "I'm starting dinner. Are you up?"

I blink rapidly. "Yeah," I reply. "I'll be down in a second."

I was pregnant. I remember the feel of a baby kicking as I watched Nick sleep. Less like a kick than a bubble popping against my side, repeatedly. I can still feel the warmth inside me as I placed my hand there. I loved that child and now I miss her—I feel certain it was a *her*—almost as much as I miss Nick. We were a family, and I made him promises—that I'd find him, that I wouldn't let her separate us again. How could we have been so much in that life and so little in this one?

I go downstairs, distress weighing heavily on me. My mother seems to interpret it as repentance. "Nothing's been done that can't be undone, honey," she says softly. "It'll be fine. Everyone knows you're going through a lot."

I lay my arms on the table and rest my forehead against them. "I haven't changed my mind," I tell her. "I'm just tired."

She sinks into the chair across from me with a glass of wine. I wonder how many she's had. Either way, it means the tears will start shortly. "I wish you would think this through," she says.

My jaw falls open. "What on earth would make you think I haven't?" I demand. I've tried to be patient with her, but this is getting ridiculous. "Why are you in Jeff's corner so much? I'm the one you're related to, not him."

Her lips go tight, a flat line that makes them nearly invisible. "It was your father's dying wish."

A small ping of guilt. I ignore it. I've had this conversation with myself enough times. "Mom, he never encouraged it until he discovered he was dying. He just wanted to know I'd be taken care of."

She is quiet, wrestling with something she's not sure she should say. "You know things," she says, her voice barely audible. "You always have. You know things you shouldn't."

I can feel my heart tapping, far too fast, at the base of my throat. We've never, ever discussed this. It's how we both wanted it and I have no idea why she's changing the rules now. I swallow. "I was just a weird kid," I reply. "I had an imagination. Why are you even bringing this up?"

Her eyes meet mine. Saying *if it was merely your imagination, it was a shockingly accurate one.* "Sometimes your father knew things too," she says, her gaze falling to the table. "Things about you. And the way he insisted at the end...it was like when you were a kid and he was so certain about your allergy before you'd ever had shellfish. He was certain about this too, and that's what makes me think you should listen to him. Because it's possible he knew something you don't."

It's the same theory I suggested to Caroline yesterday, but now that I've made my decision, I don't want to hear it.

"Jeff can't protect me from a brain tumor," I say softly. "Maybe Dad did know something, but what I'm certain of is that Jeff is no longer enough for me, and he's not how I want to spend the time I have left."

My mother knows what I'm saying makes sense. Yet I see in the way she swallows, tips her chin in a barely visible nod, that she still thinks my father was right.

~

Dinner is painfully quiet. My mother drinks throughout. She looks at me each time she pours herself a new glass, daring me to say something. I won't, of course. Her five glasses of wine will hurt no one but herself. My decision this morning hurt tons of people.

Her cell rings during dinner and she glances at it. "It's Abby," she says, not looking at me as she speaks. "She called earlier too. She said you were refusing to take Jeff's calls. Please tell me that's not true."

I rub my forehead. I napped all afternoon, but this conversation makes me want to go straight back to bed. "Mom, I said everything there was to say this morning." She gives me a baleful look and I sigh. "Let me listen to the 400 voicemails he's left and maybe I'll call after that."

She excuses herself for the night, though it's barely seven, taking a new bottle of wine with her, so I retire too. I know I need to listen to Jeff's voicemails, but God I dread it. I can deal with his anger, but I cringe at the idea of his pain. Right now, I've got so much of my own, I'm not sure I can handle his on top of it.

I shower, dry my hair, and dawdle as much as possible before I finally turn on the phone. My heart sinks when I see there are well over a hundred texts.

And stops entirely when I see the most recent one is from Nick.

Nick: Quinn, I'm going crazy. Please just answer me. I need to know you're okay.

He sent it 15 minutes ago. And he texted an hour before that. I scroll through all the messages from Jeff and discover Nick began texting me at ten this morning. Maybe he was just trying to warn me about his change of heart. Maybe he wanted to make sure I didn't show up at the lake and ruin his reunion.

Or maybe, just maybe, he's the guy I thought he was all along.

35

NICK

I already knew yesterday the risk to my career no longer mattered to me. It was only the remaining question of ethics that kept me from driving back here last night and begging Quinn to give me a chance. As her doctor, it's possible I hold more sway over her than I would otherwise. But I also know this isn't the classic case of a vulnerable patient and predatory doctor. I *know* her. My very bones remember her in ways my brain can't quite catch up with.

And when I woke this morning, I realized there was no longer time to sit around debating—I could go for it, or I could become Grosbaum, growing old still longing for someone who didn't come back to me.

The decision was made, but I never dreamed it would take me eleven fucking hours to get ahold of her. By the time she finally calls, I've spent so long worried she had another seizure that I'm almost as angry as I am relieved.

"Thank God," I say when I answer, before she's even said a word. How could she have let me go that long, unsure if she was even alive? "Why the hell was your phone off?" I demand, pacing the room.

"Why the hell was your girlfriend visiting you at the lake?" she replies. The question—and how hurt and angry she sounds asking it—stops me short.

"*What?*"

"I saw Meg," she says. Her swallow is audible. "At the market by your parents' house this morning. Talking about her *boyfriend* and his Jeep. I just don't understand how you could say the things you did yesterday and—" Her voice breaks.

I'm so confused right now. But my anger disappeared the moment I realized how upset she was. "Quinn...I honestly have no idea what you're talking about. I'm not even at the lake. I came home this morning to see you and you never answered your phone once."

"But then—" She stops and takes a deep breath. "But then why was she out there?"

I lean on the counter and run a hand through my hair. None of this makes sense. Why the fuck would Meg have gone to the lake? I saw a voicemail from her this morning but didn't check it. The more important question, to me, is why Quinn was there. "I have no idea. I didn't invite her and I haven't seen her since last week. But...why were *you* there?"

"I wanted to see you," she admits quietly. "But then she was at the market...so I left."

I'm dumbfounded. What I have with Quinn is something I wouldn't be able to replace in a year or a decade or a century—how could she possibly have believed otherwise? "I would never have done that. There is no one for me but you. Not today and not a year from now. So if you stay with Jeff—"

"I didn't," she says quietly. "That's why I came to the lake. I ended things this morning."

The relief is so sweet and sharp that for a moment I'm speechless. "Thank God," I finally whisper. There is so much more I want to say to her right now, but not like this. I need to see her face. I need her to see I mean every word of it. "Where are you? This isn't a conversation I want to have over the phone."

"I'm at my mom's, up in Pennsylvania," she says. "I'm coming back tomorrow night."

Not soon enough. Now that I've spent an entire day wondering if I've lost her, there's not a chance I'm waiting twenty-four hours to really know she's mine. I grab my keys and head for the Jeep. "Give me your address."

"In Pennsylvania?" she asks. "Are you serious?"

I've never been more serious in my life.

~

It's just after ten when I pull up to her mother's house.

I'm halfway up the walk when she steps outside the door. I don't slow my pace. I keep going until she's in my arms.

"I can't believe you came all the way up here," she whispers.

"I can't believe you thought for a fucking second I could want anyone but you," I reply. My lips press to her brow, to her eyelids, her temples, the blade of her cheek, the soft spot just below her ear, until I finally find her mouth. She tastes like mint and sugar, and I could spend a hundred years just doing this—memorizing the contour of her lips, relishing the small, solid warmth of her.

She rests her forehead against my chest. "But...can't you get in trouble for this?"

Yes, and I no longer care. "I don't think we have to worry about it too much. As long as we're careful."

She cocks a brow. "That isn't what I asked."

I'm tempted to lie because I know exactly how she's going to react to the truth. But she's *it*—the person I want forever, or for as long as I can have her. For once in my life I want to be an open book. "I could, in *theory*, lose my medical license if someone made a big enough deal out of it."

She jerks backward. "You could lose your license for *good*? But..." She trails off, crestfallen. "You can't risk that. I mean, how long would something with us even last? I might not even be—"

I pull her back to me. "Stop. We have no idea how long you have, and I'm sure as hell not going to let some vaguely possible consequence keep me away from you, so don't even suggest it." I exhale heavily. The next part has to be said, no matter how much I'd like to skip it. "But I need to be sure that this is really okay. You're relying on me to treat you, and you shouldn't feel like there are strings attached. To anyone outside of us, this situation would look kind of predatory. You're in a vulnerable position and—" My words trail off. They sound even worse out loud than they did in my head.

She slaps a palm to her forehead. "*Predatory*? Are you kidding me? I wanted you long before any of this began. Before I even knew about the brain tumor, I was trying to stop dreaming about you. And ever since you kissed me yesterday, I've been unable to think about anything else, which I can assure you has nothing to do with your ability to heal my brain."

My eyes flicker to her mouth, uncertain. I push her hair back from her face, palms on her cheeks. "Does this mean you're mine now?"

She smiles up at me. "I think maybe I always was."

I lean down, capture once more that mouth I've craved since the first time I ever saw her. But I refuse to get carried away like I did yesterday, on the dock. Tonight is our beginning and I want every step of it to be perfect, memorable. Her hands slide through my hair. "I've wanted to do that for so long," she says.

"I have a long list of things I've wanted to do for so long," I reply, my mouth moving from her jaw to her perfect neck, "but they're probably not appropriate for a first date."

She laughs. "Is that what this is?"

I force myself back from her. "Not yet, it's not." Behind her the house is quiet, mostly dark. "I haven't said this in over a decade, and I'm not sure there's anything around here that's open, but are you allowed out after curfew?"

She grins. "Yes. And I know just the place. Wait here."

She runs inside and comes back a minute later with a blanket, a bottle of wine, and two plastic cups. We drive into the hills and turn onto a gravel road, where she tells me to pull off. "We're in the middle of nowhere," I say. "I'd just like to point out that if our situations were reversed you'd probably be getting a little nervous now."

She grins at me. "You're safe. Probably." She hops out and leads me to the top of the hill where, far below us, a river winds as far as I can see, lit with starlight. I pull her close and for a moment we just take it all in. She was right—this is perfect.

"I forgot how wet it is," she says. "I don't think we can sit out here."

"I have an idea." I open the tailgate of the Jeep and spread the blanket out in back. The roof is already off and the back seats are down, so there's just enough room for the two of us.

"You're pulling me into the back of your car but *I'm* the scary one," she says as I lift her up.

"You're safe," I reply. "Probably."

She looks at me from beneath her lashes and her mouth curves upward. "That's disappointing."

Her words and that raspy little note in her voice send blood rushing to my cock. I flinch as I climb in after her, trying to will it back down to neutral. This is essentially our first date, even if it feels like our hundredth. I'm not going to try to get off in here like some sex-crazed teenager, no matter how hard it is. Literally.

She pours us each a plastic cup full of wine, and then we lie on our sides, facing each other, since there's really no other way the two of us will fit.

"I like it here," I tell her. "How'd you find it?"

She puts her wine down. "My dad and I used to hike up here when I was a kid, and later I started coming on my own."

I hear a hint of something sad in her voice and it puzzles me. I don't understand how it is that her childhood, when she describes it, always sounds so lonely. She looks like the kind of girl who would have had everything— too many friends and admirers to count, the adulation of an entire town. "Why'd you keep coming back here by yourself?"

She hitches a shoulder. "It was hard growing up here sometimes. It was hard being in my own home half the time. But coming here reminded me how big the world was, and that in a world as big as ours, there was surely a person and place for me."

"A person?"

Her lashes brush the tops of her cheekbones. "The person you're meant to be with. The one who accepts you in spite of everything and matters so much that the rest of the world matters less."

I want to be her person. I already know she's mine. "And did you ever find your place?"

"Yeah," she says softly. "That person I was talking about? I'm pretty sure it's wherever he is."

I lift up her hand and press my lips to the base of her palm. My nose grazes the inside of her wrist, longs to continue a path on her velvet skin. I stop myself. The gesture might merely be romantic with someone else, but I want so much from her right now I think I could turn almost anything into an excuse to remove her clothes. "You still haven't told me how you ended things with Jeff."

She sighs heavily. "It's a long story. Just suffice it to say he's very unhappy with me right now. He filled up my voicemail and spent most of the morning calling on repeat, which is why I turned my phone off. Based on the texts I saw tonight...he's going to need some time to cool off."

"You're not planning to go back to your house tomorrow, right?" I know it's premature but if Meg wasn't in the process of taking over my apartment, I'd ask her to stay with me when she gets back. I feel a sharp stab of desire at the thought of it. Of having her somewhere private, for an extended period of time. Her splayed out on my bed. *Fuck. I need to think about something else, fast.*

She gives a small, surprised laugh. "It's been so chaotic I'd barely thought about it. But no, I'll avoid the house right now. I guess I'll crash on Caroline's couch for a while."

"And is Caroline *Team Nick* or *Team Jeff*? I'm just trying to figure out how many more enemies I have."

She blushes. "Caroline says I should sleep with you before I decide anything for sure."

Another stab of desire. "I like Caroline's ideas. You should listen to her more."

She raises up on one forearm so she can see my face, setting the wine behind her. "How exactly is this going to work?" she asks. "So you don't get in trouble?"

I thought about it the whole way up here, without ever arriving at a perfect answer. In an ideal world we would hide this. We'd sneak around and lie to anyone who asks, but I'm not willing to do that, and I'm definitely not willing to ask it of her. "I'll tell anyone I *have* to tell that I knew you before you were a patient, which doesn't let me off the hook ethically but helps. And then, after you're done with your degree, we could—" I stop myself with an embarrassed chuckle. "Sorry, I'm getting ahead of myself."

She smiles. "You can't leave me hanging like that."

"I was going to say that once you got your degree we could

go someplace where no one knows us. So congratulations—you've turned me into the creepy guy who talks about the distant future on a first date."

Her smile widens. Even if it's creepy, she doesn't seem to mind. "I thought you were a commitment-phobe?"

She is leaning over me with all that hair falling around her face and that perfect peony mouth begging to be kissed and suddenly I can't stand to keep holding back. "Not anymore," I reply, wrapping my hand around the nape of her neck to pull her face to mine.

The kiss is gentle at first. I savor it, like the first sip of a really good wine, breathing her in and out, that smell of soap and summer. Lingering on the feel of it, memorizing that ripe, perfect mouth, and her skin, soft as rose petals.

I roll her to the side, cradling her jaw as her mouth opens under mine. That first taste of her turns the kiss into something else. Something deeper and darker. Territory I'd planned to avoid tonight but can't resist now that it's here.

My hands slide from her hair to her back to her hips, palming curves I've dreamed of touching for months. Her breasts, her waist, her perfect ass. She inhales when my mouth moves to her neck, the sound sharp and full of need. I want to drown in her response, in the way her body arches into mine, asking for more.

It continues and the world starts to narrow—to our mingled breath, to her sounds, to the need inside me that coils and grows until I can barely stand the pressure. I stop thinking of anything beyond what I want from her. Where I want my hands and mouth. Where I want hers.

Our movements become frantic. The desire for her grows vicious, swells inside me until it feels like my skin is too tight to contain me. *It's been too long. I've waited too fucking long for this and I can't keep waiting.*

I start to push her on her back, ready to take everything

from her, heedless of my good intentions—but beneath my hand I hit the Jeep's cold metal floor where the blanket has pushed away. My eyes open and reality comes crashing in, an unwelcome guest. We're in the back of my car, her back pressed to bumpy metal, my toolbox an inch from her head. My body is straining for friction, my cock throbbing and wedged between her thighs, and I've never needed to come as badly as I do right now. But this is the woman I want to spend my entire life with, and this is not how our first time should go.

I somehow force myself to stop, rolling to my back and pulling her against my chest. "Now I'm the creepy guy who tells you we're just going to look at some stars and then tries to molest you."

Her mouth curves up. "I wasn't complaining."

Her willingness is not helpful right now. I'm still fighting with myself not to pick right back up where we left off. "I don't want half measures," I tell her, pressing my lips to the top of her head. "I need everything from you. And that shouldn't happen here, no matter how badly I want to convince myself otherwise."

"I think this is all harder because it feels like we've already waited forever. It's like I've been missing you and craving you my entire life, at some level."

Yes. That's exactly what it is. Some part of me, the part that existed in another life with her, has waited all these years to get here. I'm like a man who's been deprived of water for too long. When I finally get it, I want to drink until I drown.

"If we're going to get through tonight successfully, some precautions are in order," I say, grabbing a spare blanket and wrapping her in it twice.

She raises a brow. "Your precautions involve turning me into a human burrito?"

She doesn't know about the night in Baltimore yet, but even what just happened here should be reason enough. "It'll help make sure I don't change my mind. Or at least it'll slow me down if I do."

She tucks her head into the cleft of my shoulder. She fits perfectly, as if she was made to be pressed against me like this. "You should have been right here all along," I say quietly.

"I'm just happy I'm here now," she says, nestling closer.

~

IT'S the rain that wakes us.

A light mist, fortunately, but even a light mist isn't something either of us could sleep through.

I drive her back to her mother's house and walk her to the door. So much about this feels like high school again, but high school as it should have been: spent with a girl I can hardly stand to leave. "I think I kept you out past curfew," I tell her. "If you get grounded, your mom won't let me take you to prom."

She grins. "She'll have a bigger problem with the fact that you're thirty."

I kiss her one last time and then I pull her close. "Seriously, Quinn," I say. "Don't let your mom guilt-trip you into changing your mind."

She goes on her toes to press soft lips to my jaw. "I somehow found you once in London, and then I found you here, when I didn't know who you were," she says. "And nothing can keep me away from you now that I do."

36

NICK

I arrive at my building just after five. I decide to skip my morning swim in lieu of a few more hours of sleep. In truth, what I'd like to do is just sleep until Quinn is back, and safe. It's new for me, caring like this about someone else. As if my heart is now somewhere outside my body, completely beyond my control. What will I do if we don't find a solution to the tumor? We've only been together for a few hours and I already feel like I won't survive losing her.

I unlock my door and stagger to a halt when I step inside. Meg is sitting in a chair at the kitchen table, looking at me like I'm a cheating spouse caught tiptoeing home.

"I went to the lake yesterday," she whispers, her eyes red-rimmed and raw. She looks from me to the window and stares at it blankly. "I really thought that if I just did things your way, did the stuff you like for once, you'd see how good we could be together. But you weren't there, and you didn't sleep here either. So I want to know who you were with."

I exhale both guilt and irritation. We aren't together

anymore. I broke up with her for the right reasons, and I shouldn't have to feel bad about it. I shouldn't have to come home at five in the morning with her waiting to confront me. But I don't want to hurt her either, and the way I feel about Quinn would definitely do that. It could also get me in a lot of trouble if she were to ask about it.

"I *was* at the lake," I tell her, forcing myself toward the table and taking the seat across from hers. "I must have missed you there."

"Alone?"

I should lie but somehow the truth slips out instead. "Most of it."

"So you took someone to the lake," she says, voice warbling now, heavy with tears, "but you never took me."

"You wouldn't have wanted to go to the lake."

"That's not the point!" she cries. "The point is that you never asked! I had to drag you kicking and screaming into this relationship, and this girl—this stupid, stupid girl you barely *know*—gets everything I had to fight for. She's the one you stayed out with last week, isn't she?"

My ribs seem to pull in, constricting my breathing. It looks bad. Maybe it is. I should have ended things with Meg a lot sooner than I did. I should have ended them the first time I tried, months ago. "It's not what you're thinking."

"Then what is it, Nick?" she screams, standing and pulling at her hair. "Because I figured out weeks ago that you were interested in someone. I thought it was the patient Lynn said you were spending so much time with, and I figured it would pass because we both know *that* can't go anywhere, so if it's not what I'm thinking, please tell me what the fuck it is."

I sink low in my chair and rest my head against its back, cornered and suddenly depleted. I could lie right now, but I have a feeling it'll come back to bite me in the ass. It'll be easy enough for her to find out who Quinn is and assume the worst.

"She's someone I knew a long time ago, and now she's here and"—I pause because the next words sit like something bitter, gritty on my tongue—"she's dying. So I want to spend every hour with her while I can."

Meg's mouth hangs slack. For the first time I see a hint of disgust in her eyes when she looks at me. "So she *is* a patient. Why didn't you turn her over to someone else once you realized you knew her?"

Because I don't trust anyone else to take her case. "She wanted me to treat her."

Meg laughs, an angry, hysterical sound, loud enough to wake the neighbors. "Yeah, I *bet* she did. Who the hell is she? You said you'd never had a long-term relationship."

Cornered again. *Jesus.* For a guy who's been generally truthful through most of his life, I'm getting called on a lot of shit right now. "I haven't. It's complicated...we didn't date for long, but we've known each forever."

Her arms fold over her chest as she paces. I feel like I'm being cross-examined. "Where do you know her from?"

The easiest answer would be London, except that's also the easiest to disprove since Quinn's never been. "College."

"We've talked about college a thousand times," she says, throwing out her arms, "and you never thought to mention you were *in love* with someone there?"

I pinch the bridge of my nose. "I wasn't in love with her," I say, though it feels like a lie. "I don't know. Maybe I was. But I just ran into her again, and—"

"Decided it would be fun to fuck someone behind my back while we were making plans to move in together?" she snarls.

"No. Not at all. I didn't sleep with her. I still haven't." Though God knows if we'd been anywhere but the back of my car last night I would have. Repeatedly.

Her jaw tightens and she takes the chair farthest from mine. "You're a smart man. You see what's happening here, don't you?

This has nothing to do with some random girl from your past. You're just scared of commitment. Tell me something: did this magical connection with a girl you fucking *forgot* take place before or after I suggested moving in here for a while?"

I know what she's saying. As an outside observer, I'd agree with her. But she doesn't get the fact, and I can't explain, that some part of Quinn has been living inside me this entire time. "After," I reply. "And I know how that sounds. All I can say is that it's real."

She stands, her eyes damp, pushing the chair back in with too much force. "How long does she have?"

I swallow. "I don't know. A few years, maybe."

"A few years, *maybe*? That means a year. And when that year's up, or however long it is," she says, heading for the door, "you're going to be back where you started, with the same job, and the same life. And then what?"

I flinch, unwilling to contemplate the answer. "I don't know."

The door *clicks* as it closes softly behind her, leaving only her question ringing in my head. The idea of a world without Quinn is already unthinkable. I can't imagine what I'm going to do with myself when she's gone.

Which means that, somehow, I've got to find a way to make sure she stays.

THERE'S no way I'm going to fall back asleep now, so I go straight to the hospital instead to take another look at Quinn's scans. There's got to be something I've missed. There's got to be a way to save her. It's light out by the time I've showered, but the city is only beginning to rise. Birds and the clamor of garbage trucks in the distance are all I hear as I walk on silent streets.

The night staff is still on duty when I reach my floor, heavy-eyed and paper-laden as they get ready to change shifts. A few brows are raised when I walk by the nurses' station, but they're too eager to get home to worry about why I'm here so early. I unlock my office door but freeze as I cross the threshold. There is a woman at my desk—inside an office to which only I and one other person have a key.

I grip the door handle, stunned into silence. *How?* How could this woman possibly have gotten in?

I've never seen her before but there's something intensely familiar about her. The pale blond hair, the fine-boned beauty. There's this feeling inside me when I see her face—rage, terror—that I can't begin to explain.

She takes in my shock, unimpressed, then looks back casually at the scans she has spread on my desk. Quinn's brain scans, placed in chronological order. "It looks like nature's done my work for me," she says, her mouth curving into a smile. "Hasn't it?"

Stop her, my sluggish, stunned brain commands. I lunge, but before I've reached the desk she vanishes. Only the scrubs remain behind, sitting in a pile on my chair.

37

QUINN

The woods behind Nick and Ryan's house are finally free of snow. There are buds on the trees, tiny green shoots poking out of the dirt. Once we fix the steps, we'll finally be able to get back into the treehouse.

"I can't believe your parents let you do that," I say, watching Nick hammer a nail into the wood.

"My dad had a treehouse when he was a kid," he replies. "And he built the whole thing himself."

"Does he still go in it?" I ask.

"Adults don't like treehouses."

"I will," I insist. "I'm going to keep coming up here, no matter how old I am."

He thinks for a moment and then shrugs, as if he's announcing a decision he was already pretty certain of. "I think I'll marry you when I grow up," he says.

I bite my lip to hide the sudden burst of delight in my chest. "Okay," I tell him. "Sure."

I go home to my mother and report what Nick has said as I'm falling asleep. "Maybe I'll go to the future and see if it happens," she says. She's teasing me. The room is so dark I can't see her face, but I hear the smile in her voice.

"You're not supposed to go to the future," I remind her. The stories she tells me each night about time-traveling are always about the past, because she says jumping to the future is dangerous, and you may learn things you wish you didn't know. She promises when I'm old enough she'll take me with her, but until then, I can only live through her adventures. "Tell me about visiting the soldier. That's my favorite."

"That's my favorite too," she says, her voice a little sad. "But you'll have stories of your own someday. Better ones."

My fears creep in. She's so certain I can do what she does, but if she won't jump to the future, how does she know for sure? "What if I can't jump like you?"

Her laughter fills the quiet room. "Oh, sweet girl. Your abilities will make mine look childlike by contrast."

"But when?" I plead.

She pulls the covers up to my chin and plants a kiss on my forehead. "You'll jump," she whispers, "on the day when you need it most."

Someone has torn them apart in the past, and she plans to do it again. In order to keep history from repeating, Quinn will need to master her unusual gifts—but that means admitting to herself and to Nick why she stopped using them in the first place. He may never forgive her when he learns the truth, but Quinn is running out of options--because the clock is ticking, and it's no longer just her life that hangs in the balance.

ALSO BY ELLE O'ROARK

ACKNOWLEDGMENTS

It takes a village, apparently, to convince me my book is ready to go to print—especially one with a plot like this one—so I have a long list to thank. First my amazing beta readers, who've given me such helpful feedback and are just generally the coolest people ever: Tricia Coan, Deanna Heaven, Kimberly Ann, Amy Meyer, Katie Foster Meyer, Julie Page, Brenna Rattai, Laura Steuart, Jill Sullender, Erin Thompson, and Laura Ward.

Thanks to my sister, Kate Garner, for constant reminders not to pre-crap on things and for her outrage over three-star reviews. Next, Emily Wittig for my new covers, Janis Ferguson, whose proofreading skills are unparalleled (I hate word play, so that was absolutely unintentional), Kathy Bosman, who took this through several rounds of edits, and Julie Deaton, who gave it one last look at the end since I couldn't stop changing things until the last minute.

Thanks, finally, to my girls (or coven, depending on who you ask). Many years ago, I was lucky enough to be stuck watching toddlers play soccer with Sallye Clark, Deanna Heaven and Katie Meyer. Eleven years later they are still the people I go to with every problem and every triumph, and I'm endlessly grateful to have them in my corner.

ABOUT THE AUTHOR

Elle O'Roark (who writes contemporary romance as Elizabeth O'Roark) spent many years as a medical writer before publishing her first novel in 2013. She has several degrees she doesn't use from The University of Texas and Notre Dame, and considers herself to be a logical person but also worries birds are harbingers of doom. She lives in Washington, D.C. with her three children. *Parallel* is her first paranormal series.

www.ingramcontent.com/pod-product-compliance
Lightning Source LLC
Chambersburg PA
CBHW071156270325
24181CB00014B/1143
9781956800005